Intriguing and interesting read following Andy as he navigates his way through the highs and lows of his new career.

* * * * *

Carly McIntosh - ARC Reader

Copyright

Andy
Blackmore
Police Constable
Series

An Officer's Tale

Simpson Munro

Dedication

This book is dedicated to my children and my children's children.

Acknowledgements

I would like to acknowledge those who assisted in the process, Holly for her cover design, and Anton for his meticulous editorial skills. I thank them for adding their talents to my work.

Thanks to Jasami Publishing for their patience and understanding.

Jasami Acknowledgements

The Jasami team is integral to the production of all of our titles. They are talented, creative and hardworking. Thank you!

Cover Designer

Holly Richards

Editor

Anton Trock Lundhal

Table of Contents

The Early Years

Chapter One

I t was late autumn in 1979 when Andy Blackmore, a young cop, joined the Police Service and was posted to Bankvale, a village about twenty miles west of Glasgow. His heart sank when he first saw the office that was to become his home for the duration of his two-year probationary period and possibly beyond.

It was an old building, with red sandstone walls and old sash windows, their white paint flaking with age. When it rained, the gutters overflowed from lack of cleaning. The car park was small and tight.

On entering the backdoors of the office, blue linoleum lined the corridors that led to various rooms and small offices. The Sub Divisional Officer, being a Chief Inspector, had the first office, while the Sergeants and CID shared the two smaller offices.

The night shift was gathering to go and get some well-deserved sleep, while the early shift was preparing to take over. There was warmth, friendship, and a sense of belonging among all who worked there. They were like an extended family.

There was a buzz in the air as both the night and early shifts met up, like brothers in arms, swapping stories about what had been going on as the village slept, unaware of anything untoward that had happened during the night. This was rural policing at its best, a hub for those who kept the peace in an area known for its village mentality. An example of us-and-them culture; families in the village stuck together through thick and thin, good and bad, until one of them was murdered.

This could set off family wars, and the situation would have to be contained quickly, with the perpetrator caught as a matter of urgency. The night shift had completed that particular task within hours.

Detectives were milling around and witnesses were waiting to be interviewed; the place was alive with the human endeavour to make the case stick.

Going down the long passageway towards the cells, the cry from Cell One. "Turnkey, where's my lawyer?"

"What's he in for?" Andy asked his Sergeant. He was a tall foreboding Highlander, burley with a thick, northern accent, and grey hair.

"Murder," he replied. "It's the reason the night shift is so happy with their night's work."

Andy had started only a few weeks ago, and he felt a cold shiver go down his spine as reality struck home: this profession was not something you watched on TV or read about in the papers. He knew he would have to quickly adapt and get used to the reality of death. The man in Cell One was accused of the murder.

"Laddie," said the Sergeant. "Make sure he gets fed before he goes to court."

Andy prepared a roll with square, sliced sausage, and a mug of tea in an old tin cup, which had been probably used thousands of times over the years. Pulling down the cell door hatch to hand the breakfast to the prisoner, Andy came face to face with the accused.

Sitting in the corner of the cell was a young man surrounded by walls of cold white tiles and a red-painted floor, dulled over the years. Feeble daylight tried to break through the thick glass windows: there was no escaping. He wore a grey paper suit provided by the forensics staff, as his clothes had been taken to be examined. He looked a forlorn and lonely figure, deep lines etched around his tired eyes.

Andy shouted, "Hey, breakfast!"

The prisoner looked up, his eyes cold and calculating, and he turned his back to lie down, ignoring the offer of warm food and a hot drink. He was covered in an old grey blanket that he had been given for his stay that, over the years, had been washed into submission. The unwanted breakfast was quickly consumed by hungry cops who shared the spoils.

"Right laddie," said the Sergeant. "Let's go."

"Go where?" Asked Andy his tone sounded confused.

"Mortuary," was the curt reply.

For the Sergeant, it was just another day, but for the young officer, this was a whole new ball game - compared to his previous life as a bricklayer.

Only three months ago he'd had a relatively quiet life, laying bricks and building houses, and now he was face to face with an accused murderer, and was about to head to a mortuary to view the deceased victim. It was a complete culture shock to him.

"Laddie," the Sergeant directed upon arrival at the mortuary. "You stay here until the pathologist arrives from the city to carry out the post-mortem. Your only job is to make sure nobody else gets in here."

Yes Sergeant."

Andy surveyed his surroundings as his Sergeant left the room, leaving him alone, and pulled over a wooden chair. He sat down and looked all around, at the gleaming white tiles on the wall, and the floor-to-ceiling stainless-steel refrigerators containing the dead bodies. Behind each door lay four bodies.

The mortuary had a unique odour. It was part of the local hospital, yet seemed detached from everything and everyone. Sitting there alone, with only the dead to keep him company, Andy wondered *what have I gotten myself into. Would I survive my probationary period? Much less thirty-plus years on the job? I've never seen a dead body before.*

Shortly after he began his reflections, a gaunt, pale man arrived. He was wearing a white coat, with dishevelled dark hair, a slightly bent frame so he looked shorter that his six foot frame. He identified himself as the mortuary attendant, and his flat voice only added to his strange appearance.

Coming closer to Andy, greeted him with an extended boney hand, which Andy shook.

"Hello. Not seen you before."

Andy nodded. "I'm new to the area."

The mortuary attendant's voice was a low gravel monotone. "Do you know that people die of diseases every day that they never knew they had?"

His dark eyes searched Andy's for a moment, before his thin lips parted in a crooked smile. He suddenly walked away, leaving an eerie sense of unhappiness in his wake.

About an hour later, two men arrived in the mortuary, identifying themselves as detectives. Soon afterwards, a small, dapper, balding man arrived wearing a dark blue suit, matching tie, and a gleaming white shirt.

"Good morning gentlemen," he boomed with a smile, grabbing the relevant paperwork from the hands of one of the detectives. "What do we have this morning?"

Following a quick scan of the report and a chat with the detectives, he continued. "Okay, let's see what we've got."

The mortuary attendant pattered over to open the stainless-steel refrigerator door and slid out the long metal tray on which lay the deceased, who was covered in a white sheet. He then rolled over a trolley to slide the tray onto.

Andy stood transfixed as he watched the proceedings.

The pathologist, sensing the newness of the officer, queried, "Constable, is this your first?"

"Yes, sir."

"Well, well. We all have to start somewhere, so get yourself over here."

The two seasoned detectives glanced at each other and smiled. From the refrigeration room to the sterile, post-mortem area, Andy pushed the trolley this procedure ensured the continuity of evidence for future court proceedings. Production bags for clothing were at the ready, as well as glass vials for samples of blood and tissue for the pathologist's report in court.

With everything in position, and the smell of formaldehyde hanging in the air, the pathologist drew back the crisp white sheet, revealing the pale body to the young officer. As he looked at the deceased, his first impression was that he was peacefully asleep; there was nothing obvious to suggest that he was the victim of a brutal murder. A thin piece of string tied a label to his wrist, containing the name of the deceased.

"Right, gentlemen, let's get started, I have a few more to do today."

The pathologist queried if the deceased had been formally identified. The smaller older detective confirmed identification by the victim's parents earlier that morning.

The pathologist spoke clearly into his dictaphone, providing a full description of the deceased, then requested the constable to assist in turning the body over. Tentatively, Andy walked toward the table looking at the corpse he would have to touch.

"Listen he's dead, he's not going to bite you." The pathologist gazed at Andy to see his reaction.

Everyone laughed, except the mortuary attendant, who was hovering in the background.

Andy reached out to assist with turning over the body when the pathologist exclaimed, "Ah, there it is." He turned to the young officer while pointing to the area. "Look here, see this wound? This is the one that did the damage. See the small hole in his neck? It leads directly to the jugular artery."

The body was turned onto its back once more and the pathologist lifted his scalpel. He looked at the young officer, then drew a straight neat line down toward the stomach, the chest silently opening as the razor-sharp instrument revealed the insides. All the while, It took all of Andy's willpower to not flinch. Finally, samples were taken from various organs as evidence to be logged by detectives, then refrigerated until transferred to pathology.

It seemed like a very short time and the post-mortem was complete. Items for production at court were logged, labeled, and signed by all present. This was following the appropriate procedures for submission to the court, if required.

Cause of death: A single knife wound to the neck.

The mortuary attendant stitched up the body in a pure white linen sheet, and returned it to the refrigeration unit. The two detectives looked at each other, impressed by the young officer's reactions, and offered him a lift back to the office, which he gladly accepted.

Arriving at the office, Andy noticed his colleagues hanging around, waiting for his return, after what was generally considered to be a trying morning for someone so young in service.

"Well?" asked his Sergeant, standing with his hands in his pockets and rocking on his heels.

Before Andy could say anything, one of the detectives behind him announced in a loud, clear voice, "Sergeant, he's one of us now! All went well!"

The young officer looked up at his new comrades, smiled and shrugged.

"Laddie," bellowed his Sergeant. "Have you had a cup of tea this morning?"

"No, Sergeant."

"Right, c'mon then, I'll make you one."

Together they strolled through to the kitchen at the back of the office.Andy sat down. The Sergeant poured two mugs of tea and they sat opposite each other. The Sergeant knew exactly what was going through the head of his new young officer, as he had been there himself many years before as a young constable.

"Are you okay?" he asked.

"Honestly, I just don't know."

Silence followed as he stared into his cup, and the following minute seemed an eternity compared to the morning, which had passed by in a whirlwind.

"Right," Sergeant said in a surprisingly soft and calming voice. "Just so you know, I've been exactly where you are right now. Also, no two days are the same in this job. There's not a murder every day, so believe me when I tell you that some days are just worse than others."

Andy looked up from his cup and studied the older man's expression.

"Yes, Sergeant," he finally said.

"So what did you learn this morning?"

The young officer thought for a moment. "Well, the mortuary attendant did seem a bit strange."

The Sergeant leaned back and let out a deep burst of laughter.

"Oh yes, and in years to come you'll get to know him well."

This was the icebreaker the young officer was unknowingly looking for that day. For a brief moment, they were both laughing.

"On the other hand," the young man observed. "Today I was with someone's son, someone's friend, who was murdered for no apparent reason."

"Yeah," said the Sergeant. "I'm not saying get used to it, because the day that happens is the time to leave this job, because that will be the day you stop caring."

Andy nodded, finished his tea, and left the kitchen thinking about his next early shift, just as the late shift were wandering in to start their tour of duty.

The booming highland voice of the Sergeant cried out, "Early shift! Home time!"

Andy headed into the locker room, the voices of his colleagues enveloping him in a cacophony of noise as they prepared to go home.

The senior constable on the shift came over and held out his right hand. "Welcome," he said with a broad smile.

The two shook hands and nothing more was said.

In that small red sandstone building with flaking paint, leaking gutters, a small car park, and blue linoleum lined corridors, the family had just inducted a new member.

On the drive home, Andy listened to the radio. The music was soothing, until it faded into the news bulletin with the lead story on the murder in the village. The newscaster stated that a twenty-five-year-old, local man has been arrested and charged with murder and is due to appear in court.

Holy shit, he thought to himself. He's only a year younger than me and facing the prospect of a long time locked up in a prison cell, all because of a moment of where loss of a human life just became a thoughtless event.

Upon entering his flat, there was an eerie silence in comparison to the bustling, noise-filled office he had just left behind. The young officer took off his uniform and got into more familiar clothes: jeans and a T-shirt. He pulled on his brown leather boots with a matching leather jacket and headed to his local pub for a quiet pint with some of the locals. He pushed the door open and wandered over to the bar.

"Hi, Andy," said Michael, the barman. "Your usual?"

"Aye," he replied, and suddenly it dawned on him that this was the first time all day someone had actually used his name.

"See there's been a murder down your way, Andy," commented Michael, who had been behind that bar for over forty years.

"Aye," answered Andy.

"Well, you gonna tell us about it, Andy? Give us all the gossip about who and why."

Andy looked up from his pint of beer. "No, I can't. Sorry."

If there was one thing he had learned quickly, it was to say nothing about the job to anyone.

After finishing his pint, he strolled from the bar to his home, made his dinner, and went to bed early for his morning shift.

Chapter Two

The alarm at 05:30 sounded like Big Ben in Andy's ear. His right arm reached out and hit the silence button. Then, turning onto his back, he contemplated the day ahead. Surely nothing could be like yesterday.

After a few minutes, he rolled out of bed and padded down the hardwood floor into the tiny kitchen to make the strong black coffee required to start his day. Reaching for the much-used kettle, he pressed the 'on' button, listening for the familiar sound of water bubbling towards its boiling point.

He strolled to the bathroom and began his usual ritual, turning on the hot water tap, wetting his face for a shave, evenly applying shaving cream, and then drawing the razor carefully over his face to ensure he did not cut himself: the familiar routine brought comfort. Then he stepped into the shower, letting the hot water pour over his head and course down his back. His mind drifted to the day before. Like a black and white film montage, the pictures played through his mind: the deceased on the cold table and the accused languishing in the cold cell. And despite the warmth of the shower, Andy shivered and thought, *Why should I really care? After all, the guy got himself into that mess.*

He showered, dried pulling the black trousers with the razor-sharp crease then dressing in the crisp white shirt with black shoulder epaulettes which identified his division and the related divisional number, and finally a plain black tie.. Sitting at his small round table with his coffee, Andy began to doubt whether he had made the right decision about leaving the building trade to join the police service.

He slung on his jacket, and wandered down the well-worn stairs of his common close, which was occupied by eight other flats. He got into his car at six-thirty, turned on the radio, and immediately the news came on the air. The newscaster was repeating what had been broadcast the previous evening.

Jesus, thought *Andy this is the last thing I want to be reminded of. He muted the radio, driving the rest of the way in silence.*

Arriving at the office, Andy walked into the backyard, opened the door to the blue linoleum lined corridor and went into the locker room. He opened his locker and withdrew his jacket from its hanger. He went through to the muster hall and sat down with the others as they waited for the Sergeant to deliver the morning briefing.

This was a small group of cops; nothing on the scale of what was deployed in the city. This was why everyone had to stick together: something Andy needed to learn quickly.

Everyone was deployed except him. "Andy," said the Sergeant. "We have a job to do."

It was the first time in since he reported for that the Sergeant called him by his first name. The shift, which consisted of ten officers — nine males and a female — had already been deployed to mobile and foot patrols in the village and surrounding areas, all except Andy.

As everyone went about their business, the Sergeant got a hold of Andy.

"Right, we're heading for court this morning."

"Oh?" said Andy, sounding confused.

"Do you remember the guy in Cell One yesterday?"

"Yes."

"Well, we're taking him to court this morning. In the meantime, go and get yourself a cup of tea, and one for me also. Two sugars, no milk, and bring it to my office."

When Andy returned with the teas, the Sergeant said,

"Right, before we go, we have to get a statement together about everything you did yesterday. I can help you with that. We also have to make sure all the labels are signed on the productions for court."

"Yes, Sergeant," replied Andy.

By 08:00, everything was checked and double-checked.

"Okay," said the Sergeant. "Let's go get him."

After being handed the heavy metal keys, Andy approached cell one and slipped the largest one into the lock of the steel door. He turned it to the right, and, with a thud, the mortice recoiled into the chamber and the door unlocked. Lying on a thin mattress on the concrete floor, covered by the worn, washed-out blanket, the prisoner stirred.

"Billy, get yourself together. Time for court," Andy said.

As if used to the proceedings, Billy stood up, folded the blanket, and lifted his mattress. Brushing his way past Andy without a word, he placed his mattress into the large cupboard, while the blanket went in the wash bucket for the next occupant of the cell.

Billy sat on the hard floor and pulled on his boots, delivered by relatives to the office late the night before, as he had had nothing of his own to wear. He looked up at Andy, then stood up, turned around, and put his hands behind his back, expecting the handcuffs to be attached to his wrists.

"Billy, turn around, face me please, and put your wrists together."

Andy applied the handcuffs securely to Billy's wrists. Billy stared at Andy in disbelieve trying to understand why Andy did not follow the usual procedure of hands-behind-back.

"Okay, we're off to court," the Sergeant informed the bar officer. "Shouldn't be too long, if anyone is looking for me."

In the backyard, the van doors opened and Andy joined Billy in the back for the short journey to the court cells. Not a word was exchanged between captive and captor during the entire journey.

The van came to a halt and Andy overheard through the intercom, "How many onboard?"

"One prisoner," stated the Sergeant.

The large, black gates at the back of the court opened and, as the van pulled forward, Andy looked out the rear door windows and watched as the ornate gates closed automatically.

As the back doors of the van swung open, Andy climbed out and took hold of Billy's handcuffs. He led him through the doors towards the cells of the large, blonde sandstone building that had been standing for over a hundred years.

"Welcome back, Billy," the court officer sneered.

The Sergeant handed over the relevant paperwork and the property bag, which contained a few remaining articles of personal property, such as a watch, ring, and neck chain.

Andy took his first look around the area that would become a familiar sight for him in years to come He noticed the police officers were similar in both age and service, riding out their last years as they headed towards their pensions.

"Cell Four for him," said the court officer. Andy followed Billy into the designated isolation cell and removed his handcuffs.

As he was making his way out of the cell, Billy asked,

"Hey, what's your name?"

"Andy," he replied without hesitation.

"Thanks, Andy."

"What for?"

"For treating me like a human and not judging me already. I won't forget this."

He nodded, closed the door, and, this time, turned the key to the left for the bolt to slide into the keeper.

"Right, laddie," the Sergeant said.

Ah well, thought Andy. *Back to being laddie.* With a wry smile, he got into the van, and the two of them made their way out the gates back to the office.

"Sergeant," he asked in a quiet tone. "What's the story with Billy? Everyone seems to know him."

"Aye," said the Sergeant. "He's been in and out of trouble all his life, in children's homes, the young offenders' institutions, and then prison. It's a way of life for him." After a pause, he continued. "Oh, a piece of advice. Never turn your back on him, he'll stab you in the back as quick as he looks at you. He's not just bad, he's downright evil."

Chapter Three

A ndy had been a city boy all his life, brought up in the tough East End of Glasgow. The tenements of the main street went on for miles; shops formed the ground floor, while flats extended three stories high. The stench of traffic fumes filtering into the air was something he had got used to over the years of living there.

His high school, which was in a large, red sandstone building like so many others in the area, was full of kids from various areas who rarely mingled due to the gang violence which invariably spilled into the school and the playground. Teachers struggled to keep control at times. Stabbings and slashings kept many away from school after the weekend battles, something Andy avoided like the plague.

Andy's weekends and summer nights were spent away from the gangland battlegrounds. It was not something he or his mates longed for as their territories were marked out in the blood of their foes. His weekends and summer nights were spent playing football in the parks, on the streets, in the backcourts of the tenements. The backcourts served as playgrounds, where footballs were kicked around every day and night, with the clothes poles and washing lines used by aspiring goalkeepers who awaited the call of one of Glasgow's big football clubs: calls that never came for so many. Many a ball got burst on the broken bottles that littered the area, causing the game to be abruptly abandoned. The bin shelters with concrete roofs made for great goals as well.

Then there were the winter nights under the streetlights that shone down like beacons; the pretence that they were playing at Hampden, Ibrox, or Celtic Park, just like thousands of other kids around Glasgow. This was not the place where enemies were stabbed or slashed, but where lifelong friendships were forged with a side-foot pass or a flashing header into the goal.

A lot of Andy's friends were the sons of police officers, and they lived in a block of flats which were known as 'the polis hooses'. Red brick with white, roughcast pebble dash; those were smart flats compared to where Andy lived.

Did this aspect of Andy's childhood — the scores of police officers he got to know in his teenage years — influence the direction his later life would take? Looking back many years later, Andy decided that the man he admired most was Big Billy Green, an officer of the law when

Andy was very young. Big Billy seemed to be about ten feet tall in his dark uniform as he strode down the street where Andy's grandparents lived. Billy was an imposing figure on the streets. He always arrived home in uniform, and on rainy days his raincoat seemed longer than usual, his cap held onto his head by its chinstrap.

"Have you been behaving today?" he used to bellow, knowing Andy would scurry up the garden path and into his grandparents' house.

When he left school at fifteen, there was nothing Andy didn't know about the streets and staying safe. He had avoided the gangs, and tried to remain out of trouble and support his family after the death of his father a few years earlier.

He went to college to learn basic bricklaying, and when he finished a year later, he got himself a job as an apprentice bricklayer. His job was tea-boy: making tea for the bricklayers and their labourers. The good thing was that he was earning wages, as well as getting tips from the brickies and labourers on a Friday.

A few years later, at eighteen, he was well into learning the trade of a bricklayer and was once again attending college one day per week to get his advanced building certificates. Andy often met up with Jim, whose brother was a road manager and had a rock band who had headlined at Woodstock in 1969. This friendship blossomed as the cement was mixed and the bricks were laid, and the music was the daily topic as the radio blasted.

Jim had told Andy that his brother was due to visit soon, as his band was doing a world tour. A couple of weeks later, the two long-haired, dishevelled teenagers travelled to the Usher Hall in Edinburgh. Backstage passes lay in wait for them at the ticket office, and Jim introduced his brother Brian to Andy. The two of them got on great due to their mutual love for music. Brian suggested that they all meet up with the band at a nearby bar after the gig.

"Okay," Andy agreed, the stage was all set for the gig.

Next door, down in the bar of a dank Edinburgh establishment, Jim and Andy were having a drink as others around them began to gather. Andy started to get a gut feeling that there was something different about the clientele from what they were used to in Burns Howff, back in Glasgow. Unbeknown to him, that gut feeling was to stand him in good stead in his next career,

Andy and Jim were having a beer in the bar as it filled up before the concert.

"Jim," Andy said. "There's something not quite right in here."

"What do you mean?" asked Jim.

"Take a look around you." Jim scanned the area but saw nothing. "Jim," continued Andy. "You have two women dancing over there, right? One is playing with the other's tits. And over there, two guys are dancing with their hands on each other's arses." Realisation slowly dawned on Jim. "Jim, ya wee prick, you brought us to a gay bar!"

They casually finished their beers, left the bar and, chuckling, headed into the Usher Hall.

This was a friendship that lasted for years until Andy left the trade; they worked together on sites, building houses and factories where people went on to live and make a living. They shared their love of music and worked 'in house' with some of the world's biggest bands in Glasgow, laying bricks by day and rocking by night. Party nights after gigs were a regular event to the point of exhaustion. Work by day, a party by night, and to hell with everything else.

Andy was Jim's best man at his wedding a few years later, but somehow, they lost touch as their lives went in different directions. Andy thought to himself, *Where have those nine years gone? The fun, the laughter, the growing up, the girls. Gone but not forgotten. Childhood friends remained close by.*

It was his own decision to join the police service. He got up one morning and decided *I'm not going lay bricks until I'm a pensioner.*

However, the decision to get a trade had been a good one, because if anything went wrong during his probation period, he had something to fall back on.

Andy's thoughts turned to the weekend. He would head for the gym, as he had some serious training to get in. This was a training session that was about to have a major impact on his life.

Chapter Four

On Saturday morning, Andy headed for the gym a few miles from his flat, as he had only been living in the nearby village since his appointment to the police service, and besides, it was good to get away from the past week's events. Living in the flat and being away from his mates was not the greatest move he had made, but it had to be done.

Andy was six feet two inches of solid muscle, due to his past in the building trade, and his training as a rugby and football player. For years he played for East End clubs, he also had a love of martial arts, but he didn't disclose his black belts in judo and other martial arts to his new colleagues. With his fair hair and blue eyes, women couldn't resist his rugged good looks, so he was never short of girlfriends, but, at the moment, he didn't have anyone serious in his life. Yes, he had lots of female friends, but that's where it ended.

Following a session in the weights room, Andy went into where he felt most at home, the swimming pool. He pounded out length after length. Eventually coming to a slow, gliding halt, he leaned back against the edge of the pool. To his left he noticed a woman watching him. Andy nodded, smiled in her direction, and thought nothing more of it. Then he noticed her long straight dark hair, and slim figure encased in a bright red swimsuit, which made only a small ripple as she slipped into the water from her seated position.

He continued to watch as she approached him underwater, coming up nearby.

"Hi." She greeted him with a smile.

"Hello," Andy now noticed her beautiful, ice blue eyes. Nothing else mattered to him. Andy believed in the old cliché that eyes are the windows to the soul.

Small talk followed about how often they enjoyed visiting the swimming pool, and the sports centre as they stood leaning against the edge of the pool. Within a few moments, it was obvious there was a mutual attraction between them, but neither was ready to admit that yet.

"Listen," said Andy, who had a rather wicked sense of humour at times. "I've been in here so long I'm starting to wrinkle. I could look about sixty years old in five minutes. Do you know, we've been chatting for about fifteen minutes and we've not been introduced yet? My name's Andy."

"I'm Catherine," she replied.

"Pleased to meet you," he said as they shook hands. "Hey, would you like a coffee or something before you leave?"

"Yeah, why not," she smiled.

Andy left the pool to get dried and changed, then shortly afterwards sat staring into his coffee in the sports centre café. He heard the chair opposite being drawn back and he looked up.

"Hi," he said.

"I'll have a coffee please, no milk" Catherine requested.

She watched closely as he got up from the table to place her order. Andy was wearing a tight, blue T-shirt showing off the muscles on his torso. His jeans hugged his muscular legs. Andy was always well-groomed, and he took pride in his appearance.

A short time later, after chatting about their likes and dislikes as newly-acquainted people do, Catherine said she had to leave. As she got up to go, she commented,

"You haven't told me what you do for a living. So?"

"Neither have you."

"I, er, work in a shop."

Andy paused before saying, "I'm a bricklayer." He hesitated again, which was unlike him. "Hey Catherine, maybe we can catch up here again sometime?"

"Yeah," she replied, looking thoughtful.

Andy watched as she left the sports centre in her white tracksuit and trainers, and got into her red Audi, which sped off into the distance as she waved to him.

A waitress in a blue uniform came over to Andy's table and cleared the cups away.

"Andy," she asked. "Did you ask her out or not?"

"Pardon?" said Andy, dumbfounded.

"Well," the waitress said. "I heard her saying your name and watched you looking into each other's eyes. Geez you're slow man." She laughed as she walked away, carrying the tray of used cups.

Later that evening, Andy went back to the East End for a night out with his mates. Nothing was going to change as far as they were concerned. The banter was just what he needed after the week he had been through, so their cheeky comments about his new profession were all taken in good humour.

But Andy could not get Catherine out of his head; there was just something about her. Would he see her again? So, she worked in a shop – but where? So much for being a police officer, he thought. That night he stayed with his best mate and confidant, Gerry, and as they had one last drink Andy confessed to him that he had met a lady that day by the name of Catherine.

"Oh, aye?" said Gerry with glee. "Details please."

"She's pretty, and she works in a shop.That's all I know," Andy replied.

"Some cop you'll make," Gerry laughed.

The following morning, Andy headed back to his digs, did his washing, and pressed his uniform: crisp, white shirt ironed to perfection, and trousers pressed with a crease down the legs, sharp as a razor. Even his tie got a quick pressing. His uniform was hung up on the hanger and his well-polished boots sat neatly on the floor, ready for work the following evening.

Andy was back in the gym on Monday morning, before his night shift, not in the pool but at a martial arts class he had joined; this was pure chill-out time before the possible rigours of a nightshift. His black belt hung from his waist, with two markings indicating he was a second dan black belt in his chosen field.

After class, Andy sat at the small, round, Formica-topped table sipping his coffee in the café, the waitress watching him closely. Andy was observing the comings and goings from the centre. He sat on a wooden chair that gave him a clear view of the main door, and the doors to the swimming pool, gym, and racquet courts. He suddenly became aware of a presence at his side.

"She's not in today," the waitress said.

"Oh," Andy replied casually. "And who would you be referring to?"

She smirked, "The lady you were sitting with the other day. Oh, and by the way, she was in here yesterday and sat on this seat with the same look that you have on your face right now."

"And what look would that be?"

"Let's just say she seemed to be watching for you the way you're looking for her, right?"

"What's your name?" Andy asked.

"Louise," she answered.

"Well, Louise, for all I know she may be married with a load of screaming kids running about the house right now."

"Well, Andy, only one way to find out, isn't there? And if you ain't fast, you could be last. I am going to let you in on a little-known secret. I have a list of guys' names the length of my arm wondering the same thing you are. I'd guess that you are top of her list, and that she is possibly single," she said, throwing a smile and wink in his direction.

Andy rose from the table and lifted his kit bag.

"See you, Louise!" Andy shouted as he strolled out of the centre, heading for his car.

Sitting in the driver's seat, Louise's words about the possibility of Catherine being unattached were ringing in his ears. He had his doubts, as nobody with her looks was likely to be single, but Louise was right: inquiries had to be made.

Chapter Five

T he night shift began at eleven o'clock. Winter nights were setting in, and the heavy coats were being brought out from hibernation in the lockers, ready for wearing. Andy and the rest of the shift filed into the musty room once again for an update by the Sergeant on the weekend's happenings. Everyone listened as the crimes and offences were read out: minor assaults to assaults of severe injury, breaches of the peace by their dozens, housebreakings were down on previous weeks, and traffic offences were also down.

The mobile patrols were read out and the foot beat patrol followed. Andy was paired with Joe for the full week, to get mobile patrol experience. Joe was a fount of knowledge, and probably had the most comprehensive list of 'touts' in the area. Joe ultimately became a major influence on Andy.

"Just to let you all know," the Sergeant said, "Billy made no plea or declaration, when he appeared in court the other day, concerning the murder. He was remanded in custody pending a further appearance this week."

Working the nightshift was boring for Andy. Cars were stopped and people on the street were spoken to: absolutely nothing happened. There was peace in the village. As they patrolled the village streets and surrounding areas in darkness, his geographical knowledge expanded. Most things look so different in the dark.

On Friday night, Joe looked up into the sky and said,

"Hey big man. Full moon tonight. Gonna be fun."

Confused, Andy asked,

"What?"

"This is the night of the 'headbangers' " Joe replied. "So fasten your seat belt, it's gonna be a rough ride."

Andy hadn't a clue what Joe was talking about, but, before daybreak, he would understand. Joe had just over ten years' service. He was known to everyone, and everyone was known to him.

As the van reversed out the backyard, "Control to Zulu 1!" came over the radio.

"Answer it," Joe shouted. "That's our call sign."

"Aye, okay," said Andy. "Erm, go ahead."

"Fight in Smiths Bar, Main Street, one person injured."

"Roger," Andy replied.

"Right you," said Joe. "I drive, you answer the radio. I can't do everything."

Arriving at the bar, Joe led the way. There was one man with a slight facial wound. Joe spoke to the barman.

"Right, let's go," Joe said to Andy when he was done. Even more confused, Andy sat back in the van and asked, "What happened there?"

"Report it back as 'matter resolved.'"

A few more 'matters resolved' happened on the street that night, with domestic disputes between couples, all of them the worse for wear from alcohol. Mates fell out over the most trivial things and just wanted to be idiots for a while. They were sent up the road to their homes.

Call after call, to various occurrences, was resolved on the spot. A night shift on a Friday, and not a prisoner to show for all the calls they attended.

"Listen," Joe said to Andy. "You'll have noticed we've not jailed anyone tonight so far."

"Aye," said Andy.

"Well, these people don't forget when they have a lucky escape from jail. It can be useful in the future. Don't get me wrong, I'll lock them up if need be, and they all know that." Another lesson for Andy.

Andy was thinking of a cup of tea or something to eat as break time approached, when the next call came through,

"Control to Zulu 1."

"Go ahead," responded Andy.

"Report of a serious road accident at the roundabout on the dual carriageway."

For the first time in Andy's short career, Joe hit the buttons for the blue lights and siren. The reflection of the revolving blue light shone on the houses on either side of the road as the siren wailed through the streets, filling the night air. Late-night vehicles, mostly taxis, gave way as they raced to the scene. Adrenalin was pumping through Andy's veins. They were the only vehicle attending before assessment. This was the moment Andy had been waiting for: the lights and the siren. On their arrival, Andy was confronted with carnage through the windscreen of the van.

"Andy!" shouted Joe. "Tell control we're here."

"Zulu 1 to Control. Time of arrival," Andy blurted out.

"Roger," came a calm reply.

Four cars were wrecked, lying over both carriageways, and people were trapped in the wreckages with no way out of the tangled metal. Sirens could be heard in the distance, heading in their direction, as Joe and Andy got to work. The Fire Brigade, equipped with cutting equipment, were pulling up nearby, and three ambulances stopped close to the scene. Paramedics were going to each vehicle to assess the situation.

"Andy," Joe called. "Get over here."

Andy rushed over to the contorted vehicle.

"This man is critical according to the paramedics. Go with him in the ambulance."

The firemen released the unconscious driver with cutting equipment, and he was passed to the Ambulance Service. Andy got into the ambulance and, as they sped to the hospital, blue lights flashing and siren wailing, he watched admiringly as the paramedics worked on the seriously injured driver..

On arrival at Accident and Emergency, nurses and doctors — by then alerted to the collision — were on standby, waiting with trolleys to convey the injured to the respective trauma areas for assessment. To Andy, who had never attended a serious road collision, it looked like all hell had broken loose in A&E, but, to the medical professionals, it was controlled chaos.

Broken bodies started being rolled in, one by one, shortly thereafter, and suddenly Andy snapped into life, getting details of the injured and a list of their injuries, where possible. Fellow officers, not known to Andy, entered the area, and Andy approached them to offer all the information he had. It saved them hours of waiting around and having to interrupt the doctors for information.

Among the chaos, Andy heard a female voice nearby.

"Ward One has two beds available and Ward Two has one bed available; I'm phoning around hospitals to see what's free."

I recognise that voice.

"What about the maternity unit?" asked a consultant.

"I don't think they're busy, let's try there," Andy overheard her saying.

After what seemed like an eternity, a calm began to descend in the A&E unit. Survivors of the accident were dealt with one by one, the most seriously injured getting priority and heading to wards for overnight observations and further treatment, if required. The driver Andy had escorted with the paramedics had been rushed into the theatre with serious head, chest, and leg injuries.

Andy heard the female voice again from the next room. He looked through the open door. He saw a slim woman sitting at a desk, trying desperately to get beds for the injured anywhere she could. She put down the telephone and put her head into her hands, totally unaware of Andy's presence.

"So this is what you do when you're not in the shop," Andy said, as he looked at her in her bloodstained, nurse's uniform. She turned and looked up.

"Oh, Andy! So, this is what you do when you're not laying bricks." They smiled at each other.

As Andy turned to leave and let Catherine get on with her work, he said,

"Hey, you owe me a coffee."

Catherine looked over at him and said,

"Yeah, I suppose I do." She looked exhausted.

Among the bloodstained wipes and the bandages that lay on the casualty department floor, doctors were filling in patient reports to be sent to the wards. Nurses cleaned up, porters were rushing about, assisting wherever they could, and police officers were taking witness statements.

Andy waited for Joe to arrive at the hospital. After a while, he plucked up the courage to go back to the office where Catherine was sitting. Leaning on the doorpost, he quietly said,

"Listen, when are you back in here?"

She paused for a moment then said,

"Tomorrow night."

"Okay. Who knows, maybe we'll be back. See you."

"Yeah, see you."

Denise, a colleague of Catherine's, squeezed past Andy as he left. Once he was out of earshot, she whispered to Catherine,

"Oh my god, who's that? He's gorgeous!"

"That's Andy, he's new here." Catherine said nothing further on the matter.

"Andy! Let's go!" said Joe, who had arrived at the hospital to collect him. "Traffic boys will take care of the collision. Just give them what you have later."

Andy glanced at the clock on the wall: It was almost 04:00. He could murder a cup of tea or coffee.

"Where to now?" asked Andy.

"Up to see Joan and her man. They're boxing again. She usually wins." As the van made its way into the large, sprawling housing scheme built on the side of a large hill, Andy saw the white, roughcast exteriors of terraced houses, built to accommodate the overspill from Glasgow in the 60s; it was known locally as Spill Hill.

As they pulled up outside the open door, shouting and swearing could be heard from inside. Without stopping, Joe went upstairs to the living room, followed by Andy. Andy surveyed the wreckage strewn around the floor: broken bits of a table, a chair, and a plate with what looked like the remains of a dinner. The stench of alcohol and cigarette smoke filled the room.

"Joan, Bobby, this is Andy," said Joe.

"How you doin' Andy? Do you see where that bitch hit me wae that plate wae ma dinner on it."

Andy looked at Bobby and saw blood trickling from his head onto his shoulder. "You cut?"

"You should be a detective," Bobby retorted.

Joe sniggered quietly and took a step backwards. "All yours, Andy."

"Why did she hit you, Bobby?" Andy asked.

"Coz ah came in pished fae the pub," he replied.

Andy turned to Joan and asked if there was going to be a repeat performance tonight, to which she said, "Naw."

"Your call," said Joe.

"Bobby, are you going to make a complaint of assault?"

"No chance," Bobby replied.

"Okay, let's leave it at that then. But if I have to come back tonight, then you're both getting locked up," Andy said. Joan and Bobby looked at each other in silence as Andy and Joe left the house.

They got into the van.

"Good move there, Andy. We're rarely away from this house. It's the way they live," said Joe. Andy shook his head. Radio traffic was busy as other officers were deployed to calls from the public.

"Let's see if we get long enough for a cup of tea," said Joe, as they headed to the office.

Andy radioed the control room to report the call "matter resolved."

"Nothing outstanding at the moment. Go get a break," came over the radio.

"Roger," Andy replied, grateful.

Johnny was the bar officer responsible for the welfare of the prisoners in his custody. He was having a busy night, as the cells were rapidly filling up, not thanks to Andy or Joe. As they sat there having a cup of hot tea and a sandwich, Johnny came running into the kitchen.

"That's a call for assistance on Main Street from June, who's out patrolling the streets on her own." She was the sole female officer on the shift.

Andy and Joe grabbed their jackets and ran to the van. Within seconds it was out of the yard at high-speed, tyres screeching as they gripped the road. They could see June under the streetlights ahead with three men nearby. The van came to a halt beside them, and June immediately said to Andy and Joe,

"Watch him. He's got a blade."

Andy, first out of the van, stood alongside June. She had her baton drawn to defend herself against a possible attack. As Joe stepped onto the pavement, he said,

"Pat, what are you doing?" Joe stepped back, as he knew something was not quite right when Pat failed to respond to him.

The blade flashed under the streetlights as Joe also drew his baton. Pat's two mates were not locals, as they were unknown to Joe.

"Touch him and you're getting it,

"Oh really?" Andy asked, a small smile on his face.

June and Joe looked at each other, noting that Andy did not have his baton drawn.

"Andy, get your baton out," said Joe.

"It's okay, Joe," he replied calmly. "So, you're Pat."

"Aye, I am."

"I'm Andy. Now, be a good boy and hand me the knife," Andy, watched Pat closely for any movement.

"Try an' take it, ya prick," Pat teased waving the knife while the other two were goading Andy.

"Hey big man, try it," taunted one of them. "Try an''take it from him and he'll slice you in half."

More assistance arrived at the scene.

"Pat, look around you. My gang is bigger than your gang now. So are you going to hand me the knife or not?"

"Naw, this is for you big man!"

Before any of the officers could move, Andy held the knife safely in one hand, with Pat on the ground, held down by the other. Andy placed his knee softly on Pat's rib cage and whispered into his ear,

"Tell your pals to kneel now, or I'll crush your ribs." Nobody else heard what Andy had said. Pat screamed following a slight movement by Andy.

"Kneel before this asshole kills me!" Pat shouted at his mates. They obediently knelt on the pavement, and were handcuffed before being put into separate vehicles and taken to the office. Andy handed the knife to Joe.

Andy nodded to June to handcuff Pat in the same manner who had to be carried to the van. June joined Pat in the rear of the vehicle as Andy and Joe got into the front seats.

For the first time, Andy noticed a seriously concerned look on Joe's face.

"You okay, Joe?" asked Andy, calmly.

"I'm 'no okay with what you did to him."

"Oh, don't worry Joe. He'll be fine in a few minutes, trust me."

With the van safely parked in the yard, Joe opened the rear doors to take out the prisoner.

"Joe," said June. "He's hardly moved since we put him in here."

"Is he breathing?" asked Joe.

"Of course he is!" interjected Andy. "Right you, jail time." Andy reached into the rear of the vehicle, placing his hand on Pat's shoulder, who immediately sprang to life, albeit a little wearily.

June and Joe looked at each other as Andy took Pat down to the charge bar to be charged with several offences: possession of a knife, assaulting a police officer, threatening behaviour, and breach of the peace. Joe stepped back and said,

"Andy, he's all yours to charge. You're reporting this one to the Procurator Fiscal." All the officers who responded to the call for assistance were looking on as Andy cautioned and charged the accused with the relevant crimes and offences without any errors.

Andy's Sergeant was looking on. Listening while leaning against the stone wall, his jacket open, no tie to be seen, and smoking a cigarette with the ash ready to drop off the end. As he listened to the charges the Sergeant made a decision.

"Custody case and court for that little shit on Monday. His pals can go with him. Andy, lock him up."

Andy took Pat down the cell passageway, followed by June. Andy ushered Pat into the cell, then said quietly, "Pat, apologise to Constable Brown for your behaviour tonight and threatening her with a knife.

Pat stared at Andy. "I, or should I say we, are waiting.""Andy, leave it," June pleaded.

"Nope," replied Andy.

Pat looked at June and blurted out,

"I'm sorry for what happened, Constable Brown."

"Good boy," said Andy. June turned away and walked down the corridor as she heard the keys being turned. Andy saw Joe talking to their Sergeant.

"Right, kitchen confab time. Get yourself in there," the Sergeant said to Andy.

"Do you want me to make the tea?" Andy asked.

"Sit on your arse, Andy."

"Why didn't you draw your baton, Andy?" asked Joe, the colour slowly returning to his face.

"There was no need," said Andy. He looked at both men seated opposite him. "Sergeant, Joe – Pat was out of control, I was under control. I held the advantage the whole time." The Sergeant and Joe looked at each other, bemused.

"Right, but he lunged at you. You could be wearing that knife right now inside you," Joe's tone was icy but Andy could tell he was seething.

"No, Joe." Andy paused and thought for a minute, the silence was deafening. "Listen, please," Andy continued. "Pat was threatening me – us, the guys on this shift. What I did to him was in self-defence. None of you dared to touch him until he was in handcuffs. If there's any comeback, then I'll take full responsibility."

Joe slumped back into his seat.

"What did you say to him when he was on the ground?"

"Not a lot," replied Andy.

"Okay, try this: what did you do to him that virtually put him out of the game?"

Andy looked at Joe.

"Not a lot, and he'll be fine. Someday I'll tell you what I said, but not now."

"So, when will you tell me, Andy?"

"After the trial, if there is one, but I doubt there will be. The less you know right now, the better. Trust me."

The Sergeant and Joe rose from their seats and left the kitchen, leaving Andy sitting there. A few minutes later, Andy heard voices in the corridor as the early shift arrived, and again the night's events were relayed. Andy strolled down the corridor, stopping as he heard Joe recounting the knife incident to the early shift, followed by,

"Ah don't know what he did, but it was impressive, and I'm glad he's on our side."

"Andy," the Sergeant barked. "Get the crime report done and sign the production label for the knife. The rest of you, home time." Andy never let on that he had overheard Joe's conversation.

"All right, Andy? Nice one son," said the elder statesman on the early shift.

"Yeah, I'm fine, thanks," he replied.

"Turnkey!" cried Pat from his cell, after Andy had left the building. The early shift bar officer went down to the cell and dropped the hatch. He looked in.

"What is it, Pat?"

"Who's the guy that locked me up last night? Is he still here?"

"No," replied the bar officer. "He's probably tucked up in bed, nice and cosy."

"Leave a note for him. I want to see him when he gets back here."

The bar officer wrote a note and banged it into the shift 'dookit' for Andy's attention.

Andy crawled into his bed just after nine in the morning. He was now a believer in the night of the 'headbangers' . He thought about Catherine, and wondered if she had also managed to get through her shift.

Andy's actions that night would spread like wildfire through the office and the village, there was no doubt about that. What would be the repercussions for him, or even Joe, as they patrolled the area together?

Chapter Six

A fter a lazy day around the flat, Andy made his way to the office to start another night shift. As he got out of the car, he looked up into the clear sky and saw that the full moon was starting to wane.

Checking his appearance in the full-length mirror in the locker room, he walked through to the muster room and sat down. He was handed an envelope by Stevie, another member of his shift. Opening the envelope and unfolding the small piece of paper, he saw five words:

'Pat wants to see you.'

Joe walked in and sat beside Andy.

"Alright boys?" he said to everyone. Andy gave Joe the piece of paper, which he looked at. "Fine, we'll deal with that after muster," said Joe, handing the paper back to Andy.

With everyone present, and the events of the previous twenty-four hours relayed to everyone by the Sergeant, the teams were formed the same way as the previous evening, and Andy was paired with Joe again.

"Sergeant, this letter was left for me," said Andy, as he showed him the note.

"Pat speaks to nobody," the Sergeant said. "Well, laddie, you better go see what he wants. Joe, go with him." Before they went to the cell, Joe advised Andy to listen and not interrupt Pat, as this was a first.

Andy dropped the hatch on the cell door.

"Fancy a cigarette, Pat?" he asked.

"Sure." All the other cells were empty, as his two friends had been transferred to headquarters to separate them. He opened the cell door and took Pat to a soundproof interview room. From his pocket, he gave Pat a cigarette and lighter that Joe had given him.

"Pat, I got a note saying you wanted to see me. Why?"

Pat slowly lifted the cigarette and lighter from the table. Andy watched as Pat placed the cigarette between his lips and placed the flame from the lighter to the end of the cigarette, a small hiss and flame as lit the cigarette.

Pat said nothing, just a small creek as he rocked back and forth on his chair. He stared straight at Andy, then glanced over at Joe, whom he had known for a long time.

"Joe, I'm not a grass, you know that," Pat finally stated.

Joe nodded.

"Right, here's the deal, Andy. I'm out on bail just now, and likely to go to jail for a couple of years, for this and other things. I got a wife and a couple of kids. I'm thirty-five. This is a shit life for them, and they need me here. Don't think we don't know who you are. The word is already out about you, that you're a fair guy. So, Joe, you know I hate drugs and druggies. Sooooo…"

Joe immediately took the lead.

"What are you offering, Pat?"

"A deal."

"Pat, you're going to court on Monday, so whatever's going down has to be tonight or tomorrow at the latest. After that, all bets are off."

Another draw on the cigarette, one hand on the table, his forefinger tapping the tabletop: Andy could almost see his brain ticking over. Silence. Suddenly, Pat said,

"Right, what I want is for you guys to have a discrete word with the prosecution, if you know what I mean. But, it can't come back to me."

"In return for what?" piped up Joe.

Andy recognised that this was a cat and mouse game.

"A turn going down in the next couple of hours."

"I take it you know it's not me you're dealing with," said Joe. "It's him." He pointed to Andy. "He was the one that brought you in last night, so it's his case. He's the reporting officer. Your freedom or length of the sentence depends on him, Pat."

"Okay," Pat said, looking at Andy, let's see if my mate was right. You guys go for a break, about two o'clock. There's a red car coming into the village with 'smack' in it. There'll be two guys in the front. The passenger will throw a bag out the window at the pub door on the corner that will be collected by Tommy Smith and taken to the flats for cutting. It's all arranged. Tonight's a big one for you guys.Street value's at about 10K, maybe more, and a lot of guys are depending on its safe arrival."

Pat continued to look at Andy. "He's a pretty boy, Joe; got yourself a lady-killer there."

"Pat, pack it in." Joe knew Pat was on the wind-up.

"Hey, Andy, you got a girlfriend? Wife? Kids? Maybe a boyfriend then? Yeah, you got a boyfriend, right?"

Andy gazed at Pat and smiled. After a minute he leaned forward looking straight into his eyes. "Pat, if you think I have a boyfriend, don't sleep tonight. And make sure your ass is against the wall."

The look on Pat's face was a picture of shock and total disbelief.

"You're mental," exclaimed Pat. "You're totally mental.".

Andy leaned forward again, resting his folded arms on the tabletop.

"You have no idea how mental I can be," he said, in a tone that gave even Joe the shudders. "Let's go."

As they were walking down the corridor back to the cells, Andy asked Pat,

"Oh, by the way, who's your mate?"

"Doesn't matter," Pat muttered.

"Sergeant," called Joe. "Your office, please." Joe related the information to the Sergeant, who leaned back in his seat.

"Your thoughts?" he asked.

"Well, he's got a lot to lose, and he does hate drugs," Joe said. "They killed his brother and sister. So, what have we got to lose? Let's go for it if it's quiet and the calls don't pile up."

The Sergeant picked up the phone and called headquarters.

"Traffic Department please," he boomed.

"Inspector Weir," said the voice on the line.

"Sergeant Jimmy Black down at Bankvale office," he said. "I need you and your men down here as soon as possible. What can you give me?" He listened intently to the Inspector. "Is that the best you can do, Inspector? Well, if that's it, so be it," he said, hanging up the phone.

It was obvious to Andy and Joe that Sergeant Black was excited by the prospect of a good haul coming into the village, something to get his teeth into after a 'run of the mill' life as a Sergeant.

"Right," the Sergeant said. "Get the troops mustered again. Control room staff got onto the radios and ordered all personnel back to the office. Thankfully, no calls were outstanding for action, but the pubs and clubs had not spilled yet."

About thirty minutes later, the Inspector arrived at the office.

"Good evening, gentlemen."

Andy saw the Sergeant look behind him, and Joe turned around.

"Good evening, Inspector," Sergeant Black replied. "Inspector Smith, meet the newest member of the shift, Constable Andrew Blackmore."

"Pleased to meet you, Andrew," said the Inspector.

"Likewise, sir."

"You know Joe?" the Sergeant asked.

"Yes, who doesn't?" Inspector Smith responded, with a discerning glance.

Andy looked at the Inspector, who was only a few years older than him.

"Sergeant," the Inspector said, "what's happening? I heard over the radio you were bringing everyone in and had asked for the traffic department to be here too. Is this something I should know about?"

"Excuse me, there's a couple of things I have to see to," Joe said as he disappeared from the Sergeant's office, leaving Andy stranded.

"Well sir, I was thinking of running a roadblock at each end of the village in search of drunk drivers, and maybe catching a stolen car or two, or whatever else we may find. The reason I asked for the traffic department to attend was in case someone decided not to stop for a uniformed police officer's signal."

"Good to see a bit of initiative for once, Sergeant," said the Inspector. "I'm going to check on the prisoners' welfare, Sergeant. Then I'll be off. Good luck with your roadblocks."

Sergeant Black watched as the Shift Inspector left his office and went down the corridor. The Sergeant looked at Andy and shook his head.

"Andy, I know I shouldn't say this to you, but he is useless! Bloody useless! A University graduate, seriously he wouldn't know an angry man if he saw one."

After nearly ten years in the building trade, Andy knew what the Sergeant meant and smiled.

Joe, who had intercepted the shift personnel returning to the office, kept everyone in the kitchen as the Inspector checked on the welfare of the prisoner.

"Well done, Johnny. No complaints from the prisoner," the Inspector remarked to the bar officer as he signed the visitors' book. "Tell the Sergeant I'm away, and if he needs assistance at the roadblocks, I can arrange that."

"Yes, sir," said Johnny.

As the Inspector's car left the car park, everyone entered the muster room once again. Sergeant Black came in and announced,

"June, Georgie, take a van. You're covering the whole area tonight unless something goes wrong and you need us." The two of them nodded. "The rest of you, listen up." He looked around the room. "Has anyone seen the traffic boys?" There was no reply. The Sergeant slumped into his seat, a frustrated look on his face. Andy could almost hear his blood boiling.

"Take a seat," dictated the Sergeant. Four traffic officers strolled into the muster room without any urgency. The briefing began. "At or about 02:00, a red car is going to come into the village carrying a large quantity of drugs. I want a traffic car in the north and south of the village in case it takes off, as well as for observation purposes. If you see it coming in, don't stop it, but let us know. Andy and Joe, patrol near the pub. You know why. The rest of you, cut off the side streets in case we get a runner. Right, let's do it!" Everyone dispersed to their detail.

Chapter Seven

J oe drove down to the middle of the village where the pub was located, and parked up out of sight of any oncoming cars. The traffic officers in their cars at the north and south ends of the village were vigilant of the cars coming in.

After the bedlam of the night before, calm had returned to the radios, and mundane messages were broadcast over the airwaves: domestic disputes here and there, and car alarms activating all around the division.

Andy and Joe were sitting in their van. Not a lot was said as they waited for 'the drop'.

"Andy, what do you like to do? Because a little bird tells me you've been frequenting the local leisure centre."

"Yep," replied Andy. "I do a lot of swimming, bench presses, and weights. Nothing outrageous, just enough to keep fit."

"You're a Second Dan black belt in various martial arts, and you've been training every day since you got here. I knew last night when you took out Pat on the street, you were different from anyone else on this shift." Andy remained silent, and went into deep thought as Joe looked at him.

"What exactly do you want to know?"

"I've been in this job for just over ten years, and I've never seen anyone floor Pat like you did, and you've only been here a few weeks. What did you do to him?"

Andy thought while looking out of the window of the van, searching for any sign of the drug drop.

"Do you know what Chi energy is?" he replied finally.

"No."

"Well, that's what took Pat out. Oh, and a little tweak of a nerve on his neck. That's what caused the short term paralysis."

Joe sat there confused, wondering, what have I got here?

"D'you know something?" Joe finally said. "In this job, you can only do what you're taught at college, about holds and handcuffing people."

"Really," interjected Andy in a monotone. "Joe, I promise I won't let you down. Okay?"

There was a silence then.

"Yeah, okay," Joe replied. "But what the hell is this Chi energy?"

Andy, sensing a bit of fun with his new mentor, asked,

"Joe, how's your Chinese?"

"Do ah look like I speak Chinese?"

"I don't know. Can you tell me what sixty-nine is in Chinese?"

"Sweet and sour chicken," Joe replied, and Andy burst into laughter.

Once the laughter faded Andy glanced at his watch. It was well beyond 02:00. Andy wondered, *have I been set up by Pat in revenge?*

Then in the distance, there was movement. A sole figure walked down the street.

"Andy that's Tommy Smith, you can tell by his size and gait, he's limping, and he's just wee guy."

They watched as Tommy staggered along the street totally oblivious to their van. He veered right towards the pub as Andy and Joe alighted from their vehicle and conceal themselves nearby.

Whispered radio communications with the others confirmed that Smith was at the pub. All was set to go.

Control Room announced. "Control to all stations. There's a report of a large-scale disturbance at the shops on Spill Hill. All stations, please respond."

A response came through over the radio, as June and Georgie sped their way to the area.

"Hold positions until confirmation," Sergeant Black ordered over the radio, as a red vehicle sped into the village.

At that moment the community police officer announced over the radio to the control room that the disturbance call was a decoy.

"Tango 1 to control. Red Vauxhall Astra travelling at 60 miles per hour, heading south through Bankvale. No registration plate visible." As Tango 1 gave chase, a package was thrown from the passenger's side window.

Tommy Smith ran towards the package and picked it up off the pavement, shooting across the road like a scalded cat as Andy and Joe pursued him. His aim was to get into a nearby close and disappear through the backcourts into the darkness of the night. Time was short and his limp slowed his pace.

Andy's years of rugby training quickly prevailed, and he took Smith out in a perfect rugby tackle, locking Tommy roughly in his arms. Joe snapped the handcuffs to Smith's wrists. They hauled him to his feet and back towards the van for the journey to the station. Inside the brown paper package was a large bag of white powder.

"Tango 1 now reaching seventy miles per hour on Main Street. too dangerous to continue. standing down from pursuit. Pedestrians on the street coming from clubs."

"Tango 2 to control, we have the vehicle in sight and are going for an interception."

"Roger, Tango 2."

"Tango 2 to control. We are behind the suspect vehicle, now on the dual carriageway heading west. Assistance required urgently."

"Roger, Tango 2. Tango 1, are you available to assist?"

"Roger, control," Tango 1 replied.

The offending vehicle was eventually boxed in through a perfect movement by both traffic cars, which brought the Astra to a halt.

The passenger of the Astra was the main target, and he was taken from the vehicle and handcuffed immediately. The driver followed right behind him. They were placed into separate cars for the journey back to the office, where they would receive bed and breakfast before their appearance in court on Monday morning.

The Vauxhall Astra was checked against the Police National Computer and found to have been stolen a few days earlier from Glasgow city centre. That was good enough to keep both men incarcerated until the white powder was checked by the staff at the laboratory.

In the wee small hours of the morning, Sergeant Black called the laboratory at the force headquarters. A young woman answered the phone and listened intently, then gave permission for the package to be delivered and examined on arrival.

"Joe, get that package to HQ lab for quick analysis," the Sergeant said. "Andy, start getting the paperwork together for the crimes and offences we have at the moment. Don't record anything concerning the powder until it is confirmed as heroin, or whatever drug it may be."

As Andy and the Sergeant got the paperwork together and started writing the court report, Andy waited nervously for the call from forensics to come in. Immersed in putting everything together properly, the crimes and the offences committed he jumped with a start when the telephone rang.

"Sergeant Black here. Yes Joe. Fine, thanks." Andy looked at the Sergeant, waiting with bated breath. "Well, laddie, it's not heroin." Andy's heart sank. "It's cocaine. We've hit the jackpot tonight!" The Sergeant beamed at Andy.

"I've never done this before.How do we deal with Pat?" Andy asked.

"Cautiously," the Sergeant said. "Come with me, Andy." Silently they walked down the cell passageway and dropped the hatch on Pat's cell door.

"All good in there, Pat?" asked the Sergeant.

"Aye, fine," Pat replied. "Hope all's well with you, Sergeant."

"Yes, all's well tonight." Pat's future now lay in Andy's hands, specifically in the report he had to write about him. In order not to arouse any suspicions from Pat's fellow prisoners, Andy and the Sergeant followed the same routine with the other inmates.

"Oh, I meant to say, Andy. Billy was in court. He pleaded not guilty to murder, again. So, it's the High Court for him soon."

"Will I be required to attend, Sergeant?"

"Most likely."

The completed forms, report from forensics, and the evidence with labels attached and signed, lay scattered about. Suddenly the back door banged open and footsteps could be heard coming along the corridor.

"Inspector," said the Sergeant. "Two visits in one evening, sir."

"Yes, Sergeant," the Inspector replied. "I just wanted to congratulate your shift on a job well done tonight, and for your initiative of having a roadblock. Good work, everyone!"

"Thank you, sir," the Sergeant said.

"You know, I could do with having someone like you at Divisional HQ. I may recommend you to the Chief Superintendent."

"Thank you, Inspector, but I'm happy here."

As the two men looked at each other, Andy, remembering his earlier conversation with the Sergeant, stifled his laughter. The Inspector turned on his heels with a parting comment,

"We shall see." The door crashed shut again as he left the building.

"God help us if he ever becomes Chief," the Sergeant said with a wry shake of his head and a smile, ,. "Right laddie, let's get cleared up and go home."

As the shift was signing off, the prisoners could be heard shouting to each other, letting each other know who was 'in' for the weekend and what they had been charged with.

Andy was leaving the office when Joe returned with the package. "See you tonight, Andy," Joe said.

"Aye, I suppose so," he replied as he made his way to his car.

As he slipped the key into the ignition, Andy thought to himself, *What a week! Full moon and madness! One more night to go, and surely Sunday will be quieter.*

Andy, a city boy, didn't realise that village life did not respect Sundays, or any other days of the week.

The near future for Andy and Joe was about to change both their lives, as events would challenge and test their camaraderie and trust.

Chapter Eight

Sunday - 22:20 the last of the night shifts. Andy was sitting in the muster room, alone with his thoughts about the future as a cop. The unthinkable was being rejected at some point during his probationary period. That would mean returning to the building trade, with its lack of job security due to the lack of contracts, or the weather, especially during the winter.

He looked at the wanted posters circulated by force headquarters. Intelligence bulletins were pinned to the information boards, covered with a plain sheet of paper to prevent unauthorised eyes viewing the details.

It was now 22:40. Andy watched as his colleagues dragged themselves in for one last shift. The strain of the past seven nights was revealed on the tired and exhausted expressions.

Sergeant Jimmy Black, with almost thirty years' service on the streets, was a walking encyclopaedia on the laws of Scotland. The day he hung up his baton and handcuffs would be a sad day for the force. He could have reached greater heights in the job, but he was all for his men. This flew in the face of his bosses influencing their recommendation for his promotion. All of which had long passed him by.

Andy sat and reviewed in his mind the details he knew of each officer as they entered.

Constable George 'Georgie' Smith, another of the senior officers on the shift with 25 years' service, was married and had a son and daughter. He lived locally and had built up a fearsome reputation in the village. From day one, he had no ambition to rise through the ranks, but he too could be relied on in times of trouble.

Constable Joe McGrath, forty-one years of age, with a late start in the police force following a career in the insurance business, was now Andy's tutor officer. He was the one who had to get Andy through his probation, come hell or high water. Joe had never 'lost' a probationer in his ten-year career.

Constable June Brown, thirty-one, had five years' service and she was the sole female officer on the shift, She was well-respected by everyone, and a very intelligent and reliable officer. She usually got all the horror cases involving women and children. Above all, she gave as good as she got in the banter department.

Constable Johnny McMurdo was another of the Highlanders in the office, and was fluent in Scottish Gaelic. He was the most important man in the office after the Sergeant. He was the man who had responsibility for the welfare of the prisoners and the smooth running of the office. He also had over twenty-five years' service.

As for the rest of the troops, they trailed in one by one: Billy, Stevie, Brian, and Daniel. Each one had been a total stranger only a few weeks ago, but now his life could depend on one or all of them, in the same way as their life could depend on him.

Sergeant Black entered the room, sat at his desk, and looked at each of his Constables. "Early shift, nothing to report. Late shift, even less. They must have all been at church today," he chuckled. "This has been a good week for us. We've taken some good bodies off the street, and I'm delighted to say they are thoroughly enjoying their stay with us."

The Sergeant had a wicked sense of humour knowing that good bodies meant gangsters.

He continued. "Right. Let's make sure we have everything together before this lot go to court tomorrow."

Johnny stood waiting for the officers as they went through to the charge bar to get their radios "Sergeant, there's a report of a missing person just come in. Fourteen-year-old female, potentially vulnerable. Problem is - it's the Johnstone household up at the graveyard."

"Christ, that's all I need on the last night." The Sergeant sighed. "Whose area is it in?"

Johnny looked over at Joe and Andy.

"Sorry guys, it's yours."

"Joe, stay here with me," the Sergeant asserted. "We have to go over everything that's happened this weekend and make sure everything is tickety-boo. June, take Andy up to the house and get the details for the missing person report."

"Well, Andy," June declared as she drove. "You've certainly made an impression on the shift."

"Thanks."

"What were you doing before this?"

"I was in the building trade, as a bricklayer taking work wherever I could find it, making as much as I could, as the winter months were downtime for me and the rest of the squad."

"Oh right. So that's where the muscles come from then. Nice to have a bit of eye candy on this shift!"

47

"Geez, I was warned you were forward," Andy jested.

"Take it Joe warned you. Well he was right!" she laughed.

June drove into the darkness, passing by the local graveyard towards a long and winding road that lead to a large detached villa.

When they arrived, the villa was lit by only a few lights on the outside and one single light in a room.

"Okay, here we are. Do you want this one, Andy?"

"Er, okay, why not."

As they knocked on the door and waited, Andy scanned the area: the night was still. Nothing was moving. The door swung open, and Andy turned to see a woman standing there.

"Mrs. Johnstone?" he inquired.

"Yes."

"You, er, reported your daughter missing?"

"Yes."

"May we come in?"

"Oh, yes, of course." June and Andy were shown into the hallway of the detached villa and lead into the sprawling lounge. "What do you need, Constable?"

"Can I start with your full details please, Mrs. Johnstone?"

""Helen Johnstone is my name. I'm forty-four, and I'm a nurse at the local hospital."

"Now the full details of your daughter beginning with her name, age, date of birth, and then a complete description. Also, when you last saw her what was she wearing? A recent photograph would help, and a list of her friends, beginning with the ones close to her.

"Angela Johnstone. She's fourteen, and attends Bankvale High School. She is five-foot-four, slim build, long blonde hair, blue eyes, and she has no marks or scars on her body that I am aware of. I last saw her on Friday morning wearing her school uniform."

Andy looked at her inquisitively as she rattled off the details. "Constable, I'm used to reporting people missing from the hospital, as I work in the psychiatric unit. It's second nature to me."

She paused for a moment, "I've never heard Angela talk about friends. She's a bit of a loner, and an only child, also."

"Does she wear any jewellery?"

"The one thing she will never part with is a necklace her dad gave her with the initial 'A'. It's gold."

"You said she was in her school uniform," Andy pointed out. "So, when did you last see her?

"Since I've been working night-shifts all weekend and sleeping during the day, Friday morning was the last time I saw her."

"So, has she been home since you last saw her?"

"I presume she has but her father would know."

"Can I have the most recent photograph you have of her, please?"

"Sure, no problem." Helen left the room and returned quickly, producing a recent school photograph of Angela, which she handed to Andy.

Andy glanced up as a man entered the room.

"Hello, sir. And you are?"

"Angela's father." The man's tone was curt.

Mrs. Johnstone flashed her husband a look - her eyes narrowed.

"Sir, when did you last see your daughter?"

"Ermm, Friday. Yeah, Friday night, at about eight or eight-thirty. She said she was going out with friends."

"I will need your full details also, sir."

"Eric Johnstone. I'm forty-five. I live here with my wife Helen and daughter Angela and, for your information Constable, I'm a company director with one company, and chief executive of another. All to do with the import and export of steel. I'm also standing soon as an independent candidate at the next general election, and the last thing I need is Angela as the subject of a police inquiry - causing me grief."

Andy worked to calm and mask his disbelief at the father's attitude. "When you last saw your daughter, what was she wearing?"

"How the hell should I know!"

It was his turn to glance at his wife. "Now, constables, I expect you will start a search for my daughter immediately with the rest of your colleagues. As you may have deduced, a person in my position has friends in high places in the police, so I shall expect you to report to me or my wife with the progress of your inquiries. Daily."

"Can I ask you both something? It's almost midnight on a Sunday evening, and neither of you has seen your daughter since Friday. Why the hell was she not been reported missing before now?"

An awkward silence followed.

"We just thought she was out with friends," Helen spoke up, finally. "At a sleepover, or something."

"One last thing. Can we search the house, and any outbuildings?"

"Certainly."

"Why do you need to do that?" demanded Mr. Johnstone.

"Just a matter of course, sir."

Andy and June went through the house methodically, room by room, starting at Angela's. Eric Johnstone was right behind them the whole time. June stood at the door as Andy went through the wardrobe and dressing table, looking for anything that might indicate where Angela had gone. Andy looked up and saw June talking to Eric Johnstone, who he could not see, and he quickly pulled back the cover on Angela's bed before putting it back again.

"Thank you for the photograph and your cooperation," June told the parents once they were done. "Hopefully, we'll have Angela back to you soon."

As the officers were leaving the house, Andy's blood was still boiling after Eric Johnstone's comment about his 'friends in high places'. Andy being Andy, he turned and walked back to Mr Johnstone.

"Sir, the next time you're having drinks with your 'friends in high places', don't forget to add that your fourteen-year-old daughter had not been seen for over forty-eight hours before your wife reported her missing. It will be on my report for them to see. Goodnight folks."

June got into the car, followed by Andy, and drove off. Only shortly after they had driven off, she parked on a dark road not far from the house. She switched off the engine, looked at Andy, and gently banged her head on the steering wheel.

"Andy, Andy, Andy. Joe was right, you have all the makings of being a nightmare or being brilliant. You can't say that to a guy like him. It'll go straight back to whoever he knows."

"Good. Because it's going on the missing person form."

She scowled at him.

"June, I know I'm new here, but I've worked with some hard people who've been in jail over the years, and I've listened to them. My mates' fathers were nearly all cops, and I heard them talking in their houses. Now, in my humble opinion, this one stinks. And here's what you didn't see while you were talking to him at the door of her bedroom. I pulled back her bedcover, and the sheet on the bed was heavily stained around the centre. I think she has a boyfriend or... Also was no sign of her school uniform anywhere in the bedroom. Finally, her mother said she was a loner, then said she was with friends at a sleepover."

June listened in shock.

"I don't believe you! You have some balls, I'll give you that."

Headlights on and engine purring, they headed for the office. Andy held the photograph of Angela, tapping it gently on the fingers of his other hand, being careful not to damage it, as it could be the last photograph ever taken of her.

When they got to the office, Andy was filling in the missing person forms when Joe turned to him,

"The Sergeant is looking for you."

Andy went to the Sergeant's office.

"Shut the door," barked Sergeant barked. "Sign those labels there and there for the cocaine drop." Andy did as he was told. "Right laddie, keep up the good work, you've done well this week. Be careful, though, what you do to people when subduing them. If you don't use the methods taught at college, it could get you into trouble with the Complaints and Discipline Department. Do you follow my drift?"

"Yes, Sergeant." Andy knew exactly what he meant.

Heading back to the front office, he was ambushed by Joe and June.

"Hey, you." Joe pointed at Andy. "The kitchen. Now."

Joe pulled him in there for a confab. "June told me what happened tonight with the missing kid, and what you said to her father. What have you got to say for yourself?"

"Not a lot." Andy looked at the two of them. "Joe," he murmured, eyes pointed at the floor. "I was taken aback when we left the house. I didn't expect to be taken down a dark road by a mature, female police officer, headlights extinguished and the engine turned off. And worse still, I didn't expect her to bang her head on the steering wheel. But I must admit it was rather different than being out with you, we've never done that before."

"June!" Joe exclaimed. "You never told me you took the new start down a dark road. Bloody hell, you normally wait a few months!"

"I know," she fired back. "But have you seen those muscles?" The confab was over, and everyone was laughing.

"Be careful big man," Joe advised him.

Day by day, Andy felt that the camaraderie with the other officers on his shift was getting better, but he had a long way to go yet.

"Andy!" called the Sergeant. "Has that missing person form been submitted yet?"

"I have it!" Johnny McMurdo shouted back. "And it's currently being circulated force-wide."

"Right. June, take Andy back out with you for the rest of the night, and no stopping on dark roads. Joe, you have court in the morning. Finish what you're doing and head home for a sleep after the tea break. It's quiet tonight." The Sergeant strolled down the corridor with what was becoming a familiar look to Andy: his jacket open and a cigarette hanging from his mouth, ash falling everywhere.

The Sergeant walked into the front office, sat in his reclining chair and put his feet up on the large oak desk crossing his legs and putting his hands behind his head. He reflected on the success of his officers' efforts, and the people they had in custody for court the following morning.

A car was heard to draw up outside in the early hours of the morning. Sergeant Jimmy Black never budged as he took a long draw on his cigarette as the front door opened and in walked the Shift Inspector.

"Good morning, Sergeant. Nice to see you looking so relaxed. How many men do you have on shift tonight?"

Having released a few of the men for sleep before the court the following morning, he turned to the Inspector.

"Well, sir. Enough for the tasks in hand."

"Good. The other offices are a bit short tonight on manpower, so if anything happens I'll give you a call." Little did he know that only four of the ten were out and about.

Outside, Andy and June sat in a car parked on the street, waiting to see if anyone of interest would drive through the village.

"Well, Andy, our first night out together was eventful," June remarked.

"Yep."

"You're not the most talkative type, are you?"

"Nope."

"Andy, are you winding me up?"

"Yep." He chuckled.

"Are you married, or have a girlfriend?"

"No and no."

"So, what's your plan for your days off?"

"Probably hit the gym and do a bit of training."

"Oh aye. What's that thing you're a black belt in? Joe told me about it."

"Origami," he answered with a straight face.

"Aye, ah knew it was something foreign." She laughed.

06:30

Thirty minutes before their finishing time, a call came.

"Zulu 1, return to the office to see your Sergeant."

"Roger, control," June replied. They sped back to the office and went into the Sergeant's office.

"Right, see this form? It has no friends or associates listed for further inquires to be made this morning by the early shift."

"Sergeant," Andy began, looking at the Sergeant. "This is what I found strange. Her mother said she was an only child and a loner, then a short time later they thought she may have been at a sleepover."

Sergeant Black looked at Andy, then June.

"And your thoughts are?"

There was total silence in the room until Andy broke.

"Let's find her."

"Yep," June agreed.

Andy and June were dismissed as the early shift arrived. They were in the locker room alone.

"So, what's your plans for your days off, June?"

"Not a lot."

"What does that mean?"

"Nothing."

As they strolled out onto the street, Andy looked at June.

"See you for the late shift, June?"

"Yeah, Thursday for me. I've got a day off."

"Okay." He watched her walking towards her car. There was something very attractive about June, a woman older than him by six years. Small, slim, with short blonde hair, June was certainly attractive, and she had a great sense of humour.

Andy unlocked his car and got in. The engine kicked to life.

When he looked up, he noticed for the first time that between the houses he could see the hill and road leading to the graveyard and the Johnstone villa. In the daylight, he could see that the villa overlooked the graveyard. The long winding road had been deceiving in the darkness.

Where are you Angela? Where the hell are you? he wondered as he drove off, rest and relaxation pending.

Chapter Nine

I t was 10:00 Monday, Andy's day off. Three hours after finishing a night shift, he was at the gym, pounding the pool, length after length. Andy's mind was working overtime as he thought about Angela: fourteen years old and missing. Dragging himself out of the pool, he headed for the sauna. The heat made the sweat drip down his forehead and chest. He gently poured water onto the heater, creating more steam to circulate around the Swedish-built, timber-lined sauna, until it was misted in condensation.

Lying on the upper timber bench seat alone with his eyes closed in the sauna, sweat pouring off his torso, the door opened and closed. Andy never flinched as the person sat down on the lower bench.

"Hi Andy, how are you?" asked Catherine.

"Shattered, to be truthful, Catherine."

"Me too. This has been a horrible weekend, between one thing and another."

A calm silence descended.

"I knew I'd find you here this morning," she said finally.

Andy said nothing for a while. Then, he jokingly remarked, "Catherine, this is the one place I can totally chill out, and you happen to be here."

"Sorry, Andy." She sounded hurt. "I'll go. It was wrong to seek you out here."

"I didn't mean it that way." Something seemed to have gone astray with his sense of humour. "I'm glad you're here. You know, I don't really know anybody outside the office in this godforsaken village, except for a few of the locals, , and I happen to like you."

"It didn't sound like that. "Listen, I've got something to tell you. Someone close to me is missing."

Surely not was the first thing that flashed through Andy's mind,

"Andy I need to speak to you."

He sat up and slipped down onto the lower bench gazing into Catherine's eyes. They seemed so sad.

"Fancy a coffee?"

She nodded.

Andy went into the changing room. That whole situation in the sauna was strained, to say the least.

Surely it was a coincidence she knew someone who was missing the same weekend Andy got his first missing person report.

Andy watched Catherine stare into her skinny latte as they sat in the café. She was stirring it round and round with her spoon. Her eyes were transfixed on the coffee spinning in the slender, fluted glass cup. Andy sat with his chin on his folded hands, waiting for her to break the silence on what was troubling her.

People were being served at the counter, cups were being rattled, groups of women were chatting, and local school children were heading to their swimming lessons, but as Andy looked at Catherine, there was total silence, like a television on mute.

Catherine looked up at Andy. One tear followed another forming a trickle down her cheeks she wiped the tears away.

"I feel stupid." She glanced around self-consciously. "Andy, there's something about you. I don't know what it is but there's something in you that I trust."

"What is it?" His tone was gentle, almost a caress.

"My sister's daughter is missing."

"Catherine, I've not got the experience for this. I've only been in this job for a couple of weeks."

"Yes, I know. But there's something about you that I've never felt before in a person."

They sat in silence again for what seemed like an eternity. Andy edged his chair back while sitting at the table.

"Can I ask something?"

"Yes."

"What's your sister's first name?"

"Helen." Catherine looked at him strangely. "Why?"

"Helen Johnstone?"

"Yes. How the hell do you know that?"

Andy told her that he'd taken the missing person report. He also told her that he'd spoken at length to her sister and Angela's dad, Eric.

"What do you mean? Eric, Angela's dad? Did that dick say he was Angela's father? He's no more Angela's father than I am."

"Catherine, we can't discuss this here. In fact, I'm not sure I should even be speaking to you about this. Do you have your car with you?"

"Yes"

"Okay, we can go and talk off record. Where should we go?"

"How about your place?"

"Sure, no problem, just follow me."

As both cars left the sports centre, Catherine followed Andy, tears streaming down her face.Her gut feeling told her this was the guy who would find her niece.

Andy pulled up outside his red sandstone flat, making sure there was a parking place for Catherine beside him. As they entered the secured common close, with its well-worn, grey concrete stairs, Andy led the way up to the third floor.

"You alright with this?"

"Yes," Catherine replied, as she slipped her hand into Andy's and gripped it tightly.

Andy unlocked the door and led Catherine into the top-floor flat. She surveyed the surroundings and commented.

"I'm impressed."

"What's that supposed to mean?"

"Well, it's clean for a lad's pad."

"See, if you go over to the kitchen worktop, there's this thing called a kettle. Click the button and the water will boil. Make up some tea or coffee, or whatever you like."

"Right." Catherine laughed knowing Andy was trying to lighten her mood.

Andy went into his room to change out of his tracksuit.

"Brilliant view from here!" called Catherine, as she looked out of the bay window at the road and the green rolling hills.

"Yeah," he agreed as he came back in. Andy was back in his familiar light blue jeans and a tight T-Shirt, no shoes or socks. It was his flat after all.

"Tea or coffee?"

"Coffee please, one sugar. I like mine without milk, so don't forget that in the future, Catherine."

"What future? First thing's first - I love my sister, and will do anything to protect her, is that understood?"

Andy nodded. They sat facing each other on the long couch.

"Good, now listen please as I will say this only once. Helen is a good bit older than me. She married Eric ten years ago, and she already had Angela, who was four when they married. I'll give Eric his due, he's brought her up like his own. He doesn't have any other kids, nor was he ever married before he met Helen, and he's always treated Angela as his daughter.

Catherine paused to sip the coffee. "He's had numerous directorships in various companies. You know he could be heading for Parliament at the next election and Helen has a great future in psychiatric nursing. This thing with Angela could destroy all that if it goes public."

Andy was totally out of his depth, not used to dealing with people of wealth and power. He was relying on his East End wits. Suddenly a fuse blew in Andy's thought process, and suddenly he snapped.

"Your niece is missing. When I left the office this morning, she hadn't been found. You come looking for me, and all you can think about is her parents' careers? That's the same attitude I got from them last night. What's wrong with you people? There's a kid out missing for God's sake!"

"I realise that! And yes that is what is most important - to find my niece! I don't know why but I felt I could trust you."

"You've worked in the hospital for years. You must know lots of cops, so why me?"

"I told you I don't know why - I just feel that you might be able to help my sister - and help me."

"Okay. You only have to be honest upfront with me and the inquiry team."

"Yes."

Andy rose from the couch and paced the floor, coffee cup in hand, his gut-churning.

"What shift are you on tomorrow?" he asked.

"I'm off tomorrow, why?"

"Because we should meet up again if your niece hasn't been found. Gym, same time?"

"Yes. Are you kicking me out?" Catherine got to her feet.

"Yep. But before you go, please give me your home phone number."

Andy looked down and drew Catherine into a warm and gentle embrace. After a moment he pulled away to quickly produce pen and paper. She wrote down her home phone number and handed it to him. As she was standing at the door, Catherine leaned forward and kissed him on the cheek.

"Thank you," she whispered.

Andy watched her leave down the stairs before he closed the door and sat down.

I can't believe what I just did. He sat on his couch with his head in his hands. I fancy her like crazy and I've just booted her out the door, still not knowing whether she's even single. These thoughts were racing through his head, but they would have to wait, given the circumstances.

Pulling on socks, shoes, and a leather jacket, he headed for home. No matter where he was living, home would always be the East End of Glasgow.

Within thirty minutes, Andy was home. He drove slowly through the tenement-lined streets, which held memories both pleasant and unpleasant. Within minutes, he was in the more 'well off' area. Truth was, in Parkton, nobody was more well-off than anyone else. It was just that some folks had more luck in being allocated a four-in-a-block house with a smart garden and flowers blooming in the summer. While other flowers were choked by the fumes from the cars on the main road.

As Andy drove along the narrow streets and looked at the grey, roughcast houses. Only a few years ago, he had been playing football on this street. He looked at the 'police houses', wondering who lived there now. Turning right, he was in seriously familiar territory: the street where his grandparents had lived, where he would play as a child.

The windows in the houses were all updated with double glazing, and the gardens were smart and tidy. Engaging first gear he remember odd numbers to the left, even numbers to the right.

As the car came to a halt at 32 Gatefield Street, everything became too much for Andy. He had been in and out of that house since the day he was born, up until the death of his grandparents six years apart.

Who lives there now? Andy recalled the great, the good and the sad times he'd had in that house with his family: birthdays, Christmas, New Year. He'd had it all there. Andy was beginning to wish he had never gone down that particular street.

He finally arrived at his destination a minute or two later. Knocking on the door, he awaited a reply. Slowly the door opened. An old, grey-haired woman stood there.

"Mrs. Green." Andy waved. "I'm really sorry to disturb you, but can I ask, is your husband Billy here?"

"Yes, he is. Who are you?"

"Mrs. Green, you probably don't remember me. My name is Andy Blackmore."

She moved closer, looking at his face, and realisation slowly dawned. "Andy... your grandparents lived up the street a bit. Come on in son, come on in. Billy's in the living room." She guided Andy to the living room

"Billy, look who's here! It's young Andy Blackmore."

"At last," Billy huffed. "I've been looking for him for years, on account of him and his mates' football hooliganism."

Andy sat down on the sofa. He could have cried. Billy was a fearsome sight, walking down the street in his black uniform and long flowing raincoat, with a moustache like a Sergeant Major in the army. Now, he was a mere shadow of himself, in his eighties. He was sitting in a large worn leather armchair, staring out of the window. He turned to look at Andy.

"Billy - Andy is here to speak to you."

"Aye, is he here to be charged with a breach of the peace?" Annie looked at Andy who nodded at her.

"Yes, sir."

"Stand up when speaking to me," barked Billy.

Annie laid a cup of tea on the small, highly polished table.

Andy snapped to attention, as did Billy. Word perfect Billy charged Andy with a breach of the peace. "Have you any reply?"

"Yes, sir. I need your help."

"What's your occupation?"

"Police officer, sir."

Billy looked at Andy quizzically. "Sit here then."

Andy took Billy's limp hand as they sat opposite each other. Andy recognised that the man he was terrified of as a child was in his last years, and showed the signs of suffering from early dementia.

"Mr. Green, you have no idea how much influence you had on my life. When I was a child, we were all terrified of you. But now, as a fellow officer, I need you."

Andy took a massive chance by relating the story of the missing teenager. Billy was staring out the window when Andy finished, and Annie shook her head from side to side when he failed to respond.

Andy stood to leave, and apologised to Mrs. Green for his unannounced visit.

"Has the police service been in touch with you to offer assistance?" he asked her.

"No."

"Well, they will be soon, Mrs. Green. I will get in touch with Headquarters and advise them of your situation. I am sure that the retired police officers association will have someone come out and visit you."

As Andy opened the living room door, Billy called out,

"You've not been dismissed, Constable." Andy stood still. He could see Billy's old cop-brain working.

"

Remember leave no stone unturned. And I mean no stone."

Andy gave Mrs. Green a gentle hug on his way out.

"I'll be in touch. Take care now."

As Andy headed westwards to his flat, Billy's words rang in his ears. The old cop, who had terrified him as a child, may have acted as his mentor for the last time. If this was the case, Andy was the proudest man alive, especially if Billy was right.

Andy got back to his flat later than he'd hoped to, and the red neon light on his phone was flashing, indicating that he had a recorded message. He pushed the play button.

"Andy, it's Catherine. Call me when you get in, please."

It was nine o'clock. Not too late. He hit the redial button. Andy listened as the phone at the opposite end of the line rang and rang. Just as he was about to hang up, a male voice answered,

"Hello?"

"Hi, could I speak to Catherine please?"

"Who's calling?"

"Andy."

"Andy who?"

"Hey, is this a quiz? If Catherine is there, tell her Andy is returning her call."

"Catherine, it's for you!" the man shouted.

"Hi, Catherine here."

"Catherine, it's Andy."

"Oh, Andy, great to hear from you! How was your day at the gym?" Catherine's voice sounded strained and artificial.

"Catherine? What's going on?"

"Sure, no problem. Not doing anything anyway. See you shortly."

The line went dead.

Andy sat and waited for a visit from Catherine, but at midnight he headed for bed. Something was not right about this whole thing.

No visit, nothing! Who was that man who answered the phone and sounded so annoyed? A husband, a boyfriend? I don't need this.

Chapter Ten

D aylight streamed through the window of Andy's third floor flat as the alarm rang. It was just after nine. Andy lay on his side, covered by his duvet, and looked at the clock. Get up, training calls.

By ten, he arrived at the gym and looked around the car park, but there was no red Audi in sight.

He got changed into his Karate gi, wrapped his black belt around his waist, and headed into the dojo. At this time on a Tuesday morning, there were only about a dozen people training in the dojo. Andy ploughed through his katas like a man possessed.

"Andy." His sensei approached him. "What's up?"

"Sorry, I don't know what you mean." Andy continued his kata.

"Maybe you should take a break before you injure yourself. The way you're training this morning…"

Andy bowed before the sensei and left the dojo in silence.

Sensei Yamachi, instructor and friend to Andy for many years, helped get him to where he was as a second dan black belt. He knew something was wrong with Andy as he watched him leave the dojo and head towards the changing rooms.

Light streamed through the skylight window in the room, which was lined with wooden benches and orderly grey lockers. Andy opened his locker and pulled out his sports bag, throwing it onto the floor and slamming the door closed, the sound reverberating around the room. Initially, he sat down. Then, for some reason, he found himself lying on his back, entwined hands resting on his forehead, and staring at the ceiling. He didn't even hear the door open.

"Andy?"

"Yes?" He was still staring at the ceiling.

"No matter what troubles are around you, stay focused."

"Yes, Sensei."

Slowly, he rose from the bench, showered, and changed into his denims and T-shirt. Then, he headed to the café.

"Coffee, no milk, as requested." Catherine was sitting at a table, smiling at him. "See, I didn't forget."

Andy shook his head. "What are you doing here?"

"I'm here to see you."

"Why?"

"Because I have to."

"Have they found Angela yet?"

"No. No they haven't."

"So what was that all about last night Catherine? I returned your call and I end up with some angry guy on the phone. Then I get a fake conversation with you, and a parting comment of 'see you shortly'. What the hell was that?"

Andy's annoyance was obvious, and he looked Catherine straight in her eyes. "Well?"

Catherine got up to leave.

"Enjoy your coffee, Andy."

"Catherine, sit down or this is over before it even starts. It's your call."

She sat down again.

"It's difficult, it's always difficult, the situation I'm in." After a pause, she continued. "The guy that answered the phone was my brother."

"Okay."

"You have to meet him to understand."

"Right."

Coffees finished, Louise the young waitress came over to the table

"Well?"

"Well, what?"

"Geez Andy, ask her out for God's sake."

After clearing the table, Louise walked away.

"Who the hell does she think she is?" Andy chuckled.

"Emm, my cousin Louise, actually." Catherine laughed.

"This village is like a scene from Deliverance. Everyone's related! All I have to do now is start playing the banjo on a rocking chair."

"So, are you going to ask me out or not?"

"Well," hedged Andy. "Would a thirty-five-year-old lady like a date with a twenty-five-year-old guy?"

"Yes, she would."

"How about tonight, but only if she's unmarried and unattached?"

"Yes to both, and I would love that, but should we? Should I?"

"It will be a much needed distraction for just one evening."

"Okay." Catherine agreed.

"Great, I'll pick you up at around seven, if that suits?"

"Yep, I'll be ready."

"I need an address. Always helps when collecting someone on a first date."

Catherine wrote the details on a napkin.

"What's this?" said a familiar voice.

Andy looked up. "Oh, hey Joe."

"Hey Andy, hi Catherine. So, what's this then?"

"Coffee," Andy replied curtly. "What are you doing here, Joe?"

"Well, this is what happens when you've got kids. Swim time. Speaking of which, I should get going. Bye Catherine. See you, Andy."

"Cheers, Joe," Catherine said. Andy noticed her watching Joe as he walked away. Then, she got to her feet as well. "Okay, see you tonight Andy." And with that, she disappeared around the corner.

Andy, being the punctual type, arrived at exactly seven o'clock', dressed in a grey suit and tie, white shirt, and gleaming black shoes. He knocked on the door. When itopened, his opening remark was, "Stunning."

Catherine wore a black top under a red suit, and black shoes.

"Come in," she purred, as Andy stepped into the comfortable, little ground-floor flat.

"Who are you?" someone behind Andy demanded. He turned around and looked at a man much taller than him.

"Hi, I'm Andy."

"What are you doing here?"

"I'm—"

Before he could finish his sentence, Catherine interjected, "Andy's a friend of mine. Don't worry, I'm safe with him. Andy, this is Barry, my brother."

"Pleased to meet you, Barry." Andy held out his right hand to shake Barry's, but he just stared at him. Andy wondered Barry had some sort of learning difficulty.

Catherine came around to stand in front of Barry and took his hand. "Barry, listen to me, I want you to go to bed when the alarm rings at eleven, do you understand?"

"Yes." He watched Andy his eyes wide with child-like curiosity.

Shortly afterward Catherine and Andy left the flat.

"Let's take this car to your flat and leave it there," Catherine suggested once they reached the street. "We can get a taxi into the city. I just need a good night out."

Andy did as requested and they made their way into Glasgow city centre by taxi, to the restaurant that Andy had booked for them.

Catherine ordered the Salmon Wellington, while Andy went for the mixed fish plate.

"Andy, this is my first real date in ten years."

"You're joking." Andy raised an eyebrow.

"No, I'm not. Who would want to go out with me, and have to cope with Barry as well? I've looked after him since Helen married Eric. There's nobody else to take care of him."

"So you don't have a boyfriend, or a secret lover?Nobody?"

"No."

As they exchanged stories about their childhoods, they had dessert with coffee.

"Can I have the bill please?" Andy asked the waitress.

"Certainly, sir."

"Andy, can we go Dutch, please?" Catherine piped up.

"No chance. But if you insist, I'll let you buy me a cocktail at a little bar I know nearby."

"Done."

As they left the restaurant, Catherine took Andy's arm and drew herself close to him as they walked to the nearby cocktail bar. In the corner, a man played the piano, serenading the customers. Andy and Catherine sat chatting about music and movies - avoiding anything any work-related subjects.

Behind Catherine, a large television showed a photograph of Angela. The subtitles indicated that she had not yet been found and police were increasingly concerned for her welfare. Catherine was totally oblivious to the broadcast.

"Hey, how do you know Joe?" Andy asked to distract himself from the screen. "Or is that a silly question?"

"Well, yes, it is." She smiled. "You know the police are rarely away from the hospital, so I just got to know him over the years."

"You know, I noticed something at the sports centre today."

"Oh, what was that?"

"When he walked away, your eyes followed him.

"Must have been your imagination." Her tone was nonchalant. "Can we head off now?"

Soon, they were out on the street, waiting for their taxi.

As they got into the taxi, Andy requested, "Alexander Place first then Westfield Place, Bankvale please."

Once they were en route, Catherine leaned forward to speak to the driver.

"Just go straight to Westfield Place, please." Catherine wrapped her arms around him in the back seat of the taxi. "Nightcap at yours, please?"

"Brandy okay for you?"

"Sure," she purred.

The living room was already aglow from a small lamp Andy had put on a timer.

"Music, Catherine?"

"Yes, that would be nice."

"Genre?"

"Oh, anything smooth, please. Or how about we just put the radio on?"

"Check out my LPs, you might find something there," he suggested, wanting to avoid the TV or radio, in case it broadcast news about Angela.

"You like the blues. That'll do me then."

Andy took out two crystal brandy glasses from a box.

"Ice?"

"Yes, please."

Ice cubes chinked in the glasses as the brandies were poured. Andy handed Catherine her glass before sitting on the couch beside her. She kicked off her shoes, swung her body around, and lay against him. She put her legs up onto the couch and placed her bare feet on the armrest.

Andy wrapped his arm around her body, and felt her fingertips trace the length of his arm.

"Do you know how long it's been since I've done this? It feels like forever. I need more of this, Andy."

"You can stay tonight if you want. You take the bedroom. I'll camp out here."

"You know, you're a gentleman, Andy."

As the brandies were finished and the blues was fading, Catherine leaned over and kissed Andy gently on his lips..

"Bedtime," she announced, standing up promptly. "You can join me if you wish. As you said recently, your call."

When Andy went into the bedroom minutes later, Catherine was already under the duvet. He joined her and turned off the lights. Catherine snuggled into Andy.

"Please hold me, Andy," she whispered. "All I want is the feel of your arms around me."

Andy held her and kissed her forehead.

Nothing was said as he felt Catherine relaxing into his arms and nodding off into a gentle sleep.

Chapter Eleven

A ndy awoke around nine. Catherine was sleeping in his arms, her head on his chest. She slowly started to stir, opening her eyes. She kissed his chest, gently.

"Would you like breakfast?" Andy whispered into her ear.

"Tea and toast would be nice, please," she murmured.

"I'll be a few minutes then." He placed a kiss on her cheek.

A few moments later, Andy returned to the room carrying two mugs of tea and toast unceremoniously piled on a plate and all were placed on a bedside table. He pulled back the duvet, slipped into bed beside her, and handed her a large mug of tea and a slice of toast

"There's something I need to ask you," Catherine mumbled through the toast in her mouth.

"Okay." Andy took a bite of toast.

"Not that I'm objecting, in any way, but do you always make breakfast naked?"

"Erm, come to think about it, yeah."

"I look forward to seeing you make it again, in that case."

"And when do you suppose that will be then?"

"How about Saturday and Sunday? You're on a late shift, there's no excuse."

"That would be nice. But listen, I'm a very private person. I always have been. So I've no intention of telling anyone about us just now."

"I understand. Neither have I, to be honest."

"I've left out clean towels in the bathroom if you want to have a shower before you go."

"Thanks, that would be good."

Catherine finished her tea, walked naked to the bathroom, and closed the door behind her. A short time later, she reappeared, hair and body wrapped in towels , and lay on top of the duvet beside Andy, staring at the white ceiling.

Andy rolled onto his front under the duvet and looked at Catherine.

"Penny for your thoughts."

"These thoughts would cost you a lot more than a penny." She grinned with devilment. Andy leaned over and kissed Catherine, slowly. "Oh, you're a mind reader as well."

"I better get you back to Barry, or I'll never get to work today."

Shortly after, Andy dropped Catherine off at her flat.

"Thank you, Andy. Until Saturday?"

"I look forward to it."

It was half-past one and, as usual, Andy was in the office well before his start time. He read through the intelligence bulletins about the local worthies.

The Sergeant interrupted his work. "Andy, can I have a word before the shift arrives?"

Andy followed the sergeant

"Come in here and shut the door." Andy did as requested. "What happened at the Johnstone house the other night could have annoyed the bosses."

Oh, I know.

"Mr. Johnstone just made it clear that he knew high-ranking police officers. He also made demands about reporting directly to him on the search for his daughter. So, I suggested that next time you saw them, discussing why he failed to report her missing for forty-eight hours."

"I'll clear it up." The Sergeant shook his head. "But no more throwaway lines, Andy."

"Yes, Sergeant."

The 14:00 briefing took its usual format of a round-up of events. The Sergeant reported that Pat had been released from custody by the Procurator Fiscal, pending further enquiry. The 'deal' had a successful outcome.

Finally, the Sergeant produced the missing person form with the photograph of Angela Johnstone attached. He scanned the end of the form for new information, which stated that there was still no trace of her in the village, and that she did not have any close friends.

"She has a bank account," he read aloud. "But that hasn't been used. Her passport is still in the house, and there's no clothing missing from her room. Her purse is missing, and her parents thought that she may have about twenty pounds with her."

The Sergeant announced the same teams, pairing together June and Andy again.

"You two, come with me," the Sergeant commanded. "June, weren't you meant to be off today?"

"Yeah, but I have an appointment next week, so I'll take the day off then."

"Right. Let's make some inroads into this missing person case. Get down to the school and see what you can find out. And keep me in the loop."

"Sergeant. June. I need to speak to you both," Andy announced as they went into the Sergeant's office. "Eric Johnstone is not Angela Johnstone's father." June and Sergeant Black both stared at Andy.

"And how long have you known this?" the Sergeant demanded.

"Since Monday. I heard it when I was at the gym. I'll write the information on the back of the form."

"You have no evidence, so write reak-ins 'Information has been received'. Start it that way and you're covered if it proves to be false."

Andy updated the form.

On arrival at the secondary school, Andy and June made their way to the public reception area.

"How may I help you?"

"I'm Constable Brown and this is Constable Blackmore. Would it be possible to see the headteacher, please?"

"Can I tell him what this is about?"

"Certainly. It's a missing person enquiry."

"Oh, alright."

The receptionist spoke to someone on a telephone before turning to them.

"Go along the corridor there, first door on the left. Mr. Sweeney and Ms. Berger, will see you there."

"Thanks for your help."

As they entered the office and closed the door, they introduced themselves to the staff.

"Are you the Andy Blackmore that went to school with me in the East End of Glasgow?" Ms. Berger inquired.

"Yes, Susan, I am. Small world, huh?"

"It certainly is."

"Is this about Angela Johnstone?" the headteacher, Mr. Sweeney interjected.

"Yes, sir. It is," June confirmed.

"It came as a total shock to the school, staff and pupils alike. Most of us heard about it on the news. Her parents hadn't contacted the school to say why she was absent. Angela's a very bright girl, liked by all the staff, and, unlike some here, she's never caused a minute's problem. Though, some of us have noticed that she's a bit of, well, a loner. "

As Andy took notes, June noticed that Ms. Berger could not take her eyes off Andy.

"Can we see Angela's locker?" June asked Mr. Sweeney.

"Yes, she will have. I'll check with reception as to its location and number." Mr Sweeney picked up the telephone.

"So, Ms. Berger, what can you tell us about Angela?"

"Erm, not a lot. I've only arrived here recently, sorry."

"Locker 4B, fourth floor," announced Mr. Sweeney, putting down the receiver.

"Thank you."

"No, not at all."

"Ms. Berger, can you show Andy where it is?"

"Sure thing. C'mon Constable"

June watched them leave the room.

"So, Andy Blackmore," Susan Berger mused as they walked down the corridor. "The last time I heard about you must have been around ten years ago, when you left school and became a plumber."

"Bricklayer, actually," he corrected her, as they got into the lift. "And what about you, Susan? What did you do?"

"Oh, I stayed on at school, then university. And then I went into teaching and got the deputy head job here. I started just after the summer holidays." They exited the lift on the fourth floor and went down another corridor.

"Here we are, Andy." Susan handed Andy the locker key. She leaned against the lockers, looking at him as he opened the door. "Well, I must say, it seems like you've looked after yourself since I last saw you."

"I try to."

"Are you ever in the East End, Andy, or is this home now?"

"No, I'm there a lot. It's still home."

"I'm still living up in Springhill Road."

"Same house?"

"Yep."

When Andy opened the white locker, all he saw inside was a rain jacket hanging on a hook. He searched the pockets but found nothing. On the top shelf were a few pens and pencils. Andy reached in and took out a book. Turning it over, he saw that the front cover read, '***My Diary***'. It was small, leather-bound with a gold lock on the front.

"Do you mind if I take this downstairs, Susan?"

"No, not at all."

Andy closed the door and locked it. He handed the key to Susan, and they returned to the headteacher's office.

"I think this may be the only thing of any significance in the locker." Andy showed June the diary.

"It's locked," June pointed out. "Get Ms. Berger to sign a production label for the diary, in case it's required."

Both officers looked on as Ms. Berger signed the label.

"Thank you both for your assistance." Andy handed them a contact card with his number on it, and he told them to contact him or June if they heard anything of interest.

"See you, Andy."

"Bye Susan." Andy turned to Mr. Sweeney. "Goodbye, sir." Andy closed the door behind them, and wondered about the contents.

"So, Susan. Old school friend?" June quirked an eyebrow.

"Not really, we were just in the same class."

"Well, I think that might all be about to change." June grinned.

"Behave yourself." Andy smirked.

Back at the office, June and Andy went straight to the Sergeant's office, where he was sifting through a mountain of paperwork and shift rotas.

"Get anything?" he grumbled.

"Yes, Sergeant. A diary from her locker at the school." Andy handed it to him.

"The CID is aware of this one, and the Detective Chief Inspector is getting his ear chewed off about why they're not involved. So, he's sending down a couple of guys to coordinate things."

"Mr. Johnstone getting his pals moving then, Sergeant?"

"Listen, that's all sorted, so watch what you're saying," the Sergeant warned him.

"I might have a key to fit that diary's lock, Sergeant," June spoke up and handed him the key.

"Oh, from your own secret diary June?" teased Andy. Sergeant Black just shook his head. With a little fumbling, the clip on the lock fell open.

"Now, let's see what we have here," the Sergeant muttered. After flicking through the pages, he closed the diary and handed it back to June. "You better put this through the production book, and both of you sign the label."

As they were lodging the potential production, June and Andy looked through the contents of the diary.

The entries began innocently enough, during the summer of 1978:

Long summer. I'm bored. Nothing to do except hang about the house, looking out of the window watching the gravediggers. Mum and Dad are always working.

Entries over the next months were few and far between:

The Xmas holidays are coming soon. I wish I had a brother or sister to share things and hang out with.

March 1979 was written in ink:

Made some friends at school, going to visit them, better than being alone in the house. Mum and Dad never ask me if I have friends. They don't care about me so why should I care about them?

As the weeks went by, the diary entries became more graphic.

May 1979:

Had fun today. Stood at the window overlooking graveyard, teasing the workies in my bra and knickers.

In a separate entry in May:

Saw a new guy working in the graveyard. He's kind of cute. Need to find out who he is.

June 1979:

Was at the shops today, met the cute guy from the graveyard and we got talking. His name's Jonny and he told me he doesn't have a girlfriend. So we're going to the cinema on Friday. I'm gonna tell Mum I'm going out with pals, as she'd never let me go out with a guy. My first real date!

July 1979:

> *Saw Jonny tonight after he finished work. Mum was working and Dad was out, as usual. The house was empty. We went up to my room and did it. Twice. I loved it. I felt wanted. I can't wait until the next time.*

June stared at Andy, dismayed, as she realised what this meant.

September 1979:

> *Been seeing Jonny for four months. Told him I was sixteen when we met, can't tell him my real age or he'll leave me. He's my secret. Mum's working the night shift again. Dad's out with his mates. Jonny came over with Greg. They'd been drinking and they both wanted to have sex with me. I refused and put them out. I was pure raging with Jonny.*

November 1979:

> *After we shagged tonight, Jonny told me he didn't want to see me again. I panicked and told him I was pregnant. He said to get rid of it. I'm not really pregnant, but I'm not going to tell him the truth. And if Mum or Dad find out about this, I'll tell them the same. That'll teach them to ignore me.*

June stopped reading the diary.

"We have to get it confirmed that this really is her handwriting. There's nothing to say that any of this is true. It could all be a figment of a teenage girl's imagination, after all. If this is her diary, and this is true, we have to find out who Jonny is."

Joe and Georgie arrived just as they were putting the diary into the lock-fast production room.

"What you guys got there?" Georgie prodded.

"We think it's Angela's diary," June answered. "Andy found it in her locker at school. The entries in it indicate that she was in a sexual relationship."

Joe stood there, ashen-faced.

"Really?"

"Well, it might not be her diary, as there's no name in it."

"June, Andy," the Sergeant cut in. "Reluctantly, I think we have to hand all this over to the CID. It's getting too complicated, and we have to establish who that diary belongs to, not to mention the mountain of other inquiries we haven't got time to go into."

June could see the disappointment on Andy's face.

Driving around the area June finally asked Andy "Are you okay?"

"Yeah, sure,"

"Listen, Andy, this is your first missing person case. Don't get hung up on it. There'll be plenty more over the years to come."

"I know."

"Still. If one good thing comes out of this, you've been reunited with Miss Berger."

Andy smiled weakly, but said nothing.

"Zulu 1," the radio buzzed.

"Go ahead," Andy replied.

"Return to the office and attend at the CID room."

As they entered through the back door, the familiar smell of burning tobacco filled the air.

"June, how are you?" boomed the Inspector, who was smoking a pipe.

"Fine, Inspector. And yourself?"

"I'm good, but I could do without this missing girl. Who is this you have with you?"

"Detective Inspector Henry O'Brien, this is Andy Blackmore. He joined us a few weeks ago."

The pair shook hands as Inspector O'Brien took a close look at Andy, sizing him up.

"So, you're Blackmore."

"Yes, Inspector."

"I've been looking forward to meeting you. June, your thoughts on all this, please?" She related the contents of the diary and gave her opinion on the matter. "Andy, what about you?"

"Honestly, I haven't a clue what's going on with her, other than what June has said. And, I think the parents are lying."

"What do you mean?" The Inspector puffed on his pipe.

"Angela's mother says she is a loner and only child, while the father doesn't have a clue about her life."

The smoke from the pipe floated in the air. Andy could see his DI thinking deeply.

"We have to be careful with this one, given the man involved, and his alleged connections, although it may not be much. We certainly won't be jumping to any conclusions. What's their lifestyle like?"

"Helen, the mother, works Friday, Saturday and Sunday night shifts. Eight 'til eight in the psychiatric unit down the road," Andy rattled off.

"Eric is a company director," June added, "among other things. He makes his own hours, so he could be home, at work, or out at functions socialising."

Inspector O'Brien, gathered a small team of Detective Constables around him, and closed the door once June and Andy left the office.

"We deserve a cup of tea or something after that." June yawned. "C'mon, let's have a break."

They walked down the corridor to find that Joe and Georgie were just finishing a break.

"Andy, have you got a minute please?" Joe frowned.

"Sure thing, Joe."

"We need to talk, privately."

Why me? I've not been here five minutes, and all this is happening.

Andy followed Joe outside.

Chapter Twelve

I n the yard, Joe leaned with his back against the wall of the office building. He drew a packet of cigarettes from his pocket and offered Andy one.

"No thanks Joe."

"I should have known better," Joe muttered, lighting a cigarette.

"Joe, is there something I can help you with?"

"How do you know Catherine Smith?" Joe eyed him.

"I met her at the gym, or, to be more accurate, in the swimming pool. I believe you two also know each other. That's what she told me."

"What exactly did she tell you?" demanded Joe.

"That she knows most of the cops here through her work at the hospital."

"Anything else?"

"No."

"Okay, thanks. Are you, err, going to see her again?"

"Maybe." Andy frowned at him. "Joe, you know you turned pure why when you learned the contents of the diary. Why?"

Joe ignored his question and went back inside.

Andy and June had their break, and then went back out on a general patrol.

The rest of the day eventually ground to a finish.

The next few days were long, with nothing happening, and not much information being circulated by the CID about the missing person inquiry.

June and Andy were patrolling on Saturday afternoon when a call came in about a disturbance on a street in the south end of the village. There, they found two well-known local worthies, brothers Dave and Alan Jones, both in their sixties and the worse for wear, in full battle cry.

"All yours, Andy."

"Right, you two," called Andy. "At the moment, your conduct is tantamount to a Breach of the Peace, so you're both 'tin pail' material."

The two men looked at each other.

"What'd he say?" Dave piped up, swaying from side to side, holding onto his bottle tightly.

"Doesn't matter." Andy shook his head.

"Andy, send them up the road if you want to," added June.

"Right, you two, we're going to the end of the road. If you're both still here when we get back, you're coming with us."

"Right sonny, nae problem," Alan burped, the stench of wine hitting Andy's nostrils. The two men watched as the car turned at the end of the road, and before June and Andy returned, they were off, nowhere to be seen.

"Matter resolved," Andy spoke into the radio.

"I can't believe it's so quiet on a Saturday," June whispered. "This isn't normal. Anyway, what do you fancy for dinner tonight, Andy? Chinese or Indian?"

"Chinese."

"

They went to the rear of the Chinese restaurant and pulled open the back door.

"Hi June!" called the cook. "Wait a minute, be with you!"

"Okay!" she yelled back over the noise in the bustling kitchen. "Wan, this is Andy!"

"Hi, Andy!"

Andy put the palms of his hands together bowing. In twenty-five year Wan had never received a show of old fashioned respect. He smiled and responded accordingly.

"Sweet and sour chicken please, Wan," June requested.

"Beef curry and fried rice for me please." Andy added.

Within minutes, both dinners were served up in cartons.

"Fifty pence each, please."

They both handed over the correct amount.

"Thanks, Wan, see you soon," she said as they left. "He's a good guy, Wan. I always get a discount there."

By 19:30 they had consumed their meals and gone back out for the final furlong of the shift. June drove to the north of the village for a change, although Spill Hill and the south were their areas. She parked across the entrance to the local hotel, which hosted a disco every Saturday night, although it was still quite early.

"Right, let's see who we get coming in tonight," June grunted, fiddling with the handle to move her seat down.

Cars came and went: mostly taxis dropping off revellers on a Saturday night-out. Although it was early, the crowd entering the hotel seemed larger than usual, and they were all in the twenty-to-twenty-five age group.

A car drew up and June started. The driver's door opened and out stepped

"Well, well, well. Jamie Gallagher," June breathed. "The godfather of drugs round here. I didn't know he was out and about. I didn't see anything about him in the intel. Did you?"

"Nope." Andy replied.

The other doors to the car open, and out poured three more men.

"That's his brother Bobby." June pointed. "And – Jesus! That's Andy Frazer and Davy Rogers. Get the make and registration number of that car, Andy!" He did as he was told. "That's why they're all early tonight. Four major dealers from four different areas, all in one place."

Suddenly, Jamie looked right at the marked police vehicle, at June and Andy. He waved, and blew a kiss to June. Well, Andy hoped it was June. Gallagher crossed the road and approached June's door. She rolled down the window as Gallagher slapped his hands on the roof of the vehicle and leaned down.

"Hello June," Jamie mused. "Long time no see." He lit a cigarette.

"Four years," she responded curtly.

"Okay, June, now just for your information, there'll be no drugs, no nothing. Just a nice weekend out with my brother and a couple of friends." He noticed Andy. "Who's your pal?"

"Nobody you would know, Jamie."

"That wasn't the question, June."

"Okay Jamie," she sighed. "This is Andy Blackmore. Andy, meet Jamie, drug dealer and conman."

"Oh June, you'll give Andy a bad impression of me."

"Hi Jamie," Andy said coldly. "I'll make up my mind about you just fine on my own."

"Hello Andy," Jamie chuckled. "Now I can put a face to the name. Billy sends his best wishes." With that, he walked away. He only made it a few paces before spinning on his heels and returning. "Oh, by the way, June. Who grassed up about the cocaine drop last week? Whoever it was is in big trouble. That was an expensive night out for some friends of mine."

"It was the work of the Lord. You should have a word with him."

"He flicked his cigarette to the ground and walked off. "You haven't changed a bit, June. See ya soon."

What are you doing when we finish tonight?" June asked Andy.

"I'm not sure yet."

"Are you going to see Catherine?" The question took Andy unawares. "I can see why you're attracted to her, honestly, and I know you've been seen with her outside work. Joe saw you with her at the gym, and I saw you two in the city."

Andy sat in silence for a little while.

"Who else knows, June?"

"Just me and Joe."

"Look June, let me be straight with you. Nothing is going on between Catherine and I. And I had no idea that she was connected, in any way, to Angela until Monday, when she told me. I didn't know she was Angela's aunt, and I had no idea Eric Johnstone wasn't Angela's father until she told me. So that begs the question. Who is Angela's father? And who gave her the gold chain? Eric, or her real father?"

There was total silence in the vehicle, for what seemed like a lifetime.

"June, I'm sorry for going off like that."

"No worries."

Andy smiled. "June, I've got a question for you - do you know who Angela's real father is?"

"Do I have to answer that?"

"No, it's okay. I have my suspicions, but I hope I'm wrong."

The shift passed without any further incidents, and everyone got away on time.

As they left the office together, June turned to Andy.

"Hey, have a nice night."

"Thanks, June. You too."

Andy headed for Catherine's place, which was only a short drive away. He tapped the window instead of ringing the bell, as he knew that after eleven o'clock, Barry would be in bed.

"I have visitors," she murmured, glancing behind her. "I can't do tonight anymore, sorry. Will you call me in the morning?"

Andy sensed something was amiss, not for the first time, but he nodded and walked away.

It was 11:00 on Sunday, and Andy stood with the receiver at his ear, the ringback tone sounding constantly. A tired voice finally came through.

"Hello?"

"Hi."

"Where are you?"

"In my flat."

"Listen, go straight home tonight. When you finish, I'll be waiting for you. We have a lot to talk about." There was a pause. "Andy, please trust me. Tonight, you'll know everything. I promise." Her voice wavered.

Andy put the receiver back down in its cradle. He knew that Catherine was under pressure, having to cope with Barry and the rest of her family, in addition to her work. The words 'please trust me' reverberated around his head. They brought to mind the old saying, 'blood is thicker than water'.

Chapter Thirteen

It was 13:30 and Andy was in early, as usual. June was too, which was not as usual.

"Well, did you see Catherine last night?" June asked Andy, taking a seat next to him in the muster room.

"Nope. Discussion over, June. Sorry."

The shift gathered for the Sergeant's 'Sunday sermon' but the chit-chat instead concerned the pending World Cup game on Wednesday.

"I don't care what happens this Wednesday," Andy butted in. "Nothing will ever compare to the night Joe Jordan rose above the Czech defence and headed us into the finals a few years back. I was there. Never to be forgotten."

The Sergeant entered the room, followed by the Chief Inspector.

"Right you lot, stand up."

The shift stood in front of their designated chairs, and God help anyone else who sat on it. It was even worse in the canteen if a new start sat in the chair of a senior cop. "Ah, widnae sit there son" was the phrase used or"That's Big Tam's seat. Nope, ah widnae sit there either, that's Boab's seat. Sit there son, that's the typist's seat, she'll no bother."

"Attention!" the Sergeant boomed. "Produce appointments." Each officer produced his baton and handcuffs as the Sergeant went along the line. All uniforms were inspected in turn before hitting the streets: hats, tunics, sleeves, and boots. Andy was used to this after years in the Boys' Brigade, when they would parade for the company Captain in full uniform.

Finally, the Sergeant called, "at ease and please sit. For a weekend, there's not a lot happening. But, June and Andy submitted a great bit of intelligence." He paused. "Jamie Gallagher is back on the streets after a four-year prison spell."

"Sergeant," Andy interjected. "That had nothing to do with me. It was June who knew who he was, and I can't take credit for it."

"Andy!" June hissed in his ear. "It's all for one and one for all on this shift, so shut it."

"Sergeant, I'm rarely frightened, but she scares the hell outta me," Andy laughed.

"Don't worry Andy, she does the same to me." The Sergeant smiled, and the whole shift chuckled. "There were a couple of houses broken into during the night," the Sergeant continued. "A couple of assaults. If anyone's got any reports to write, they can get on with that, and if anyone's got anything else to do, go ahead. Andy, June, you're together again. Stevie, go with Joe. And the rest of you, sort yourselves out." The Sergeant left the room, before promptly returning. "Oh, and make sure the cars are clean, inside and out."

"Right Andy," June sighed. "Let's go get that thing cleaned out. Ditch your jacket."

As June, Andy, Stevie, and Joe cleaned their vehicles in the back yard, a CID car swung in. Two CID officers got out from the front, and Eric and Helen Johnstone alighted from the rear, led into the office via the back door.

"What's going on?" whispered Andy.

As they washed and dried and cleaned out their vehicle in the yard, Andy's thoughts turned to Catherine. Was she next?

"Let's get out and deliver these citations, and see if we can execute a few warrants," June grunted once they'd finished up.

A few hours later, with most of the paperwork complete, they got into the car and drove off. June parked outside a shop.

"So, what happened with Catherine last night?"

"I told you earlier, I didn't see her."

"But why not? I thought that was all set up."

"She had visitors." Andy was not in the mood for discussing this.

"Do you know who she was with?"

"No, I didn't go in."

"Andy, as a colleague and a friend, I'm telling you, please be careful. We just don't know what's going on with this kid, so please don't get emotionally involved."

"I hear you."

"Yeah, I know you hear me, but please listen as well."

"For you, I promise."

Suddenly, the radio burst into life.

"Zulu 1, return to the office, please. Report to Detective Inspector O'Brien."

"Roger," Andy replied.

As they entered the office, O'Brien was standing with the Sergeant.

"In here," O'Brien demanded in an officious tone. "Not you, June." Sergeant Black stood behind Andy, a position Andy was not comfortable with.

Silently puffing his pipe, the O'Brien leaned back and let the smoke filter through his lips and curl in the air.

"Andy," he murmured, finally. "Catherine Smith, Helen Johnstone's sister. You know her, yes? Well, of course you do, you're in a sexual relationship with her after all, aren't you?"

Andy breathed deeply, leaning forward and rubbing his hands together.

Eventually, Andy looked up.

"I was told you're the most respected Detective Inspector in this Division. I expected more from you, sir, and not that line of questioning." His voice was calm as he looked into O'Brien's eyes.

O'Brien repeated his question in the same manner.

"My reply is the same as before." Andy didn't blink. There was a stunned silence.

"Andy," Sergeant Black hissed. "Are you seeing Catherine Smith?"

"Now, that's a different question," Andy remarked. "Am I seeing Catherine Smith? We met at the gym, where we're both members. Have we had a night out? Yes. Have I met her brother Barry? Yes. Have we had a sexual relationship? That's got nothing to do with anyone other than Catherine and I. Next question?"

O'Brien was fuming.

Andy got up to leave the room.

"Oh, and by the way, Detective Inspector, rather than question me about my relationship with Catherine, maybe you should look at Eric Johnstone's affiliation with senior officers. This inquiry has sprung a leak." He opened the door to leave. "Neither June nor I know anything about what has happened here for days, so look within your own department." He slammed the door behind him.

"That is one cocky young man," O'Brien grumbled.

"Aye, maybe so, maybe so," the Sergeant muttered.

June looked at Andy as he came down the corridor.

"June, let's get out of here."

"Sure."

As she drove them away from the station, June sensed that there was something wrong with Andy. They entered the nearby countryside and got a magnificent view of the local loch. She stopped at a lay-by, switched off the engine, and got out.

"Hey, you gonna join me?" She called from the bonnet of the car, where she sat looking out on one of the most stunning views in the area. The loch was still, reflecting the rolling hills in the background.

Andy slowly got out of the vehicle and climbed up beside June.

"See, all the cops working in the city would give their right arm for this," June whispered.

Andy gazed out, the hills displayed multiple shades of green, and, as the minutes passed by, the clouds moved and the light changed.

"June, I'm finished." Andy exhaled.

"Er, what do you mean?"

"I'm finished. I'm not going to have some little, pipe-smoking Inspector question me about my private life due to an inquiry they can't solve. So, it's game over for me."

"Over my dead body. Get in the car."

"Not yet. I want you to see something."

Andy removed his hat, jacket, baton, and handcuffs. As the red ball of the sun collided with the water on the loch, casting a magnificent reflection, Andy went into his kata routine. June watched in awkward silence until he finished.

"Okay, time to go," Andy huffed as he got back into the car.

"Feel better now, Andy?"

"Yeah."

The drive to the office was silent. June pulled the car into the backyard. As they sat in the car, they both instinctively knew what the other was thinking.

"June," Andy began, "I've only known you and the rest of the guys for a few weeks, but you and Joe have been great to me, and the rest have been very welcoming. Thank you."

June watched from the car as Andy went into the office. She got out, determined to stop Andy from leaving the force, when another unmarked car drew in. She recognised Catherine in the back seat. She was with a man June presumed to be her brother, Barry.

Oh Christ, where is Andy? June hurried into the office and found him ogling one of the notice boards.

"Kitchen, now," she demanded.

"What is it?"

"Catherine and a man have just been brought in by the CID. Wait here, and don't do anything stupid."

A few minutes later, June returned.

"Andy, they're just here to give the CID statements. Let's get out of here."

Andy stared out the car window as June drove slowly around the village.

"This is not going to happen, Andy."

"Eh?"

"You resigning. It's not going to happen."

"And why not?"

"Because we're not going to allow it. Sleep on it, see how you feel tomorrow. And think about this. How best you can help Catherine? By helping find Angela. You can't do that outside this job."

An hour late they returned to the office to finish their shift, and saw the unmarked car leaving the backyard with Catherine and the man, who Andy explained was her brother Barry.

June put her hand on Andy's.

"Right big guy, let's get finished. And no more talk of leaving us, okay?"

As they went into the corridor, O'Brien was standing there.

"Andy. I had to find out, I hope you understand." Andy looked at him, nodded, and walked away without saying a word. June just looked at O'Brien and shook her head before brushing past him.

"Goodnight June," Andy called after they were dismissed for the night. He walked down the corridor with his head down. June didn't follow Andy onto the street as they went to their cars. Instead, she waited in the office.

Andy went straight home, expecting a visit from Catherine; she had said she was going to tell him everything.

Finally, around midnight, he called her.

"Hello?"

"Hi Catherine. I thought you were coming here after you finished tonight?"

"I was going to."

"I saw you when you were leaving the office with Barry earlier. Although I haven't a clue why you were there, I know they've made a connection between you and me. I don't want to give them any more ammunition to fire at us by being seen at your place."

"Andy, they couldn't have been nicer to me, or Barry. I made a statement, and I was allowed to sit with Barry as he made his. So where does that leave us?"

"As far as I'm concerned, there's no change there. It's just that our friendship is known about now. If you can live with that, so can I."

"Yes, I can." She remembered how good he looked naked.

"Good. You've helped me decide my future."

"What do you mean?"

"It doesn't matter now. Thank you."

"Andy, do me a favour please. Leave your door off the latch." Catherine hung up.

A short time later, Andy was lying in bed when he heard the door open. There was saw a small brandy waiting for her on the table with a note: 'Nightcap. X'. Only the lights from the street lit the room as Catherine stripped off next to the bed. She pulled back the duvet and lay beside Andy.

"You alright?" Andy whispered.

"I am now."

"You know, now that they know about us, they won't let me close to Angela's case."

Catherine wrapped herself around Andy.

"To me, right now, this is more important."

At 14:00 on Monday, and Andy's shift were in the muster room when Sergeant Black announced that a search of the graveyard was to be carried out in the hope of finding Angela Johnstone.

"Joe, Georgie, June and…" the Sergeant trailed off. "Ooch, why not? You too Andy. Go and assist the rest of the officers. "Search begins at 14:30, prompt, under the watchful eyes of the CID and O'Brien."

"Sergeant," June spoke up. "What's the purpose of this search?"

"My understanding is that, because of its proximity to the Johnstones' home address, the graveyard has to be searched." Sergeant Black's answer was followed by a short period of silence. "All I ask is that you guys be professional. At all times. No throw-away lines." He flashed a look at Andy. "And don't give O'Brien a reason to complain."

"Sergeant, this big mutt will be fine." June beamed at Andy. "He'll be with me."

At 14:10, the four officers selected for the search got into a marked car and headed for the graveyard. June and Andy got in the back, while Joe got in the driver's seat and Georgie took the passenger seat.

"All good today?" June eyed Andy.

Andy smiled and nodded. Joe watched Andy in the rear-view mirror.

"You're a quiet one, big man," Joe remarked.

Andy knew exactly where this was going.

"What's going on?" Georgie whined.

"Oh, Andy boy here is seeing Nurse Cathy," Joe explained.

"Cathy? Catherine Smith? From the hospital? She's never been known to go out with anyone, especially not a cop!"

"Well, Andy here has melted her heart," Joe teased.

"Wow, lucky boy! Many have tried and many have failed," Georgie mused.

"Okay guys, give it a break," June snapped.

Andy was the butt of many jokes throughout the rest of the drive to the graveyard.

"Cathy Smith, well I never," Georgie muttered, shaking his head.

The four alighted from the vehicle and gathered in the graveyard, O'Brien was already there. The graveyard was well kept, headstones old and new peppered the manicured grass. Flowers left by mourners brought life and colour to the last resting places of its permanent occupants. Four fresh graves, with soil piled around their rims, awaited new occupants on the following day.

Stones, stones and more stones.

Andy remembered, 'Leave no stone unturned, Those were the words that Big Billy Green had told him as he left his house. Is this what he meant? Andy mulled this over as O'Brien briefed everyone, including officers from the Force Support Unit who were trained for these sorts of searches. The officers stood in a straight line across the width of the graveyard, ready for the search to begin.

As the search began, the officers moved forward, slowly, looking for any sign that Angela had been there. Gravediggers watched with interest from their bothy, in case their assistance was required.

The search went from north to south, but nothing came up. O'Brien, who, according to his reputation, was a perfectionist, was not satisfied. He ordered a second search from east to west.

As they passed a fallen gravestone, Andy noticed that a large, ancient headstone had been felled over a grave. "Constable Blackmore, leave no stone unturned" raced through his head.

To everyone's dismay, the search ended with a negative result, again. The group got back into their vehicle.

"You're very quiet, Andy," remarked June. "What's up with you?"

"It's stupid," Andy muttered.

"Spill the beans," Georgie urged him.

"You'll think I'm stupid, but when we were searching east to west, there was a large gravestone lying face down over a grave. It was newly damaged. There were no old marks on it, or weeds and moss, and the top part was snapped off about three feet from the top."

"What are you suggesting?"

"To leave no stone unturned."

The four of them sat in the car and watched as O'Brien headed towards his vehicle. Suddenly, Georgie leapt out of the car.

"Sir, I need a word with you."

As the two conversed, O'Brien kept glancing at their car and shaking his head.

"Everyone," Georgie announced when he returned to their car, "get out and follow me."

O'Brien walked over to Andy.

"Is this your hair-brained idea, Constable?"

"Yes, sir."

The rest of the group froze, shocked by the comment. They walked back to the graveyard, and O'Brien went to the bothy.

"Andy," Joe murmured. "If you're wrong about this, he'll bury you, here and now."

"I don't need to dig one, there are four new ones over there." Andy pointed. "Oh, and didn't June tell you? I'm chucking it anyway and going back to the real world."

"Yer whit?" Joe guffawed when O'Brien returned with the gravediggers, interrupting the discussion.

"Boys, I need this part of the stone lifted immediately," O'Brien commanded the gravediggers.

The foreman surveyed the scene. "That's a lot of weight. I'll have to get a machine to lift it."

"Well, go get the machine. Since it is so heavy how would it have fallen over?"

"I haven't got a clue. Jonny, go get the lifter!" The foreman shouted to the gravedigger who was standing at the bothy, watching them.

Jonny began to shake.

"W-w-what are you needing that for boss?" he stammered. "There's virtually no diesel in it."

"To lift this stone."

Jonny reluctantly went to get the machine. He knew what lifting the stone would reveal.

A short time later, he returned, driving a machine that resembled a small crane with a large strap on a hook. The gravediggers manipulated the strap around the top part of the stone. The foreman signalled Jonny to start lifting.

Slowly but surely, the stone began to move. The strain on the lifting arm was obvious to all watching. When the stone was about eighteen inches off the ground, O'Brien ordered Jonny to halt the machine.

Everyone watched as he got down on his knees and looked under the raised stone.

O'Brien rose to his feet and brushed down the legs of his trousers. He took his pipe from his jacket and filled it with tobacco, and then produced a lighter from his trouser pocket and lit his pipe. Smoke billowed from his mouth as he stared intently at Andy and his colleagues.

"Lift it," O'Brien finally grumbled.

Jonny restarted the machine, carefully pulling the stone into an upright position before the stone fell back on itself, revealing freshly dug earth and a grave whose last occupant was interred over one hundred years ago.

"Mr. Jones, as foreman of this graveyard, you would have a record of the graves opened in the past few weeks, yes?" O'Brien inquired. "Do you have any records of this one being opened?"

"No, sir." The foreman spoke softly, eyes wide.

As Jonny jumped out of the machine, Joe noticed a chain that around his neck. Jonny promptly shoved the necklace inside his T-shirt.

Andy noticed a change in Joe's demeanour as his face drained of blood. He began to sense, not for the first time in this inquiry, that something was wrong with Joe.

"Mr. Jones, have your men extract some of the earth here?" O'Brien ordered.

"Certainly."

With shovels and rakes at the ready, the gravediggers slowly removed the freshly dug earth, bit by bit.

When one gravedigger placed his shovel into the earth, he sprang back.

"Jesus Christ! Davy!" he shouted. In the dirt was an exposed leg, dressed in a sock and black shoe.

"Everyone, stop!" O'Brien commanded.

June put her arm around Andy, while Joe and Georgie stood there silently. Joe clenched his teeth, dreading that the body in the shallow grave was Angela.

This had become personal for Andy, through his connection to Catherine, and he had a gut feeling that Joe had more than just a professional interest.

Within an hour, forensic scientists and police photographers were at the graveyard, which was in total lockdown: all access points sealed and secured. O'Brien instructed the four officers to return to the office to begin their statements.

"Sir," June spoke up. "We were here at the start of this, can't we remain to the end?"

O'Brien looked at them standing together; he knew they were a team.

"Yeah, alright, I suppose I owe you all that, at the least."

A large tent was placed over the grave to protect it from the elements, and to keep away prying eyes. Forensics experts were carrying out a fingertip search of the scene and gathering evidence. Floodlights were brought in to assist the forensic team.

After several hours, the body of a young, deceased female was exposed under the harsh light As she lay there on the cold, dark earth, dressed in her Bankvale High School uniform, her blonde hair partially obscuring her face, a police officer took her photographs.

As darkness descended, Andy saw in his peripheral vision a light go on in a nearby villa. An unrecognisable figure stood at the window overlooking the graveyard. Andy subtly brought this to June's attention through head and eye signals. She nodded.

At 22:00, the local undertaker attended at the graveyard to remove the remains of the deceased. The forensics team, dressed in their familiar white-hooded suits, boots, and gloves, was satisfied with their findings. They lifted the deceased into a black body bag, which they then placed in a brown, fibreglass coffin. It was brought from the tent and laid on the ground. When the undertaker moved forward to take a handle, Andy stepped in front of him.

"We can get that." Andy looked straight at Georgie.

"Sure, big man," Georgie complied, stepping forward.

"You know one of you is going to have to go with her." O'Brien remarked.

As Andy was about to get into the hearse, Joe placed his hand on the window of the vehicle. Andy nodded at him.

"She will be cared for with respect," Andy promised.

"Thank you," murmured Joe.

The hearse drew out of the graveyard while Joe walked slowly towards the gravediggers and his colleagues. O'Brien stood with the remaining officers in a small circle. Additional officers had been summoned to make sure that the area was sealed and secured for the foreseeable future, as forensic inquiries had to be completed.

"Now to find the killer." O'Brien barked.

"Jonny!" Joe called to the gravedigger. "We need a word with you, please."

He approached the officers with his hands in his pockets.

"Jonny, are you the only one who uses that machine?"

"Yeah, mostly."

"Okay. Tell you what. Gimme the chain from around your neck, Jonny."

"Wh-What?"

"Give me the chain, or I'll take it."

Jonny, shaking like a leaf, handed the gold chain to Joe. Joe stared at the chain; it had gold charm on it: the letter A.

"This is Angela's pendant," Joe informed O'Brien, who immediately instructed two detectives to take Jonny to the office for further questioning.

"Honestly, Mr. O'Brien, I didnae kill the lassie. It wisnae me, you have to believe me!" Joe pleaded.

When Joe arrived at the office, escorted by the detectives, the Sergeant was waiting for them.

"Kitchen, now!" The Sergeant commanded.

June, Georgie, Joe, and the Sergeant sat in the kitchen in silence.

Eventually, Joe produced the gold chain and laid it on the table.

"Angela's father gave her this the day after she was born," Joe spoke, softly. "He loved her mother, but things were... wrong at the time. But he wanted Angela to know she was loved. And in years to come, her mother would tell her the story."

Joe handed the chain and attachment to June, tears streaming down his face. The three officers left him alone.

"Shit, what a mess," June remarked as they walked down the hallway.

"Circle the wagons, he'll be fine."

"Remember. Andy's also in this mess."

"Yes, I'm well aware of that. They'll be fine."

"Sergeant." June pinched her nose. "Andy's thinking of resigning."

"Really?" The Sergeant stopped in his tracks. "That could take a while, as it goes through me. That resignation could get lost in transit."

June smiled. "Good."

Once again, Andy sat alone in the mortuary with a deceased person. The difference this time was that he had a connection to the body. Andy knew in his heart that this was Angela, but an identification had to be made. The door opened and in walked a detective.

"Hi Andy, I'm Brian."

"Pleased to meet you." Andy shook hands with him. The door opened again.

"Dr. MacKay, police casualty surgeon," the incomer announced.

"Constable Andy Blackmore, sir. Pleased to meet you."

"Has the deceased been touched at all?"

"Only to be brought here from the locus, doctor. And then from the coffin to the table."

"Okay." Dr MacKay unzipped the body bag. "Let's get to work then."

Gloves were worn by all parties during the brief examination of the body.

"A forensic pathologist will be attending as soon as possible. Tomorrow, hopefully," MacKay informed the police officers. "Looks like strangulation, by the marks around her neck, but a more thorough examination will have to be done to confirm that. Don't remove anything from the body. Goodnight, I'll go to the office and note down that I attended here."

A hundred pounds a call out for two minutes work.. I'm in the wrong job. He watched as the small, slender man, suited and booted, with greying hair and gold-rimmed glasses, departed.

Andy filled out the label — female, white, unidentified — and attached it to the body's right wrist. He sealed the bag with the zip. Assisted by Brian, he slid the body into the fridge.

"Goodnight Angela," he murmured under his breath.

"Come with me," Brian beckoned. "I'll drop you off at the office."

On Andy's return to the office at 23:30, Jonny was being questioned by the CID.

The Sergeant gathered his troops once again in the kitchen: June, Georgie, Joe, and Andy. The kettle was boiling, and tea bags and coffee were laid out on the counter.

The Sergeant was inspecting Andy.

"What's your connection in all this?" he asked, finally.

Andy explained his relationship with Catherine, and how that came about. What he didn't reveal was how involved he had got.

"Okay." The Sergeant turned to Joe. "And you?"

"Sergeant, can we leave this, please?"

Joe and Andy shared a look.

"And why the hell should I?" snapped the Sergeant.

"Maybe some things in life are better left alone," suggested June.

The Sergeant summoned June and Georgie to his room, leaving Joe and Andy alone.

"Joe, I'm sorry for your loss, Andy spoke softly. "I really am. To be there, at that time… I can't begin to imagine how you feel." Andy stood up from the table to leave.

"Does anyone else know yet?" Joe blurted.

Andy shook his head. "I've not said anything to anyone, although I don't think it'll take much time for them to work things out, Joe."

It was going to be a late finish for everyone, as they had statements to write. Andy rejoined June and Georgie in the Sergeant's room.

"Can I ask what's going to happen now?" Andy asked to no one in particular.

"Well," started the Sergeant, "young Jonny Laing is with the CID in the interview room, O'Brien and Detective Sergeant Anderson are on their way to the villa with the pendant to have it identified. Then it will be a case of having the body identified tonight or tomorrow morning." The Sergeant was glaring at Andy. "I hear you're thinking of resigning Andy. Can I ask why?"

Andy looked at June, who stared at the floor.

"Sorry, Andy," she murmured.

"Nah, it's fine June."

"Well?" prompted the Sergeant.

"Honestly, I've only been here a few weeks and I've seen drug drops and dead bodies. It's been a whirlwind, and I don't know if I'm coping with it all that well. I'm just drained by the speed of everything." He paused. "Then there's all this with Angela."

"This isn't just about Angela, is it? It's about Catherine too."

"No, absolutely not."

"Are you sure?"

"Positive."

"Right, here's what to do. Write out your resignation on your days off, bring it to me on Friday for your early shift, and I'll process it. Is that okay with you? It's pointless having you here if you don't want to be here."

Andy nodded. June listened in disbelief at what was being said.

"Andy, are you serious?" Andy nodded again and June just stared at him, mouth agape.

"Andy," Georgie cut in, leaning forward in his seat, his arms resting on his legs, and his hands clasped. "I haven't been out and about with you yet. There's no doubt you've had a rough start to your career, but it's not always like this. Joe and June were young when they started on this shift, and we've never failed to get anyone through their probation. And you're not going to be the first. You're not young in the true sense of the word, you're twenty-five, heading for twenty-six. You've been about. Your quick thinking and, dare I say needed in this job, so give it a lot of thought before you resign."

"Okay." They proceeded to write their statements for the CID. Andy's and June's took longer than everyone else's, as they took the original missing person report, and had been present up until the discovery of the deceased.

At 03:15, more than four hours after they were due to finish, Andy and June made their way out of the office. There was activity in the CID room, and Andy stopped to see O'Brien still working away.

"Sir." Andy cleared his throat. "The pendant?"

O'Brien looked up and saw Andy and June standing in his doorway. He nodded. "Yes, it's been positively identified as the necklace worn by Angela. Arrangements are in hand to have the body identified in the morning, but everything points to it being Angela."

"What about Jonny Laing?"

"He's being interviewed just now under caution. You two get home." He began to shuffle papers on his desk, before directing his attention at Andy. "I'm not sure I like you, but good job."

"Thanks."

As they stood on the small, quiet street outside the office, Andy looked up at the dark sky.

"How long will it take you to get home, June?"

"At this time of the morning? About forty-five minutes."

"I'm only fifteen minutes from here, so you're welcome to stay over if you want, no strings attached. Your call."

"Thanks, Andy, but no. I have my reasons."

"Sure, no problem. I just thought—"

"I know, and I appreciate it." She smiled.

"What am I going to do about Catherine, knowing what I know now?"

"Absolutely nothing." She wagged a finger in Andy's face. "And I mean it." She walked slowly to her vehicle and got in.

Andy sat in his car and watched June speed off into the darkness.

Within fifteen minutes, he was pouring himself a small brandy and collapsing onto a seat in his living room. He knew that going to bed now would be fruitless. He'd just contemplate the events of the day.

He poured another brandy, and, as he lifted the glass to his lips, the telephone rang. He stared at it, confused, before lifting the receiver.

"Hello?"

"Andy?"

"Yeah."

"It's June."

"June, do you know what time it is?"

"Aye, of course, I do," she snapped impatiently. "I just got a call from the office. When did you last see Joe?"

"When we were sitting together in the kitchen." Andy rubbed his eyes. "June, what is this all about?"

"His wife called the office looking for him. He's not gone home, and nobody knows where he is."

"Well, he's not here, that's for sure."

"Andy, cut the shit right now. This is serious."

"Sorry."

"Jonny Laing has given the CID information about the death of Angela, and they think Joe is involved."

"What information, June?"

"I don't know, but no doubt we'll find out soon enough. Sorry to bother you, Andy. Goodnight."

"Goodnight June."

Andy could feel a knot forming in his gut, and he didn't think it was the brandy.

Please Joe. No.

Chapter Fourteen

T he telephone blared, waking Andy at 10:20 in the morning. He was still in his chair, clothed in his uniform from the previous day's shift. Dazed and confused, he gathered himself as the telephone rang constantly.

"Hello?"

"Andy," Catherine breathed. "I called you about a dozen times last night."

"I didn't get in until God knows what time this morning. I'm wrecked."

"Helen's been on the phone to me. The CID was at the house and they lifted Eric."

"What? Why?"

"I don't know, Andy. I'm in bits with all this. I need to see you."

"I've not been to bed all night, I fell asleep on the chair."

"Oh for Christ's sake Andy, get your act together."

"Yeah, gimme an hour."

"Okay."

He hurriedly fried some breakfast and brewed some tea before calling her back.

"Catherine?"

"Yes?"

"I'm on my way over. Is that okay? Or do you want to come here?"

"No, you're fine, please come over."

"Okay, see you shortly." He hung up and dashed out of his flat.

"You look tired Andy," she remarked when she opened the door. Andy stepped into Catherine's flat, and as the door closed behind him they wrapped their arms around each other tightly.

"Catherine, I'm afraid I have to be at work shortly."

"Sorry." She wiped a tear from her eye. "If ever I needed someone, it's you, now. Have you seen the news today?"

"No. I came straight here."

"The police found a body in the cemetery, and they said it's a girl." She gulped. "Some guy has been arrested and is due to appear in court today, and now they've lifted Eric."

"I know, I was at the cemetery when we found her. I didn't want to tell you over the phone."

"Have they... Is it Angela?"

"The body still has to be identified, but the CID found a gold chain. It looks like her's."

"Oh God, please no, Andy." Her stomach began to churn with fear.

"Is Joe Angela's father?" Andy blurted.

Catherine jolted. "Why do you ask?"

"You don't have to answer if you don't want to, it's just that certain things happened yesterday."

"Was he also there wh—when she was found?"

"Yes, he was."

"It was a long time ago, who knows?"

"I don't know. I'm not saying anything." He chewed his lip. "Listen, I'll see you when I finish tonight, that's a promise. We can go over everything."

"Okay."

At 13:30, Andy was getting himself ready for the start of his shift in the locker room when June walked in.

"Oh, hi June. How are you?"

"Crap, to be honest," she grunted. "So tired."

"Did you manage to find out about Joe?"

"No." Have you seen Catherine?"

"Yeah, this morning. Her brother-in-law's been lifted." Andy stared into his locker.

"Why?"

"She doesn't know. Neither do I."

"Well, we could be about to find out. But before we go in there, tell me, did you say anything about yesterday?"

"What do you mean?"

"Nothing," she replied curtly. "It doesn't matter."

They went into the muster room and sat down.

"Let's see if he turns up today," June murmured.

One by one, the shift arrived, each of them taking their customary seat. Finally, the Sergeant marched in with the briefing books under his arm and sat down. One seat lay vacant.

"Let's get this briefing over with. O'Brien is coming in to speak to you all in a few minutes." The Sergeant looked around the room. "Anyone seen Joe?"

"No, Sergeant," everyone replied in unison. The Sergeant nodded.

Fifteen minutes later, O'Brien entered the room holding an unlit pipe.

"First of all, I want to thank everyone who was at the graveyard yesterday for all your efforts and professionalism, especially after the deceased was found. And thanks to this officer and his observations on the fallen gravestone,"

He made a vague gesture at Andy. There were mutterings of agreement around the room.

"As you will understand, inquiries have been going throughout the night. Last night Angela's parents positively identified her pendant as the one that Jonny Laing was wearing. Also, Angela was formally identified by her mother and her mother's cousin. Eric Johnstone is currently here, helping us with inquiries." Andy frowned at that. "Jonny Laing will appear at court this afternoon, charged with unlawful sexual intercourse with a girl under sixteen and preventing a lawful burial. Acting on information from Laing, it would appear he had been sleeping with Angela when her parents were out of the house. She told him she was pregnant, which proved to be false, as there was no trace of her being pregnant at any time according to the post-mortem. I've spoken with the Procurator Fiscal about the assistance we got from him, and he has decided that he will only go on the sexual charge and drop the latter. Jonny will likely get a couple of years of probation and community service."

Anderson entered the room and whispered something to O'Brien. "Sorry folks, I have to go. But, before I do, I just want to note that it would be a shame to lose a new cop who has the potential of becoming a really good officer. Even if he's not my favourite person on the shift." He winked at Andy.

"June, take Andy out with you today," the Sergeant ordered. "As for the rest of you, same teams as yesterday. Georgie, I'll go with you until Joe arrives."

As they were about to leave the office to begin their last shift, the back door opened and Joe walked in , dressed in casual clothing.

"Where's the Sergeant?" he piped up.

"He just went into his office." June sized him up.

"Thanks."

They heard the door to the Sergeant's office close, then open again.

"O'Brien, would you come into my office?" the Sergeant asked.

"Sergeant, I'm rather busy."

"It's important, sir."

"This better be good, Sergeant."

June and Andy looked at each other as they left the station and got into their patrol car.

"June, I've decided to stay and see out my probation. I have to get used to this way of life, and if I left, I'd probably regret it for the rest of my life."

June looked around to check that nobody was in sight, then pulled Andy towards her and planted a kiss on his cheek.

"That's great news! Welcome aboard, partner."

That afternoon was uneventful, and at break time they returned to the office. As they made their way down the corridor to the kitchen, they found that the charge bar was blocked by detectives surrounding Eric Johnstone.it

June and Andy stopped abruptly and silently observed the scene. O'Brien was charging Eric Johnstone with murder in the presence of his lawyer.

"You are not obliged to say anything in reply to the charge, but anything you say will be taken down in writing and may be given in evidence."

O'Brien asked Johnstone if he understood the caution. He nodded. Andy listened as O'Brien described how Johnstone placed his hands around Angela's neck and strangled her.

As the charge was being read out to him, Eric Johnstone saw the whole incident playing out in his head: the argument with Angela in her bedroom, grabbing her, placing his hands around her neck, choking her as she attempted to force his hands away, her body going limp as he squeezed the life out of her, letting her fall onto her bed. He had looked at her lying there, eyes open and staring at him. Then the feeling of panic had set in as he considered how to dispose of her body. When O'Brien finished reading out the charge, Eric came back to the present.

Andy felt his fingers go numb and his skin grow hot. Tears welled for Angela and her family. How was Catherine going to explain Angela's fate to Barry?

"Do you wish to reply, Mr. Johnstone?" O'Brien finished.

"I would advise against that, Eric," Johnstone's lawyer stared intently at his client.

"No," Eric murmured.

As he turned to be escorted down the corridor to the cells, Eric saw June and Andy. His eyes lit up.

"I need you two to do me a favour. Please tell Helen and Cath—," he choked. "Tell them I'm sorry."

"Eric," his lawyer warned. "Don't say anything else."

Once he was at his cell door, Eric slipped off his expensive shoes and placed them neatly together outside the door. This would not be the last time he would hear a prison cell door close behind him.

June and Andy were having their dinner in the kitchen when O'Brien came in, poured himself a cup of coffee, and sat beside them.

"We'll deal with Helen Johnstone shortly. I'd like you both to deal with Catherine as soon as possible, before this hits the streets. I don't want her to hear about what's going on based on rumours." He took a sip of his coffee. "Eric told us everything during his interview. It would appear that Angela told her mother she was pregnant, and Mrs. Johnstone, knowing that this could not be kept secret for long, told Eric, who knew that this scandal would destroy his standing in the community, and kill all his hopes for a political career. After Helen left for work, he went to Angela's bedroom, where he confronted her and demanded she terminate the pregnancy. She refused, and, in one of his sudden rages, he strangled her."

June shook her head and scoffed.

"He put Angela in the boot of his car, took her to the graveyard, where he found Jonny Laing working alone. Eric told him he knew about him and Angela, and threatened to kill him if he didn't take the blame for her murder. They dug the shallow grave, buried Angela, then, using the machine, Jonny covered it over with the gravestone. If it hadn't snapped when it hit the ground, we may never have found her." He took another sip of coffee. "What makes it so tragic is that she wasn't even pregnant. The post-mortem confirmed that."

"What about the pendant?" Andy asked.

"When Eric carried Angela to the grave and laid her down, Laing took the pendant off Angela."

"Why did Jonny consent to helping him?" June inquired.

"He's a young lad, terrified of the powerful Eric Johnstone. And he knew that nobody would believe his word against Eric's."

"What about Joe, Inspector?"

"He's taking a couple of weeks off." O'Brien paused. "I don't think this needs to go any further." Andy nodded in agreement, as did June. O'Brien finished his coffee, took his pipe from his pocket, and rose from the table. "Lots to do now."

A short time later, June and Andy went to see Catherine. Andy knocked on the door, and Barry opened it.

"Hello Andy." Barry speaking to him was a breakthrough in their relationship.

"Hi Barry. Is Catherine in?"

"Yes. She's getting ready for work."

"Can I see her please?"

Andy, who is this?" Barry spoke up, gesturing towards June.

"Barry, this is June."

"Hello, Barry." June smiled at him.

"Are you his girlfriend?" Barry asked.

"No, we work together," she replied, amused by the question. "Anyway, Andy has a beautiful girlfriend already, he doesn't need me."

"Oh. Okay," Barry said, as he went into the living room.

At that moment, Catherine came downstairs in her nurse's uniform.

"Andy, June, what are you both doing here?"

"We need to speak to you," June said softly.

June gave Catherine as much information as she was permitted to. It was a learning curve for Andy on what could and couldn't be shared.

When they broke the news, Catherine had to lean on the bannister for support.

"I have to phone work, I can't go in when this is happening, I have to see Helen," Catherine rambled, running her hands through her hair. Andy laid a hand on her shoulder.

"I'm so sorry for your loss, Catherine." June frowned.

"Thank you," Catherine choked out. "For everything. Both of you."

"I'll meet you in the car when you're ready," June told Andy before opening the door and heading outside.

"Okay, thanks." Andy took a seat beside Catherine on the stairs. June shut the door behind her.

"If you're not going into work, do you want me to collect you later?"

"No thanks, I'll go see Helen." Catherine wiped a stray tear from her cheek.

"I understand. Please call me, let me know how you're coping.I'm here for you." He kissed her on the cheek.

Before Andy got up to leave, Catherine squeezed his hand tightly. "Take care Andy." Watching him leave, she wept.

It wasn't long before June, Andy and the rest of the shift were closing their lockers after another day. They headed outside to the car park.

"Hey you," Andy called to June before she got in her care. "What did you mean earlier, when you told Barry 'I didn't need you'."

June laughed. "You know what I meant."

"Well, if I'm staying here, I do need you." June smiled.

"Yes, you do," she agreed. "Training tomorrow, is it?"

"Sure is, then home to the big city to see an old friend. To say thanks."

When Andy arrived at his flat, he kicked off his shoes and changed into his jogging trousers and T-shirt.

He poured himself a moderate nightcap and put the blues on, making sure to turn down the volume so as not to disturb his neighbours so late at night.

As he listened to Buddy Guy in the background, he heard a gentle knocking on his door.

Who could that be at this time of the night?

He opened the door to find Catherine standing there, crying. She brushed past him and swept into the living room. Andy closed the door and followed her in.

"I'm sorry, I know it's late, but I needed to speak to you. I've just been to Helen's and… I don't know what to do now. I'm at a total loss."

"Can I offer you a drink or something?" Andy felt uncomfortable.

"Water, just water, please. I—I need to get back to Barry tonight."

"I understand." Andy handed Catherine a glass of water and waited for her to begin.

She looked at him through tear-stained eyes.

"Before I start, I want you to know one thing. I've never met anyone like you, and over the past few weeks that we've been seeing each other, I've seriously fallen for you, like nobody I've known before."

"Where is this going, Catherine?"

"Where this is going, Andy is... nowhere. I've come here to end our —this relationship."

"Can I ask why?" Andy's heart was pounding in his chest.

"There's no future for us. I have Barry to look after, and I can't put that burden on you in the years to come, or however long we might have together."

"Can't I be the judge of that?"

"No, you can't. This is my decision, and if you want to have a career ahead of you, you have to go on without me. I was with Helen tonight, and she told me things that I can't keep from you forever."

"Do you mean about Joe being Angela's father?"

"Yes. That and much more you don't know about." She considered for a moment. "About fifteen or so years ago, he and Helen worked together in the insurance game and became involved with each other for a while. As a result, Angela was born. Helen left the company before Angela was born and ended her relationship with Joe. He didn't even know he had a daughter until a few years ago, long after she had married Eric."

"So, what has this got to do with us?" Andy asked, confused and impatient.

Catherine sipped her water and stared at the floor.

Andy eventually broke the silence. "Has this got anything to do with the murder?"

"Yes, it has," Catherine suddenly snapped.

"Okay."

Catherine sighed.

"Andy, can I use your phone please?"

"Er, sure."

Catherine dialled her home number, then waited for a few seconds before someone picked up.

"Barry, it's Catherine. It's late, I know, but can you do me a favour and go to bed, please? I'll see you soon, I promise. Make sure the door's locked. Yes, I do have my keys. I'll see you later. Goodnight."

Andy watched as she kicked off her shoes and took off her jacket, which she hung over the chair at the dining table. She picked up her glass of water from the table and shook it at him.

"Can I change this for a large glass of whisky, please? With ice?"

Andy walked over to the display cabinet, lifted out a whiskey glass and poured out a large Scotch. He handed it to Catherine, who was sitting on the couch, looking disheveled. She didn't make eye contact.

"Thank you." She grasped the tumbler.

"I take it you'll not be driving after that?" His question was met with silence. Catherine continued to stare at the floor. Andy sat down and observed Catherine, anxious of what was to come.

"Andy, can you turn the music off? If what I'm about to tell you will shock you as much as it did me, and it could have a devastating effect on your career, depending on what you do next." Andy rose to switch off the music. "This is the sole reason why I'm ending this thing between us."

Andy returned to the couch and sat beside Catherine.

"Listen to me," Catherine continued. "When this is all over and done with, you will be known as the guy who slept with the sister-in-law of the man who murdered his 'daughter'. That'll never go away, and I'm not going to be the one responsible for you not reaching whatever heights the future holds for you."

"If I had to choose between having you or becoming Chief Constable, there would be no contest. You'd win every time."

"I'm sorry Andy, this has to be our last night together."

As he rolled over in bed the following morning, his arm stretched out to hold Catherine, but she was gone.

Upon his return to the office, the shift was informed that Eric Johnstone had tendered a plea of not guilty to the murder of Angela Johnstone, and had been remanded in custody.

"What happens now?" Andy asked June.

"Precognitions. Then we all head for the High Court within a hundred and ten days."

Over the next couple of months, Andy was trained in precognitions and sitting in the witness box. His first time acting as a witness was going to be at the High Court.

Ninety days later, Andy found himself waiting in the police witness room of the High Court in Edinburgh, along with most of his shift, including June and Joe.

"For Christ's sake, look at him," June remarked. "Cool as a cucumber. He looks like he's on a day out with his mates."

"Well, I am," Andy retorted. "This is a nice place."

"I give up on you, Blackmore." June shook her head, smiling.

"No you don't, you love me to bits." He chuckled.

At that moment, the door to the witness room opened and the court officer entered to check that all the witnesses cited were present.

"Cool the jets big man," O'Brien murmured to Andy, watching him closely.

"First time here, sir."

"Just read your statement and memorise it. Don't expand on it. Got it?"

"Read, memorise, don't expand. Got it, boss." Andy gave him the thumbs up.

"Case against Eric Johnstone," called the court officer, about an hour later.

"Over here," replied O'Brien.

"Plea of guilty to murder accepted by the Crown," the court officer droned, like he was ordering a sausage roll at Gregg's. "Sentencing in a couple of weeks."

"I didn't expect that," commented O'Brien. "I suppose his defence counsel was trying to get a plea for Culpable Homicide instead?"

"Yeah."

"Oh well, home for me." O'Brien rose from his seat as all the other witnesses in the case followed suit.

Andy left the police witness room and was met with the sight of Catherine and Helen in the corridor; they were crying and hugging each other. Andy hesitated, but ultimately decided to follow his colleagues. He glanced at Joe, who had his eyes firmly fixed on Helen.

A few weeks later, Catherine and Helen sat hand in hand on the benches of the High Court in Edinburgh, listening to the Prosecution reveal the facts of the case to the Judge, and ask him for a life sentence to be imposed on Eric. The Defence Counsel laid out his case, but, in truth, there was very little he could say in defence of his client. His Lordship listened intently and noted everything they said. After a few minutes of silence, with only the odd whisper heard from the public benches, the jury, who had reconvened for this part of the proceedings, turned to look at the judge.

"Please stand," His Lordship boomed.

Eric Johnstone stood up, flanked by two police officers, and faced the judge who was to decide his future. Dressed in a white, open-necked shirt, grey flannels, and black shoes he looked just like any other man.

The judge began to speak. Johnstone's head bowed, he feared the worst.

"Eric Johnstone, I have listened carefully to the case for the prosecution and the case for the defence. You had before you a wonderful future. A life many would crave, but you chose to end the life of another human being for no reason at all. I can only come to one conclusion to this case, and one sentence." The judge paused for a moment as he looked through his papers; Andy could have heard a pin drop.

"Eric Johnstone, I hereby sentence to you to life imprisonment for the murder of Angela Johnstone. Take him down." Those were the last words Eric heard before he was led to the cells. As he was about to go downstairs, he glanced at the public benches, where he saw Helen and Catherine for the last time. He nodded at them as if to apologise. Helen and Catherine sat hugging each other tightly and stared at Eric as he disappeared down the narrow staircase.

News of the sentence was quickly relayed to everyone involved in the case: by telephone from the High Court, and later by word of mouth.

Joe sat in the police car with June.

"Hopefully I'll still be around when Eric Johnstone gets out," He muttered. The tone in Joe's voice, and the meaning behind his comment, was not lost on June, who remained silent.

Meanwhile, Andy, patrolling the streets alone with only his VHF radio for company, also had his mind on the sentencing. If there was one thing he wanted, it was to have Catherine back in his life. She'd made her decision for them to go their separate ways, and he had to respect that, but he also had to accept that their paths would cross by the very nature of their careers.

Andy smiled to himself.

He checked some lock fast shops for insecurities, and while he did so, he found himself thinking of Susan Berger, the teacher. The thought that he and Susan should end up working in the village of Bankvale. He knew nothing of the impact that Susan was soon to have in his life, as well as her father: retired police officer, Brian Berger. History was about to repeat itself, as a new inquiry began to unfold before his very eyes.

Looking Back

Looking Forward

Prologue

Over two years ago, at the tail end of 1979, Andy Blackmore packed away his trowel and spirit level for the last time. He had passed his entrance exams to join the police service, fulfilling a long-held, secret ambition.

His only concern was getting his long hair cut off after years of head-banging around the concert halls of Glasgow.

The walls of the barber shop were adorned with AC Milan memorabilia, particularly photographs of Giovanni's heroes, especially Baresi and Albertosi, the goalkeeper.

He sat in his regular chair, and asked Giovanni,

"Are you ready for this? Not a trim this time but short back and sides, please."

"Yeah, Andy you're joking, right?" he chided, his Italian/Scottish accent thick.

"Nope. Number four all over."

"Andy, why you do this madness?"

"Well, Gio, on Monday morning I'm going to be a cop."

"You, a cop? Andy! You never a cop, you a lay a brick and rock."

Andy smiled. "You know you're never going to forget this."

He watched as Giovanni clipped in the number four cutters. The buzzing sounds grew louder as the cutters approached his head.

"You a sure Andy? No gonna go back. When it's gone, it's gone."

Andy nodded, then watched his reflection in the mirror as his long locks fell, bit by bit, onto the floor, his ears seeing daylight for the first time in years.

Gio finished the job. "Oh Andy, the last time I saw you like this was maybe ten years ago!" He stared at Andy in the mirror.

Andy stared back, eyes wide with shock.

"Gio, what have you done?"

"Eh, I cut your hair, as you say."

"Gio, I'm only joking." Andy chuckled as he reached for his wallet.

"This one is free, my friend. I know you and your father many years."

"Hey Andy. I always wanted to do that to you."

"Hey Gio. Forza internazionale. I always wanted to say that to you."

They laughed and wrapped their arms around each other. "Good luck, Andy."

"Gio, I will always come here my friend." Andy went out the door, before promptly opening it again and sticking his shorn head in.

"Il mio amico Gio, Dio benedica internazionale!"

Gio threw a towel at the door. "Next time, it a numero due!"

Andy went to the local chippie, owned by Antonio: another Italian he had grown up with during his years in the tenements.

"Hey you," Andy called. "See that thing you wrote out for me, what have I just said to Giovanni?"

"You said you love him and want to marry him."

Andy shook his head and walked away. Antonio, a man made huge after years of eating fish and chips, was laughing heartily. He was swarthy-looking, with slicked-back hair that had remained unchanged over the years. What he actually taught Andy to say was, "my friend Gio, God bless Internazionale", also known as AC Milan's great rivals, Inter Milan.

Chapter Fifteen

A ndy had always wanted to be a cop in the city, because it was his stomping ground. He knew the backcourts, the streets, the people, and the tenements. Getting sent to the sticks (the countryside) was ideal.

Yet, looking back over his last two years, the sticks, had turned out to be the best thing that had ever happened to him. With the help of those around him, he was able to flourish into a fine policeman. His former classmates from college, who were working in City Divisions, had hardly progressed beyond the occasional arrest for a Breach of the Peace.

He had kept his word and returned to Giovanni for his haircuts, and to Antonio, who had the best fish and chips anywhere.

Andy left the East End, but the east end would never leave him.

Now that the probationary period was over, he made himself a promise: never arrest anyone for an offence that he had committed as a young man.

He was never a wild guy, like so many others. He'd had his mad moments in life, but nothing was ever nasty or evil: it was all just good fun. The police in those days hadn't been the friendliest. Andy was thinking especially of Billy Green. He held a special place in his heart, and always would, as the man who helped solve a murder case just before his death. His words, "never leave a stone unturned", would remain with him long into his career.

The night after his confirmation as a police officer, they celebrated getting to the end of a long, hard slog. Andy had arranged for everyone to meet in his local pub, as the atmosphere there was friendly towards police officers. His whole shift came out to celebrate, something that he would find himself doing for others in years to come. The one person missing was Catherine.

Andy thought *if she wanted to be here, she would be here. The relationship was not to be.*

"Andy!" June roared over the bustle. "If there was one woman you would want here tonight, who would it be?"

"You!" His colleagues roared with laughter.

"Okay, okay, in the fashion of the 'This Is Your Life' programme," continued June. "Do you remember your days at school? Do you remember recently meeting a lady who was in your class at school?"

"Em, aye." Andy suddenly felt a little uncomfortable.

"Do you remember her name?"

"Bob."

"Okay, really pissing me off that she is here." June rolled her eyes so Andy knew that she was only joking. "Let me introduce, Bankvale High school teacher, Miss Single, Not-Attached, Waiting-for-you-Andy, Susan Berger!"

Huge applause greeted Susan.

"Oh my God," she exclaimed, blushing. "This is mad! You are supposed to be respectable officers of the law"

Susan sat beside Andy and placed an arm around his neck.

"You have done well, and I am very proud of you." She stared straight into his eyes.

"Thanks." Andy laughed. "You know, we've done okay for a pair of east-enders."

"Yes, that we have. By the way, I heard all about your involvement in the Johnstone case."

"Do you remember Billy Green? The cop who lived near us?"

"Big Billy? Who could forget him? He scared me to death."

"He was the breakthrough in the case of Angela for me. It was Billy who solved it, in a way."

"Oh." Susan furrowed her brows.

Later, Andy was standing at the bar when June joined him.

"And whose idea was that?" Andy prompted.

"Mine."

"I just love you to bits. You're very special to me, June."

"Really?"

"Yeah, really. You, Joe, Georgie, even the Sergeant, who is something else. No matter what, in years to come, no matter where I go, I will never forget any of you, you know?"

"You're pissed."

"Me? Absolutely not! I'm being honest with you."

Susan came up to the bar. "Andy, this has been a blast, and, as I said earlier, I am so proud of you. But, I do have to head out now. I have a class at nine o'clock." She hesitated. "But maybe we could catch up next time you're home?" Susan gave Andy a brief hug, before turning to June to do the same. "June, thank you for inviting me."

"No problem."

June and Andy watched Susan walk out the door. June turned to Andy, and seemed surprised to see him there.

"Go after her! You'll regret it otherwise."

"Will I?" He paused. "What about you, June?"

"Don't make this more difficult than it is Andy. Go and get her."

"I'll call her. Shit! I haven't got her phone number, just the one for the school."

"You do now." June handed him a piece of paper.

"Where did you get that?"

"Susan gave it to me, for you, in case you might ask for it."

The celebration of Andy's confirmation ended with everyone heading home in taxis.

As Andy and June waited for theirs, she asked,

"What now, Andy?"

"Ten days off, as of today."

"You going to do anything special? Go somewhere warm?"

"That's the plan. Ibiza, Majorca, maybe Tenerife. My mates are all working, so I'll head out on my own. I've done it before. What about you?"

"I've time off too, but can't afford to do anything at the moment."

"Oh that's a shame." A taxi pulled up then, and Andy opened the door for himself. "Well anyway, I'll see you when I get back." They parted with a kiss on the cheek.

"Yeah, enjoy Andy."

Andy sat in his flat, pondering the long, lonely weekend ahead. Several times had he considered calling Catherine and asking her to tag along, but there was nothing there for him. He had to move on.

The following day, he cancelled his short break, and later that evening phoned the number June had given him. A woman answered.

"Would it be possible to speak to Susan, please?" Andy requested.

"Who is calling?"

"Andy Blackmore."

"Susan!" the woman yelled, her voice muffled by her hand on the receiver. " Andy Blackmore wants to speak to you."

"This is a surprise," Susan mused when she took the handset from her mother.

"I just wanted to thank you for coming to my night out."

"Oh, you're very welcome. Sorry, my stay was so short."

"Do you have any plans this weekend?"

"No, the schools are closed from Thursday to Tuesday for the mid-term holiday, but I have nothing planned."

"Would you like to go out on a long date?"

"What is a long date?"

"Friday to Monday?"

"Where? May I ask?"

"Well, I was thinking somewhere hot. My treat."

"You are mad you know? You want me to go away with you for a first date?"

"Sorry, I shouldn't have asked."

"I am flattered, honestly Andy."

"Leave it. We can have a normal evening out when I get back if you wish."

"That would be nice, thank you." She ended the call.

A few moments later, Andy's telephone rang.

"Andy, can you pick me up at the school at lunchtime tomorrow?" It was Susan. "We can see what's available. Life is too short to put things off. One o'clock would be good, but I have to be back by two."

"Certainly."

"Great. See you tomorrow."

On Thursday, at one o'clock on the dot, the school bell rang, and Susan ran towards Andy's car. She got in and looked him in the eye.

"You are mad!"

"Well, so are you." He smiled.

"Well-matched then." Susan returned the smile and winked.

A few minutes later, they arrived at the local travel agency.

"Hi, we are looking for a long weekend away. Either in Ibiza, Majorca, or Tenerife, leaving tomorrow and back Monday." Andy was straight to the point.

"Let me see what we have available." The agent scanned for options. "What type of accommodation would you prefer? A hotel, or an apartment?"

"Whatever is available," Susan replied.

"All we have is Majorca, Palma Nova. Hotel, half board, only one double room available."

"Well…" Andy trailed off.

"We'll take it," said Susan.

"Leaving at 07.00 hours from Glasgow Airport to Palma. Please be at the airport an hour beforehand. Shall I book everything for you?"

"Please do."

After a few minutes, the agent handed over the paperwork."This shows you've paid in full. Enjoy your break."

Once they were back in Andy's car, Susan commented, "you look a bit shell-shocked. I know what you're thinking. A double room on our first date. But we'll sort something out."

"Yeah, right. Only one thing to sort now. Getting to the airport."

"I finish at four o'clock. I can go home after, pack a bag, and stay at your's overnight. Then we can get a taxi to the airport in the morning, yeah?"

"Are you always this organised?"

"Definitely not, which you are about to find out."

A few hours later, Susan arrived at Andy's flat, two massive bags in hand.

"Jesus, Susan. We're only gone four days."

"Well, I want to look good for you."

They spent the evening catching up on the missing years over a small drink, before retiring for bed. Susan slept in Andy's bed, while he took the large chair for the few hours of sleep he would get before they would have to leave for the airport.

When 7:00 came, and Andy and Susan set out to enjoy their holiday. Meanwhile, there was a pending Complaints and Discipline Department interview over the arrest of Pat, unbeknownst to Andy. It was an assault complaint, and although Andy had heard plenty about that Department from other cops, this would be his first meeting with them. Andy knew a little unorthodox in the arrest of Pat, but it was certainly not an assault under Scots Law.

Chapter Sixteen

U pon landing at Palma Airport, Andy and Susan went through passport control and out onto the concourse, before boarding a bus to their hotel. Palma Cathedral soon came into view; a magnificent building on the right-hand side of the road, with steeples pointing at the sky: a landmark they both knew well from previous visits.

On arrival at the hotel, they checked in, and were handed keys to their room on the tenth floor.

Balcony doors opened onto a magnificent view over Palma Nova. Warm air and sunshine entered the room, something they were not used to during October.

They unpacked before going out to explore the area and get their bearings for later in the evening. They held hands walking along the promenade; it looked like been together for years.

"Hey, pal," coaxed a lad with a Scouse accent. "Interested in a timeshare? Great value."

"No thanks, mate."

"Free drinks and a gift if you go," he shouted after them as they started to walk away.

"I said, no thanks."

"Okay, keep yer hair on."

"Honestly can't be bothered with them," Andy muttered, shaking his head.

Back at the hotel, Andy offered the shower to Susan.

"Thank you."

"I'll wait on the balcony."

A short time later, Susan shouted to Andy that she was finished in the bathroom. She was sitting at the dressing table, using her hairdryer, when she caught Andy staring.

"What?" She gazed at him in the mirror.

"Just thinking how fantastic you look, even like that."

"Thank you." She smiled. "Just wait until I'm finished."

Andy stepped into the shower.

"For God's sake!" He yelled when he turned the water on. "This water is freezing!"

"Oh yeah, forgot to tell you about that!" Susan laughed.

When Andy came out of the bathroom,Susan was standing there, waiting for him. She was only slightly shorter than Andy, and her shoulder-length brown hair framed her oval face. Tiny specks of gold dotted her hazel eyes. Black trousers hugged her slim figure, and a stylish white blouse matched her pearl earrings.

"Wow, you look amazing," Andy breathed.

"Thank you."

They had dinner at the hotel, and then went into town, where they drank at a bar into the small hours of the morning, before eventually returning to the hotel. Sitting on the balcony looking over the bay — the lights shining from the street and reflecting on the water around the bay —Andy drew Susan to him and gently kissed her.

"Took you long enough, Andy."

As he closed the balcony door and drew the curtain, Susan switched off the bedside light. And in that moment, the issue of who slept on which side of the bed was forgotten as Andy got in beside Susan.

All throughout the flight home, as the plane passed over France and England before swinging out over Ireland and heading into Glasgow, Andy and Susan chatted about the next stage in their relationship.

When they started circling over the city, the familiar sight of the Campsie Hills of East Dunbartonshire came into view. Then, as the plane began to descend, Andy felt as though he could touch the high-rise flats of Drumchapel and Yoker and scoop water out of the River Clyde.

Finally, they landed with a thud. The noise of the engine increased as the plane slowed down and turned in towards the docking area.

After disembarking, Andy and Susan stood in the main hall of the airport with their luggage at their feet. The atmosphere between them was strained: silence lingered for a couple of minutes.

"What do we do now?" Andy finally piped up.

"Hmm. How about you go to your place and I go home? Then, you dump your bags, get in your car and come for dinner, so I can introduce the man who has been sleeping with their daughter for four days to my parents."

"I would like that, but can you think of a better way to introduce me?"

"You'll just have to wait and see. One more thing, dinner is always at six pm sharp. And Mum hates being late with dinner."

Back in the east end, this time in Springhill, Andy parked his car outside the Berger family home. He had managed to grab some flowers at the local garage for Mrs. Berger. It was the least he could do, given he had been away with her daughter before even meeting either of the parents.

At 17:45 exactly, Andy rang the doorbell. After a tense few seconds, a tall, slim man with greying hair answered.

"Can I help you?"

"Em, flower delivery for Mrs. Berger."

Taking the flowers from Andy, the man closed the door without another word.

Right, plan B.

Once again, he rang the doorbell, and the same man answered the door.

"Oh, have you forgotten something? Do I need to sign for them?"

"No, sir. Is Susan at home? I'm Andy."

"Susan!" he bellowed, before turning his back on Andy and retreating into the house. Then, Susan appeared.

"Andy! Come in." Susan led him into a dining room. "Mum, Dad, this is Andy."

"Pleased to meet both of you." He smiled.

"Oh, right," her father huffed. "I'm Brian, and you must be the person who was away with our daughter this weekend. Did you have fun?"

"Yes sir, we had a great time."

"Thank you for the flowers, Andy!" Mrs. Berger squealed.

"And where are my flowers, considering I kept you entertained for days?" Susan teased, smiling.

Andy wondered what would be coming next.

"Let's sit," Susan suggested.

At six o'clock on the dot, homemade vegetable soup was laid on the table.

"Thank you, Mrs. Berger." Andy bowed his head.

"Call me Sandra, please. Think you're a bit old to call me Mrs. Berger."

"Thank you, Sandra."

"So, Andrew," Brian barked. "I understand you were in Majorca with my daughter this weekend."

This was the moment Susan was dreading; her father had cost her boyfriend after boyfriend, and she was never allowed to have a proper relationship with anyone, even at her age.

"Yes, sir."

"I never even knew she was away until my wife told me."

"Really?"

"This is not something I approve of, you hear?"

"Dad," Susan groaned.

"Leave it, Susan," Andy commanded. "Please continue, sir."

"I like to know where she is, at all times."

"Okay." Andy raised an eyebrow. "The night before we went to Majorca, she spent the night at my place."

He did not mention the fact that they never slept together. Brian threw his wife a look of disapproval.

"Then we flew from Glasgow to Majorca and had four great days together."

There was an awkward silence, penetrated only by the sound of Sandra slurping her soup..

"So, what do you do for a living Andy?" Brian suddenly interjected. "What are your aspirations in life? Why should I allow you to see my daughter? Oh, and before you answer, I should note that I was a police officer for over thirty years, so be careful what you say in my presence. I can detect a liar a mile away. I finished as a Chief Superintendent, you know."

Andy eyed Susan in his peripheral. She never cracked a light that her father was an ex-cop. Andy also glanced at Sandra, who was staring into her bowl. His feeling was that this man ruled the roost, and he and Susan would have to be strong together to over come him.

"Well, sir, that was three questions in one. Which do you want answered first?"

"Whatever one you feel capable of answering first. Then the others."

"Okay. Firstly, what do I do for a living, I breathe. Secondly, about my aspiration in life? To make Susan happy. Thirdly, why should you allow me to see Susan? Because she is like me. We're both twenty-seven now, we were at school together, and I'm an east-ender like she is. We were made for each other." Andy looked at Susan and Sandra. They were staring at him; nobody had ever spoken to Brian like that.

"So, did you detect any lies?" Andy inquired, raising his eyebrows.

"I didn't," Brian answered, red in the face.

"Good, because there weren't any."

Andy suddenly felt pressure on his right foot and saw that Susan was grinding her heal into his toes.

"Okay, Andrew." Brian threw up his hands. "You say you breathe for a living. I can accept that. Hopefully, that continues, so long as you don't hurt my daughter. Let me put it this way, how do you earn a living?"

"Well, sir, I was a bricklayer for nearly ten years."

"Oh my God, Sandra! She has found herself a bricklayer!" Brian wheezed, smacking the table with a large hand.

"I said I was. And do you know something? I'm proud I have a trade if things ever go wrong with my current career."

"Which is?"

"I'm a police officer."

Susan glanced at her father, who looked stunned, his smile gone. Her mother nearly choked on her soup out of sheer delight.

"Oh, and before you ask, I keep fit by playing football and rugby, among other things."

"Other things?"

"Yes, sir."

"Explain. Do you run, or jog, or what?"

"Yeah, I do a little of that. I am a Second dan black belt in judo, and so you will find me in the Dojo almost every morning or afternoon, depending on my shifts. If you want to object to me seeing your daughter, we can take it outside." Andy laughed. Sandra looked at Andy and shook her head.

"You are what?" Susan queried her eyebrows raised and a small smile on her face.

"Right!" Sandra interjected. "Who is ready for the main course? Square sliced sausages with mash, and cauliflower with cheese sauce."

"Magic." Andy beamed at Sandra. "It's been years since I've had that."

"Right," Susan commented, walking behind her mother into the kitchen. "Let's wind this conversation back a bit, shall we?"

Andy followed her.

"Are you telling the truth, Andy?" she whispered.

"About what?"

"Your hobby."

"It is not a hobby, it is a way of life. And yes, it is the truth."

"Sandra, that was magic," Andy announced once he had cleaned his plate. "Thank you so much."

"You're very welcome, and please come again soon. You're a breath of fresh air around here."

Susan felt reassured knowing she would have her mother's back.

Brian spoke up after wiping his mouth with a napkin. "Where do you work, Andrew?"

"Bankvale."

"Oh, Susan works there in the school."

"That's actually how we reunited. It was during an inquiry I was involved in. She assisted us with it."

"Is your Divisional Commander Hughie Burch?"

"Yes, I believe so."

"Hughie and I served together in his younger days. We were in the lodge together. Are you a traveller, Andrew?"

Andy knew exactly what he was referring to. It was about being a Mason, but was not going to rise to the bated question.

"I am a traveller. I love the Canary Islands."

"What do you mean by the fact you believe he is your Divisional. Commander?"

"Wouldn't know him if he walked in this door right now. I don't have a lot of time for senior officers who spend their time being promoted through the offices without getting their hands dirty."

Susan shifted uneasily in her seat. Andy noticed, promptly shifting the conversation toward Brian's hobbies, now that he had retired.

"Nowadays, I prefer a life of leisure and pottering about the garden."

Andy smiled and checked his watch.

"Susan, I better be heading out. Mrs. Berg— I mean, Sandra, thank you for dinner. Mr. Berger, it has been a pleasure meeting you, sir."

As Andy stood up, so did Mr. Berger.

"Call me Brian," he uttered, almost reluctantly. He extended his hand. "Look after my daughter and you will be fine with me."

Andy shook his hand. Susan was stunned, this had never happened before with anyone she had brought home.

Susan saw Andy out the door. They had a quick kiss.

"I'll call you," he promised.

"Please do."

Susan retreated to the living room and sat down.

"I like him," Brian announced. "I like him."

"Well, don't scare him away, Brian," Sandra warned.

"He won't scare easily." He turned to Susan. "Well, young lady, what have you got to say for yourself?"

"He is special, very special. And all weekend he treated me with absolute respect."

"Do you love him? Does he love you?"

"Dad, this is very early days to be speaking that way."

"Well, my betting is he is very, very fond of you, to say the least. I think you have found someone, a soulmate, and that is special indeed."

Susan went to bed, happy that her dad had finally accepted someone in her life. Now it was just a matter of seeing how things developed in their relationship.

Christmas was rapidly approaching.

Andy hoped he had not made a mess of things with Susan's parents, for Susan's sake. But did he care himself? No. He couldn't wait to get back to work in a couple of days.

The following morning, Andy discovered that his answering machine had a lot of missed calls. They were all from Joe and June, asking him to call them. They did not disclose a reason, but they both sounded anxious.

"Joe, it's Andy. How are you?"

"When are you due back in the office?" Joe fired back.

"Uh, I have a couple of days yet, so Friday, early shift."

"Okay, this is the score. You're getting a visit from the Complaints and Discipline Department."

"Has someone made a complaint about me?"

"Someone saw the way you took hold of Pat that night he had the knife and has complained to the boss. He had to pass it on."

"Oh okay," Andy answered casually. "No problem. I'll see you Friday then."

"We've all been interviewed while you were off, but we can sort it on Friday before they arrive."

"Thanks, Joe."

Well, this is going to be interesting,.

He knew that a complaint of assault was a serious matter and could lead to all sorts of consequences, including an appearance in court.

He also had to consider Susan in all this, and decide what he would and would not tell her.

Chapter Seventeen

A t 16:00, Andy was outside Bankvale High School in time to see Susan get into her car. He swiftly blocked her path with his car before she could move off. As he left his vehicle and approached hers, she rolled down the window.

"Excuse me. Can I detain you for dinner tomorrow night?"

"You certainly can officer."

"Good. My place, after you finish. You are free to go now, thank you."

Susan watched as he returned to his car and drove off. Just then, she thought she might be in love. She had never felt this way in such a short time before, but everything was so relaxed and natural with Andy. She knew in her heart that she wanted to be with him.

After work, she went home to find her mother alone.

"Look at you," she mused, beaming at her daughter. "I remember that look. That's what your father looked like when he met me."

"Oh Mum, behave."

"Susan, you better not lose this one. I will work on your father if he gives either of you grief. But somehow, I don't think that is going to happen this time."

"Thanks, Mum." Sandra kissed her cheek.

"When are you seeing him again?"

"Tomorrow night for dinner."

"Good! I am pleased for you both."

"Mum, why are you looking at me like that?"

"I think I might start looking for a hat."

"Oh my god, Mum we're not getting married yet!" They both laughed.

"Why all the hilarity?" Brian looked puzzled as he came through the door.

"Nothing!" They replied in unison.

The following evening, Susan arrived at Andy's expecting to go out for dinner. To her surprise, he had a table set for two.

"You cook?"

"Yep. Well, I try. Should be about an hour until it's ready."

"Great."

"Can I offer you a drink?"

"I'm driving, so I'll have a lemonade if you've got it?"

"Sure, coming right up."

She saw a small blue box lying on one of the place settings. Her heart started to pound. There's no way he's going to propose so soon! After one weekend away.

"What are we having?"

"Oh, just a little something I rattled together."

She watched as he boiled rice, and cringed when he strained it. He then shovelled the rice into a large dish. Opening the oven, he revealed his prize possession: a Moroccan tagine.

"There you go," he announced as he carried it over and placed it on a mat. "I have taken a real chance making this." He lifted the lid, and a plume of steam rose to reveal an aromatic Moroccan lamb stew.

"Is that lamb?"

"Yes."

"That poor little lamb was wandering about a field a few weeks ago, and now we're about to eat it?"

"Oh right. I know I took a chance on this one, sooooo it is either that or Rice Krispies."

"Lamb for me, then."

"Hells Bells, I haven't a clue what I am going to do with you."

"Oh, should be good experimenting then." She had a devilish look in her eyes.

"Before we start dinner, that blue box is for you."

"O-okay."

"Would you like to open it?"

Susan lifted the box from the table before slowly prying it open, only to gaze at a brilliant diamond. It was set in a golden heart pendant which lay on a bed of dark blue velvet.

"Oh my God," she breathed, holding the box in one hand and covering her mouth with the other, trying to hold back tears.

"It's stunning! But what is this for?"

"For being mad. For trusting me and going away with me., For being you. I have never been in this situation before, where someone has swept me off my feet the way you have."

Andy stood up from the table and took the pendant from Susan to clip it securely around her neck.

He gazed at Susan once he sat down again. "Are you sure you're okay?"

"Yes, oh yes. I am. Christ, what is happening here?" She wiped a tear from her eye.

"What is happening is that we are about to eat Mary's little lamb."

Susan laughed through the tears, smiling blearily. they began to eat.

"Andy, can I have a glass of wine please?"

"No, you're driving,"

"I am not going to ask again," she teased. "Make it a large one."

"Are you sure?"

"Very. Do you know, in one visit, you won over my Mum's heart."

"Really?"

"Yes."

"Well, I must admit she won mine over with that dinner. But it might be inappropriate for me to ask her out and see her daughter at the same time."

"Is there anything you can't do? Black belt, cop, bricklayer, and cook?"

Once they finished dinner, Andy announced, "coffee to be served over at the couch. Also, I was thinking, if I've won over your Mum's heart in one visit, how about you?"

"Andy this weekend was pure magic. I have to tell you, being there with you was something special. When you came to school about the Angela Johnstone case, I knew who you were instantly. And I felt that you sort of remembered me. June was watching me like a hawk. She must have found my suspicious, gawking at you. But I just couldn't believe how you turned out from the kid I knew at school. You know June is mad about you, don't you? But, to answer your question, when you blocked my car yesterday and asked me to dinner, my heart melted." She sipped on her coffee. "Do you want a laugh?"

Andy quirked an eyebrow.

"No, no, forget it."

"No, go for it,"

"Mum is going to look for hats."

"Why? Hasn't she got one?"

Susan chuckled. "Nah, think she is just looking for a new one for next summer."

"Looking for a hat in December. Women are mad." He took a deep breath. "You know how we've done things kind of back to front? As in going away before we dated? Could we get some orderly fashion into this? Would you be my date to the office's Christmas night? It's in a couple of weeks."

"Hmm." She tapped her chin with a finger. "There is one condition. No matter what shift you are, you have to go to mine after."

"Why?"

"Because I want to introduce everyone to the man in my life who, after such a short time, means everything to me."

"Done deal Susan, done deal." Andy pulled Susan close.

As they listened to Buddy Guy, Andy's thoughts turned to the complaint made against him.

"Andy, we have to take a look at your music tastes."

"Okay, but absolutely no jazz. What time do you want the alarm set for in the morning?"

"Seven. And get used to it."

Chapter Eighteen

A ndy's short break with Susan seemed a lifetime ago.Andy, June, Joe," barked Sergeant Black. "Kitchen confab time." The kettle was boiled, and Joe prepared four mugs of tea and laid them on the table.

"Andy, the suits are coming after you for assault, big time, because of the way you took on Pat Callaghan and virtually paralysed him. You know this results in an official interview. There are two possible outcomes to this complaint. One, you get the sack. Or two, you get the sack, plus jail. Callaghan didn't file the complaint. Someone saw you in the village. Anyone you've fallen out with?"

"Nobody that I know of, Sergeant." Andy tried to remain calm and nonchalant.

"Right, this is the situation. You are entitled to have someone in the room with you during the interview. Who do you want?"

Andy thought for a minute. "Well, Joe was there at the time, and so was June. I presume they have both been interviewed, so, if you don't mind, that leaves you or someone else from the shift who wasn't there. But I don't want anyone to bother over something I did."

"Joe, June, leave us," commanded Sergeant Black. They discussed Andy's options. If he was being interrogated, then he had the right to a lawyer. Though maybe he was being interviewed in general about the incident. Andy would have to wait and see.

They both returned to the office just before ten o'clock.

"You okay, Andy? Have they been in yet?"

"Yes and no, June."

"I've said it before," Joe spoke up, "but you can be like ice sometimes. I don't know how you do it."

"He's just frightening at times," commented June as they walked away.

"Let's see how he gets on when they go for him."

"Sergeant," Andy called. "I'll be outside if you're looking for me."

"Why are you going outside Andy?" Joe asked.

"To prepare."

Joe and June finished their break and went into the muster room. They both stared out the window overlooking the yard.

"What is he doing, June?"

"Haven't a clue."

Andy stood stock still, one hand over the other, breathing slowly.

"He's crazy, June."

"Yeah. But he's also kind, and a beautiful person."

"June?"

"Joe, leave it. There is only one woman for him and it's not me."

Suddenly, the door to the yard opened and the Sergeant stepped out. He gestured for Andy to come inside, who nodded before following him in.

Andy went to the Gents toilet, keeping the two Chief Inspectors by the front door waiting. He looked in the full-length mirror and heard the ghost of his friend Billy Green. "If you look good, you feel good."

Andy made his way into the Inspector's office, followed by Sergeant Black.

"Take a seat, Andy. I am Chief Inspector Grant, and this is Chief Inspector Mahoney."

"Well, if you are Chief Inspector Grant and you are Chief Inspector Mahoney, then I am Constable Blackmore."

Sergeant Black cringed at this reply. Neither Chief Inspector responded. Here was a young officer, with just over two years of service.

"Gentlemen, do you have something to ask me? Rather than doing my job, I am using up the public's money doing this."

Mahoney's lips tightened. Andy could tell that Grant was the calmer one.

"Right, you," Mahoney spat. "What did you do the night you arrested Pat?"

"Pat?"

"Pat Callaghan," Chief Inspector Grant clarified.

"Oh, we playing good cop, bad cop?"

"Andy," Sergeant Black cautioned.

Andy held up a hand. "Sergeant, I'm good. Gentlemen, let's go for it."

He remained calm, hands resting on his lap.

"It is alleged that you assaulted Patrick Callaghan, using methods not sanctioned by the National and Force Training methods, which constitutes a possible assault."

"Whoa, whoa, whoa, let us be clear here. It's either an assault or it isn't. You said I assaulted Patrick, then you followed that up by saying it's a possible assault. I am sure you both know the definition of assault in Scotland. I do not I into that category. I protected myself and my fellow officers, and there is not a judge in Scotland who would convict me. Remember, there has to be criminal intent, and there was none on my part. Remember he was the one holding a knife and threatening to use it."

Andy stood up. "This interview is over. I shall send you both a statement concerning the incident. You're both on a fishing expedition. Try the loch, it's full of them."

Andy walked out of the room to see Joe and June at the far end of the corridor. He winked at them. Sergeant Black left the room immediately, followed by the two Chief Inspectors.

"We want that statement on our desks in seventy-two hours, Sergeant," Mahoney huffed. He side-eyed Andy.. "One of these days, he is ours."

"Yes, sir." Sergeant Black showed the Chief Inspectors out, before returning with a sour expression. "Joe! June! My office, now!"

They discussed Andy at length. Sergeant Black asked if they had made an error allowing him to complete his probation. Was he a ticking time bomb?

June was first to respond. "Sergeant, this is no kid. He's from the east end of Glasgow, brought up in the tenements. He lived in the backcourts, and had to rely on his wits. We can't change him now."

"Joe, your thoughts?"

"I agree with June on this one, it's still early days, but I have to say that I would rather have him on our side than not."

"Meaning?"

Joe considered this for a moment, staring at the floor. "See if the day ever came that we are in serious bother, I would want him beside me."

"One hundred per cent," agreed June.

"So how do we reign in his east end attitude? He admires both of you. He's likely to listen to you."

"We keep it, but refine it," suggested Joe.

Sergeant Black contemplated what to do. "Refine him then. And tomorrow, we get that statement. You know, every so often someone comes along in this job that you know is special in some way. I like this guy, although I do not know why. So, say nothing. I have never seen someone take on Complaints and Discipline bosses as he did. So young in service, to be so calm and cold, it's like dealing with an iceberg."

June was smiling as she and Joe left the office. "Wonder how he is going to take to his new nickname."

"Eh?"

"Iceberg."

"Well I'm not telling him."

They found Andy sitting in the kitchen, mulling over his tea. June sat first, then Joe.

"Well, young man," Joe started, "we have been given the unenviable task of refining your east end manner, which we think is not going to be such an easy task. But if you want to get your pension, you're going to have to change." He paused before adding, "oh, and June has something to tell you."

"No, I don't."

"Yes, you do."

"Andy you know how everyone, well, almost everyone, has a nickname on this shift?"

"Yes?"

"Well, someone made a comment that you are like an iceberg, so that's your nickname from this day forth. It will stick with you forever."

"Iceberg?" Andy considered this, shaking his head and smiling.

"So, to more pressing matters." June was eager to change the subject. "The Christmas night out is all booked. An overnight stay down the coast in a four-star hotel. Problem is that Stevie and his wife aren't able to go now, but they still have to pay for the room and the party night."

"Can you leave that until tomorrow?" Andy requested. "I might be able to help out there."

"Uh-oh, what are you up to this time?"

"Nothing. Just have to check something, then we may be able to sort things out." He stood up. "Well, as I'm the spare man today, it is foot patrol in the town centre for me. See you guys."

Iceberg. Wait until I tell Susan that one. Andy walked down the corridor with a smirk on his face and shaking his head.

A couple of hours later Andy was rounding a corner which lead to the car park behind the shops, when he saw a vehicle with two males inside watching staff coming and going from the local chemist. That door, Andy knew, often lay ajar when the staff were in, making it easier for them to get to the rubbish bins.

The men could not see Andy from their position, as he had partially concealed himself behind the large rubbish bins used by the shopkeepers.

"Zulu 169 to control, over."

"Go ahead, 169."

"Can I have a PNC check on a black Ford Cortina, registration number JYS 391 J?

"Aye." There was a short pause. "Control to Zulu 169, come in."

"Go ahead."

"Can you give me the registration number again? What you have given me refers to a yellow Ford Escort."

Andy repeated the number as before.

"Where is the vehicle?"

"Rear of the shops in the town centre."

"Maintain a static watch on the vehicle. I'll get someone to join you."

"Zulu 169 to control. The car is on the move out of the car park."

"Roger. Is there any vehicle in the vicinity of the town centre shops?"

Everyone was attending other calls so there was nobody available to intercept as the vehicle drove away. Andy spotted a white, oval sticker with the letter D in the centre stuck on the boot of the car. Despite a search by other officers, the vehicle could not be found.

Andy submitted an intelligence report, noting his observations.

Susan stopped off at Andy's place on her way home from school.

"Susan, this is a lovely surprise."

"Glad you approve."

"You checking to see if I have a harem in here?" Andy laughed.

"Don't even joke about that, silly. I just have something to ask you."

"Fire away."

"Will you go with me to teacher's Christmas party?"

"Yes, of course. I was going to ask you the same thing for ours." He hesitated a moment. "Susan, I haven't mentioned to anyone in the office about us being away."

"That's fine."

"Stevie and his wife— oh I should explain. Firstly, our night out is in a four-star hotel down the coast and is an overnighter. But, as I was saying, Stevie and his wife can't go, so there are two tickets and a double room available. I have to let June know tomorrow."

"Great! Say yes. They have to find out about us eventually." Susan kissed his cheek. "I'm heading home now Andy, are you okay for tomorrow night?"

"Yes, but I have the early shift on Sunday," he moaned.

First thing Saturday morning, Andy was hauled into the Sergeant's office. They prepared a statement for Complaints and Discipline, then sealed it in an internal envelope for delivery to the Force Headquarters. Soon afterwards, Andy was back in the town centre.

Over the past couple of years, the shopkeepers had gotten to know Andy better, and so he was more than welcome in any of the shops for a cup of tea and a chat.

One shop he liked was the newsagents.Big Jessie Keegan worked there. She was in her mid-forties, rotund, with a ruddy complexion and short-cropped black hair. She was also a divorcée with four children and lived up on Spill Hill. If someone sneezed within a ten-mile radius, big Jessie heard it. Trust was a big issue for Jessie, but as time went by, she grew more and more at ease with Andy, as he had always been honest with her from the first day they had met.

"Fancy cream cakes for breakfast, Jessie?" shouted Andy through the open door of the shop.

"Aye, why not? You will have to do the teas. I'm too busy."

"I'll go get them." He knew the last thing Jessie needed was cream cakes.

Returning with three bags from the bakers, Andy went into the back of the shop, switched on the kettle, and laid out three mugs.

"Hey Tony, I got you a cream cake too."

"How did you know I was here, Andy?"

"I saw your reflection in the mirror above the door."

"Geez, Andy. Good thing I wasn't doin' anything with Jessie." Tony laughed.

"I heard that! You've no chance."

"Hey Jessie, what 'bout Andy?" shouted Tony.

"Now yer talkin'." The air was filled with laughter. "And Maggie here says she's next."

"Behave yersel' Jessie, and don't give Maggie any ideas."

"Oh, I don't. She has enough of her own where you're concerned, Andy."

"Jessie, you'll be terrifying the boy," Maggie chided.

As Tony went to the front of the shop, Jessie went to get her tea and cream cake.

"Andy," she whispered. "Keep an eye on the chemist's shop, would you? One of my daughters works in there. The word on the hill is it's going to get done."

"When?"

"Tomorrow, it's the only one open in the area, and this place is dead on a Sunday."

"Thanks, Jessie."

"My daughter is working tomorrow. That's why I'm telling you."

"Does she know it's going to happen?"

"No, I don't want to frighten her. Try to get it stopped before it does."

"Sure, I'll pass everything on when I go back to the station. Thank you, Jessie." He patted her shoulder.

He left the newsagents, knowing that, if this robbery was on, he had to make sure Jessie's daughter was safe. He could not let her down. The problem was that, with this type of crime, anything could go wrong.

Chapter Nineteen

Back at the office, Andy relayed the information to Sergeant Black, who immediately phoned through to the Divisional CID. "Sergeant Black here. Ah, Detective Inspector O'Dowd. How are you this fine day?"

"Good, good," replied the DI.

"Listen, we have a bit of information you might be interested in. Are you coming down this way?"

"Yes, I was coming down to the office later."

"Great, we shall see you then." Sergeant Black put down the telephone and turned his attention to Andy. "Did Jessie say who was involved and if they would have any weapons on them?"

"No, she didn't."

"If this comes off, we'll give Jessie a few shillings to spend on her children. Get your break early, then we'll see what the DI has to say about this. Also, what about the matter of the black Cortina yesterday? Could this all be linked?"

Andy was considering Sergeant Black's questions when June walked into the kitchen, followed closely by Joe.

"Any information for me about the Christmas night out?" She quirked an eyebrow.

"Yes. I'll take Stevie's tickets and room. We just have to get rid of my ticket and the single room, if that suits you."

"Brilliant. A mate of mine was going to take your ticket if it became available."

"Magic. We're all sorted."

"Who are you bringing with you, Andy?" Joe smiled.

"Susan."

"As in Susan Berger?"

"Yep, the same Susan that I was in Majorca with."

Andy walked off.

"You okay, June?" Joe whispered.

June shrugged. "Of course I am, why wouldn't I be?"

Sergeant Black found Andy in the kitchen. "Andy, the DI is here now. Come on and fill him in on what you've heard." Andy relayed all the information he had been given, as well as what he had observed, regarding the black Ford Cortina with the false number plates. The DI drew a pipe from his pocket, filled it with tobacco and lit up.

"What are your thoughts on this one, Andy?" He asked finally..

"Well, sir, everything adds up. Could be a runner."

"I agree. I'll make arrangements and be back here at six o'clock tomorrow morning. I take it you guys are early shift again?"

"Yes, sir."

"Sergeant, your whole shift has a six o'clock start. I'll authorise the overtime since they're starting before the normal time."

"Fine, sir. I'll inform them when we finish later."

Later on, Andy was passing the newsagents when he saw Jessie behind the counter. He nodded a greeting, which she acknowledged with a quick smile.

At the end of the shift, Sergeant Black rounded everyone up to inform them of the early start, which was greeted by a chorus of moans.

"Don't blame me, blame Andy," he declared as he walked away.

Susan arrived at Andy's flat near seven o'clock in the evening, dressed casually in jeans, a t-shirt, a leather jacket, and black boots.

"Sooo…" Susan trailed off. She received a blank stare from Andy. "Christmas night out?" He smiled.

"It's all arranged, and we are no longer a secret." He hugged her.

"How did June take it?"

"Eh?"

"You know she's mad about you."

"Oh.."

"You'd have to be blind not to see that."

"Susan, she's a colleague and a dear friend, and that's all it is on my side."

"Alright. Anything else you would care to share with me?"

"Me?" He pulled her into his arms again.

"Don't be funny, I'm being serious." Susan wriggled free.

"You've lost me."

"This might be none of my business, Andy, but you had a visit from two senior officers when you went back to work, no?"

"Wait a minute, how the hell do you know that?"

"Do you have to ask?"

"Of course! Your father, the brotherhood, the masonic lodge!" Andy rolled his eyes.

"I'm sorry, Andy, but he still has a lot of contacts, and he is very protective of me."

"Looks like he's still investigating whether I'm good enough for his daughter, eh?" He smiled.

Susan stared at Andy, knowing this was the truth.

"C'mon Susan, let's go out. Oh, before I forget, I'm up at quarter to five tomorrow morning."

Susan rolled her eyes. "Looks like I am making my breakfast then."

They sat in Andy's local pub, listening to the band play covers of some of his favourite songs. Susan slipped her hand into his and leaned on him.

A young man approached them, wringing his hands together. "Hello Miss Berger. You might not remember me, I'm Robbie Jones. You were my teacher for a few years at Wellbank."

"Of course I remember you, Robbie! How are you?"

"Fine, thanks."

"So, Robbie, what became of you? Are you working?"

"Sort of. I manage. It's so nice to see you again. I'll leave you with your friend. Enjoy your evening."

Andy watched as Robbie Jones rejoined friends. He also noticed them looking over in their direction.

"Andy, are you alright?"

"Yeah, I'm fine." But, as he continued watching the small group, he came to a decision. "Let's get out of here. It's a bit loud."

"Sure."

"Goodnight Miss Berger!" Robbie called from his table, waving. "Goodnight Andy!"

"Goodnight," they replied in unison.

They stopped at the local off-licence kiosk to purchase a bottle of white wine. When they got back to Andy's flat, Susan kicked off her boots and curled up on the couch. Andy handed her a glass of wine, and once he sat down, she snuggled into him.

"Susan, how well did you know Robbie Jones?"

"I don't, I was just being polite. I only did a placement at Wellbank School when I was a student."

"Susan, how did he know my name? You never introduced me."

"I don't know."

Andy felt uneasy and wanted to change the subject. "Now that my probation is over, I've been thinking of buying a flat of my own. I was just planning on renting this one until I could be sure things would work out here. would you like to go flat hunting with me? Maybe I could get one we both like?"

"After only a few weeks you're asking me to move in with you?"

"No, I'm not that presumptuous."

"Oh, so you're not asking then?"

"Well, maybe it's something we can think about in the future."

"Yes, we can, if that's what you want."

"You know you would have to leave your father at home if you moved in with me."

"It's a deal then." They laughed.

Before leaving the flat the next morning, Andy gently kissed a sleeping Susan and whispered, "I love you." As he closed the door, Susan smiled, engulfed by the feeling of being loved.

The chemist shop was due to open at ten o'clock, before closing at four in the afternoon. DI O'Dowd had made a detailed plan and marked on a map exactly where he wanted all his CID officers, as well as the traffic vehicles. This would be a long day for everyone. Sergeant Black's officers were to maintain a standard Sunday routine, to not raise suspicion. Beat officers, including Andy, would walk the town centre and surrounding area as usual. Both mobile patrols would remain in their respective areas, and everyone would be on the lookout for the Ford Cortina. DI O'Dowd was very clear that under no circumstances was the vehicle to be stopped coming into the town.

"Any questions?"

"Sir, what about the staff in the chemist shop?" asked one plainclothes officer.

"I spoke to Mr. McIntyre yesterday and he is aware of the circumstances, so he knows that he will have a few extra customers today. I also told him that the safety of the staff is paramount to this operation, Anything else?"

The question was met with complete silence.

The officers who were meant to watch the chemist shop were deployed immediately to take up their points around the town centre. In his peripheral, Andy saw two officers open a metal strongbox and pulled out two handguns, which they quickly concealed into their shoulder holster under their jackets.

The early shift cleaned their vehicles, as usual, before taking to the streets.Andy went out on foot patrol in the town centre on his own.

Tony was stacking mountains of the Sunday newspaper, waiting for his delivery boys who were due to arrive shortly.

"Tea, Tony?"

"Yeah, thanks."

From the surrounding areas, the first of the boys arrived on their bikes, followed by a few girls. They all handed their money over to Tony, who gave them the papers at less than face value, they made their money from the papers and plus tips.

"Hey Andy," called one of the kids. "You on your own? You wanna buy a paper? Would you give us a hand?"

"They're good kids I have here," Tony commented. "Sometimes you wonder how they go wrong later in life."

"Mmm," Andy replied, finishing his tea. "Well, I have to go check the properties and make sure nothing has been broken into during the night."

"Take care out there."

Acting as if he was being watched, Andy went around each shop in the town centre including the chemist's, which was secured from back to front. Following the Sunday routine, he then checked the shops on either side and lastly the bank.

Locals began to appear on the streets, some heading for church, some heading for the chapel, but most heading to Tony's for their Sunday papers and the statutory Scottish hangover cure, Irn Bru.

Andy saw a grey transit van pull into the car park behind the chemist shop. The driver got out and walked towards Tony's shop. Andy followed him in.

"Can I have this packet of mints, please?"

"Long walk for a packet of mints," commented Andy. "Considering you could have parked outside. It is Sunday after all."

"I park where I am told to, Constable." He glanced around, making sure nobody else was in the shop. Then he stared at Andy, as if sending a coded message.

"I suppose you have to do as the gaffer tells you."

"Aye, it's handy for the job today. Saves lugging materials about."

"Double time on a Sunday. I remember it well. Don't have to do that in this job."

"I know." The man left the shop.

"Is everything okay, Andy?" Tony piped up.

"Yep, all is good. See ya, Tony."

The silence on the radios that day was surreal: everybody waiting to see if the information would turn out to be true, and if Andy's observations from the day before would bear fruit.

Patrolling the streets, Andy's mind wandered to the night before, and that slightly suspicious meeting with Robbie Jones. Was it a ploy to lead Susan into a trap? To see if she knew who he was? Did her little white lie about remembering him prove to be fateful? Was he just a genuine guy being polite? Andy's gut feeling ruled out the latter. He didn't think that was the end of it, and when all this was over today, he would, at the very least, inform his Sergeant.

At around nine o'clock in the morning, Andy got a call on his radio.

"Zulu 169, return to the office."

"Roger."

He returned within a few minutes.

"Andy," called one of the civilian assistants, Margaret. "Phone your home number. Someone called Susan wants to speak to you."

Andy called his home number and listened until he was transferred to the answering machine.

"Margaret, when did Susan call here?"

"About fifteen minutes ago. Is everything okay?"

Andy hung up and dialled again, with the same result. "Susan, if you get this, call the office right away."

Margaret could tell something was wrong as Andy leaned on the desk and stared at the floor.

"Margaret, I'm going on my break in the kitchen. If she calls back, please tell me."

"Sure, no problem."

A few plainclothes officers were sitting in the kitchen having a break, as well as June and Joe.

June looked up from the table. "I can always tell when something is bothering you. Is everything okay with you and Susan?"

"I don't know, I just don't know," Andy sighed as he took a seat next to his colleagues.

"You fell out already?"

"She hopes you have," quipped Joe.

"Joe, piss off," she fired back, attracting the attention of the other officers.

"Sorry," Joe winced sheepishly.

Andy then started to relate the incident from the previous evening.

"Andy," Margaret interrupted from the doorway. "Susan's on the phone." Andy followed her and picked up the receiver.

"Hi." Susan sounded fine. "Just wanted to say I have no keys to lock your door, so I will just close it behind me. Hope that's okay? I am heading home now. Sorry, I missed your call, I was in the shower. And just to let you know, I feel the same way."

"Christ, I thought something happened to you."

"Why would you think that?"

"Doesn't matter. Please leave a message on my machine when you get home safely."

"No problem. Love you, Andy Blackmore."

"Speak to you soon, Susan Berger."

As he hung up, Margaret asked, "is that Susan Berger, the Deputy Headteacher down the road?"

"Yes."

"She's a lovely girl. You be sure to hang onto her."

He went back to the kitchen and sat down, breathing a massive sigh of relief.

"All good?" enquired Joe.

"All good."

Andy began relating the events of the previous evening to Joe and June again, this time telling them the whole story.

"Hi, do you mind if I sit here?" Someone interrupted again, this time a plainclothes officer. He extended his hand and Andy shook it. "By the way, I'm Mike."

Before Andy could answer he sat down. "How do you know Robbie Jones?"

"I don't."

"I'm sorry, I couldn't help overhearing your conversation with your colleagues. How does your girlfriend know him?"

"She doesn't. She pretended to, just to be polite. But he knew who we were."

"Doesn't surprise me in the slightest. He does his homework, for one so young."

"How do you know him? And is Susan in any danger?"

"Robbie Jones is a cocky little drug dealer. He thinks he is invincible, supplying drugs all over the place. As for your Susan, I would think so. He is trying to rattle your cage, since you lost him a lot of money recently."

"Right. it all makes sense now. The cocaine, the assault complaint , the meeting in the pub last night."

Mike looked at his watch and stood. "I have to head out now, you take care, Andy."

Joe and June just looked at each other.

At about nine-thirty in the morning, a car parked behind the shops in the town centre, and the chemist, Mr. James McIntyre, stepped out of his vehicle. He was a small man in his sixties: slim and balding. He walked directly through the lane to the pedestrian precinct at the front of his shop, raised the electronic shutter, unlocked and opened the front door, and immediately locked the door, as was his normal routine.

His demeanour did not hint that he was aware that something could happen at his shop.

Over the next twenty minutes, a reduced Sunday staff arrived. Only a few shops around the chemists were open, and pedestrians were few and far between.

Andy had gone back out on foot patrol a few minutes earlier and saw Jessie's daughter arrive by her usual route. She was let into her shop by a member of staff.

At ten o'clock the shop was open for business. The only things moving outside were the birds on the street, pecking away at the crumbs left by the Saturday night revellers.

As time passed by, the whole village, from one end to the other, remained eerily silent. Andy remembered experiencing such silence in his younger days in the east end; when the streets went quiet, everyone knew something was going to happen and they stayed well away from the area. Even the roads were distinctly empty for a Sunday.

"Foxtrot Charlie," someone murmured over the radio. "As described. Coming from the south."

"Roger," another voice responded.

"Moving to Charlie 10."

"Roger."

This prevented Andy and all others from hearing what was going on, as the radio channels were outside their frequency. He sussed out the language used and knew that the robbery was about to unfold. Andy was desperate to see what was happening, and although he knew a shortcut he could take to get a good view of the scene, he resisted the temptation and continued with his normal patrol.

Suddenly, another voice buzzed over the radio. "All stations return to the office,"

When Andy arrived at the office, he saw Sergeant Black at the back door, waiting for the arrival of his shift. Everyone was told to go to the muster room upon arrival. Georgie was back last and took his seat.

"Three men are in custody right now, concerning a conspiracy to commit armed robbery at McIntyre's. They are on their way to headquarters to be questioned by the Serious Crime Squad officers, who were here earlier. I can also tell you that a sawn-off shotgun and a machete were confiscated as two of them left their vehicle. Neither was used. Any questions?"

"Do we know who they are?" enquired June.

"We don't.. The late shift will be in shortly. Find yourselves something to do for a little while, then go home. Andy, a minute."

Andy followed the Sergeant to his office and closed the door behind him.

"On your way home, drop in and see Mike," ordered Sergeant Black. "He spoke to you this morning. He said you'd understand."

"Sure thing." Andy was a little puzzled.

"Go now. Don't want you wasting your free time."

"Thanks."

When he arrived at headquarters, Andy parked and before heading inside to see Mike.

"Hi, Andy. I want you to see something. When we go down the cell passageway, say nothing. Just look through the observation glass and walk away."

Confused, Andy did as he was asked. Sitting alone in the cell was Robbie Jones.

Andy circled back to Mike and nodded. They went outside.

"It should be a long, long time before you or Susan see him again."

"Thank you," Andy sighed.

"My pleasure. Couldn't let anything happen to my old boss's daughter now, could I?"

Andy smiled before walking back to his car, shaking his head.

"Andy, tell the boss I was asking for him."

"Who will I say?"

"Mike, just Mike."

During his days as a bricklayer, Andy always knew what he was going to do before he got to work.. Being a policeman was entirely different. No two days were the same. Where was tomorrow going to lead him? Unbeknownst to Andy, there was a surprise in store for him from the unlikely source of Detective Inspector O'Dowd.

Chapter Twenty

ergeant Black announced that Chief Inspector Yardley from Divisional Headquarters would be in to address the shift at 08.00 and that he wanted everyone to be present, no excuses.

On the button, the Chief Inspector entered the muster room, followed by Inspector Smith.Immediately, the whole shift stood to attention. The Chief Inspector instructed everyone to take a seat and as they did. He surveyed the room.

Sergeant Black sat with the officers of his shift, facing the lectern as the Chief Inspector leaned over it. Behind him, Inspector Smith was smirking, as if he knew something nobody else did.

"Well," the Chief Inspector began, "this has been one of the most successful periods here that I can remember in the past few years. The kind of criminals we, or should I say, you have taken off the streets recently has been commendable. The Divisional Commander has sent his thanks. The success has not gone unnoticed." He paused for a few seconds. "As a result, Sergeant Black will be transferred to Headquarters as of January the first. A promotion parade is being held in a few weeks, and I expect a new Sergeant to be appointed here."

Inspector Smith looked at the Sergeant and nodded. The Sergeant glared back. Stunned silence filled the room.

"The shift as a whole has been exceptional, and Detective Inspector O'Dowd has requested that the next secondment to the CID is filled by Constable Andrew Blackmore. Now that the complaint of assault against him has been investigated thoroughly and dismissed, this move has been sanctioned by the Divisional Commander, effective from January the first, for six months."

"Well done, Andy," shouted an officer, followed by several more.

Andy's shock was tempered by the news that their Sergeant was moving on. A sense of disappointment filled the room, as well as a few groans.

Chief Inspector Yardley invited Inspector Smith to say a few words. He stepped forward.

"I can only reiterate what the Chief Inspector has said in respect of the work done by this shift under my leadership and Sergeant Black's. I congratulate Constable Blackmore on his secondment, and I am pleased to welcome Sergeant Black to Headquar–"

"Wait a minute, Chief Inspector," the Sergeant boomed. "Just hold on a minute, I am not at headquarters yet."

"Is there a problem, Sergeant?" asked the Chief Inspector.

"One that can only be sorted in my office, sir."

"Oh right. Well, in that case, you may dismiss the shift and send them out to their duties, Sergeant."

"Thank you, sir."

Everyone rose to their feet. "Shift attention. To your duties. Fall out." Quietly, one by one, the shift filed out of the room in silence.

Chief Inspector Yardley turned to Inspector Smith.

"Smith, leave me with Sergeant Black, please."

"Certainly sir, I'll return to Headquarters if it's all the same to you. I do have other offices to visit today."

"No problem Inspector. I'll get a lift back to the office from someone."

"See you soon, Sergeant Black."

"Tea or coffee, Chief Inspector?" Sergeant Black prompted as they headed toward his office

"Coffee. No milk, no sugar."

Sergeant Black left the room to make the refreshment. Johnny, the station officer, stood by the charge bar and indicated with two fingers on his lapel that the Inspector was still in the front office. Sergeant Black nodded.

"Right, Johnny," said the Inspector. "I'm away this time, bye Margaret."

"Nice to see you again, sir."

Sergeant Black strolled back into his room with two cups of coffee, which he laid on the desk. He sat in his chair opposite Chief Inspector Yardley, saying nothing.

"Jimmy, what's the matter? I've known you for a long time. Something is decidedly bothering you."

"I have just over a couple of years to go. I want to finish here after my thirty years is up."

"Or?"

"Well, sir, let's not go there yet."

"Jimmy, does this have anything to do with working in the same office as Inspector Smith, by chance?"

"I have a great bunch of people here. Better to be happy here than miserable there."

"He came to us from the city via the shires. He is on his way up and we have no option but to babysit him through his time here until the next year or so."

"Well, sir, you know me. I will not let this happen."

"Thought so. In fact, I knew it. Just leave it with me for a few days. We have time."

"Certainly."

"Now, who can take me back up the road? Or will I have to walk?"

"Let's see who is available." He rose from his chair and looked out of the window. A car lay unused.

Andy watched the Chief Inspector stride across the car park towards him. He leaned over and opened the passenger door.

"Okay Andy, let's go."

"Um, seatbelt, sir?"

"Good to see you were paying attention. Don't want to be stopped by the police, do we?"

A good part of the journey was carried out in silence.

"How do you feel about coming into headquarters to work with the CID, Andy?"

"I've had little time to think about it. I have a lot to thank my shift for, sir."

"In what way?"

"Since I arrived, they've all been great to me, especially June. And Joe, Georgie, and Sergeant Black."

"What's so special about Sergeant Black?"

"Well, sir, I can only base it on gaffers I had in the building trade."

"Go on."

"The Good, the Bad and the Ugly."

"And he falls into which category?"

"Beyond Good. He is respected by everyone and is a true leader. He inspires loyalty."

"Do you think he can be replaced?"

"Nobody is irreplaceable, but I doubt I'll ever get another Sergeant like him." Andy paused before adding, "will that help you decide if he is going to HQ, or staying where he is, sir?"

"Geez, I was warned about you and your forthright manner."

"I hope that helped, sir."

"Yes, it certainly did, Andy."

Another comfortable silence followed as they neared the gates leading into the large, three-storey, 1960s-inspired building. But there was nothing inspiring about it; it had a cold and empty feeling, unlike the Bankvale office, which was full of character.

"Just here will do, Andy. That is my parking space."

"No problem." As Andy parked the car, the Chief Inspector reached for the door.

"Oh, by the way, how is Susan?"

"Pardon, sir?"

"Susan Berger. I believe you are seeing her?"

"Yes, sir. Err, she is fine, sir. Why do you ask?"

"Let's just say you have a Guardian Angel at the moment."

Andy switched off the engine.

"Right, I helped you out this morning, now it's your turn. Spill the beans."

"Andy, up here nothing gets past us. We know who's who. Just like you said, 'The Good, the Bad and the Ugly'. And for one so young, you flew quite close to the sun with Complaints and Discipline."

"That's bullshit and you know it," snapped Andy.

"Really?"

"They had no case. You know it, and they knew it."

There was no immediate response from the Chief Inspector: he stared out the windscreen.

"Andy," he finally started. "We know all about you and your family. We know about your martial arts achievements, the history of the brotherhood in your family throughout the many years. So why did you not join the Lodge?"

It was Andy's turn to stare out of the window in silence. He felt the gaze of Chief Inspector Yardley.

"Must be something big, Andy."

"Yes, sir."

"Do you want to talk about it? I'll see if I can help."

"Far too late for that, sir. The damage is done." Another silence followed before Andy added, "what you can do, sir, is tell your Berger I have to walk this path my way and, at the moment, and hopefully in the future, with his daughter by my side."

"You have lived up to my expectations, Andy." Chief Inspector Yardley beamed. "Like you, I have no Brother Berger or any other. But I'll pass your message on to him."

As the shift started to drift back into the office to finish another day, Sergeant Black ordered everyone to the kitchen.

"You all heard what was said this morning. Cutting a long story short, I am going nowhere. I had a call from the Divisional Commander himself, reassuring me that is the case. What this means is that I am stuck with you lot."

"Ah well, Sergeant, we all have a cross to bear," piped up Georgie.

The officers were dismissed, and as they all drifted away, the Sergeant could see smiles plastered on their faces.

Andy was last to leave. Sergeant Black nodded to him and he returned the gesture.

"Oh, by the way," Sergeant Black called to Andy before he could get too far. "We have to have a quick chat before you go."

"Certainly, Sergeant."

They went into his office.

"Give this to Jessie." He handed Andy a plain envelope.

"Sure thing."

"Tell her to get something for the kids."

"No problem."

"Everything okay with you?"

"It will be. Just got someone to sort out. Not in a bad way."

Andy was in the gym going through his katas, punching and kicking the air, trying to calm his mind. He had to speak to Susan, and was not looking forward to it one bit. Her father, Brian, was the least of his problems.

Andy met up with Susan after she finished work, and she followed him to his flat in her car. Upon arriving, he made tea while Susan settled into her usual position on the couch. Soon, Andy joined her, sitting on the couch with big, tea-filled mugs.

"Susan," he began. He had to approach this gently. "I think your father might be interfering with my job, and I'm going to have to speak to him. What I don't want is for this to come between us."

"What makes you think he's interfering with your job?"

"Things that have happened over the last few hours. Things said which have me thinking."

"Okay." Susan scrunched up her eyebrows and took a careful sip of tea "Take it up with him, Andy, and don't worry, it will not come between us. I promise you."

Andy kissed her gently on the cheek. "My weekend off is coming up. I'll speak to him then, if that's okay?"

"He does this all the time." She sighed. "This is why I have never had a long-term relationship." Susan   kissed Andy on the cheek. "We shall be just fine."

"You remember this Saturday is the Christmas party night."

"Yes, I do, and mine is the following weekend."

"And I have that time off."

The following day, the shift learned that Robbie Jones had been remanded in custody along with his mates from the south side.

The rest of the early shift was a quiet affair. Andy dropped by the newsagents and quietly passed on the envelope to Jessie. He told her to get something for her kids for Christmas and proceeded to make tea for the staff as usual.

When the early shift finished, the party organiser, June, reminded everyone not to be late to the office party. "It starts at four o'clock start! And a late finish, so be fit."

"See you Saturday night!" Andy gave her a thumbs up.

"As long as I get a dance, big man."

"Marked on my dance card, June."

As June watched Andy walk away, knowing she would not be working with him for six months, if ever again, she felt her happiness for him mix with sadness and a little regret. And that was not all that was on her mind as the party approached.

Chapter Twenty-One

S usan was working until four o'clock on Friday afternoon. Andy made his way to her house. That was not the plan, but he felt compelled to clear the air with her father.

He pressed the doorbell and waited. The door opened and he was greeted by Susan's mother,

"Hi, Andy! Susan's not here."

"I'm actually here to see your husband".

"Oh, well please come in. He's not here just now, but he's due home soon." She sighed and rolled her eyes. "What has he done this time?"

Andy followed her into the house, and he caught her up in the kitchen for a few minutes before they heard the front door close.

Brian Berger strolled into the kitchen and flinched when he saw Andy standing there with his wife.

"Hello Andrew," Brian Berger greeted him flippantly.

"Hi."

"What are you doing here? Susan's still at work."

"I know. Hence the reason I'm here now."

"Okay, let's go sit down. Sandra, don't you have things to do?"

"Sandra, please sit with us," Andy interjected before she walked away.

The three of them went to the living room and sat down. Andy waited for Brian to make the first move, which he did.

"You have something to say, so just say it."

"Firstly, I have a message for you. Mike was asking for you."

"Oh, how do you know Michael? Good guy that one."

"I met him the other day. Secondly, and more to the point, have you been speaking to anyone about me?" Andy's face was impassive.

"Well, Andrew, I care for my daughter a great deal and I don't want to see her getting hurt, in any way. It doesn't matter to me that she might think her old man interferes in her life a lot."

"Could you answer my question?"

"Brian a-answer his question," sputtered Sandra, before sinking further into her seat.

"Yes, I have been speaking about you," Brian conceded.

"Through your contacts at the lodge?"

"Without me, you would have been back on the building site by now." Brian's face grew red, and a vein popped on his forehead.

"Really? For your information, they had no case. nNothing at all. The whole thing was a set-up, and if you don't believe me, just ask your old buddy Mike." Andy leaned forward. "Now, as for the lodge. The brotherhood is not going to happen for me, so let's get that straight now. If I get anywhere in this job, it will be entirely my doing. My choice. It is not going to be on the strength of a handshake."

Andy leaned back in his chair while Sandra stared at Brian. Complete silence filled the room.

After a while, Andy continued, "and finally, you say you love your daughter and care for her? Well, so do I. Please don't make her choose between you and me. That would be cruel, and I would never come between a father and daughter."

Sandra's heart was pumping fast; it felt as if it was going at a hundred miles an hour. She smiled nervously at Andy.

"Well, Brian what do you have to say to that?" questioned Sandra.

"You keep Susan happy, then I'm happy," Brian yielded grudgingly.

"As for the job?"

"You're on your own from here on out. Your guardian angel has left the building." Brian stood up to indicate an end to the conversation. "Are you staying for dinner? Susan will be home soon."

"I am happy to accept your kind invitation." Andy smiled, his tone hinting at sarcasm.

Andy followed Sandra into the kitchen. "Can I wash up?" He pointed to the pile of dishes in the sink.

Sandra smiled and nodded.

Brian walked into the kitchen and glared at Andy. Sandra waited on an explosion.

"I am gonna tell you something Andrew. You got some bottle, coming here and confronting me, and telling me about your feelings for my daughter." He turned and walked away.

Andy felt a momentary pang of conscience. He wished Sandra had not been present during the confrontation.

Suddenly, the front door burst open and in walked Susan.

"Hi Mum, hi Dad!" She called from the hallway. "What a day! Kids everywhere." She entered the kitchen and stopped in her tracks when she spotted Andy. "Oh hello Andy. What are you doing here?"

"Well, Andrew, tell her." Sandra bumped Andy's elbow with her own, a smile on her face.

"Just getting a few things sorted, once and for all."

"And... are they sorted?"

"Hopefully we have reached an agreement."

"Who reached an agreement? With who? about what?" Susan asked, her puzzled eyes darting from her father to her mother to Andy, and then back to her father.

Surprising everyone, Brian answered first. "This young man declared his love for you, so I'm happy with that.I have a feeling that he will take care of you. I'll also let him get on with his career without interference. As for joining the lodge, he has made his decision, which I respect, and I rest my case, as their lordships say."

That actually sounded genuine.

Susan turned to look up at Andy. "What was your case? To bring this on?"

"I think it was my final summing up, to be honest." Andy was revelling in the situation

"Which was what?"

"I told your father that, just as he love you, so do I."

"Really?"

"Yep."

"Good job, because I am mad about you. I love you to bits." She gave him a huge hug.

"Susan," Sandra interrupted. "Shall I order a new hat?"

"Bit soon Mum, but it's always worth looking."

"Oh, you going somewhere nice, Sandra?" Andy asked, knowing full well the meaning of the phrase.

"Oh for God's sake Andy, wakey, wakey."

A couple of hours later, dinner finished, Andy decided to hit the road. He stood by the door facing Susan, his hands in hers.

"See you tomorrow for the Christmas party," he murmured. "Have you got everything you need?"

"Yes."

Brian cleared his throat.

"Susan, pack what you need for tonight and tomorrow night. You two go and have a great time. Maybe it's time I realised my little girl is no longer a little girl."

Susan was as stunned as Andy by the comment.

"Sandra came and hugged Andy before he made his way to his car.

"Dad, I will always be your daughter, no matter what." Susan smiled up at her father. "Andy is a good man, and he loves me."

"I know. But someday you will realise it's hard to let your child go. I guess it's time I finally did."

"Love you both!" Sandra waved to Andy.

"See you Sunday. Love you too!" Susan called heading to Andy's car, waving her goodbyes as the front door closed.

"Well, what now Brian?"

"Retirement, travelling, and whatever else comes our way." He locked the door for the evening.

Sandra wondered if her husband could actually ever let go of his only daughter. She had always felt he would not let her go that easily, especially to someone like Andy Blackmore.

On Saturday afternoon, Andy turned his vehicle into the car park of the sprawling Oceanview Hotel, just after three o'clock. He and Susan matched in their jeans, shirts, and comfortable trainers.

Carrying their evening wear in a folding suit bag draped over his left arm, and pulling along a small overnight trolley case, Andy opened the front door of the hotel for Susan. The hotel foyer was elegant, made up of a wide-open space dotted with curved sofas and a chandelier that illuminated the high ceilings and marble floors.

Andy did not see anyone he recognised, so he went straight to the reception to check in.

"Good afternoon, sir," the receptionist greeted him, before nodding to Susan. "Madam. How may I help you?"

"Blackmore and Berger. We are part of June Brown's booking."

"One moment please. Yes, here you are. Unfortunately, a maid reported damage to your room by guests from last night's party. So..." The receptionist smiled conspiratorially. "We have upgraded you, at no extra cost, to the honeymoon suite. If that is okay with you both?"

"Oh, I suppose so." Andy feigned a disappointed tone and returned the sly smile.

"Ignore him, please. Of course it's alright." Susan swatted at Andy, clearly not in on the joke.

"Excellent. Honeymoon suite it is then. If you just fill out these forms, and here is the key to your room. Number 304, on the top floor. Enjoy your evening, and your stay."

As they made their way towards the lift, more of Andy's shift arrived, wives and girlfriends accompanying them.

"We'll catch up with you folks shortly, once we dump the bags," Andy called to his colleagues.

"No problem, big man. See you in the lounge," replied Joe.

The door closed behind them, and the lift started to rise to the third floor. As the elevator slowed to a halt, Susan planted a quick kiss on Andy, right before the doors opened. They found room 304 and Andy opened the door, stepping aside to let Susan enter.

"Thank you kind s—oh my God look at this," Susan squealed, all in one breath.

The two of them stared in silence at the luxurious room. Finally, the two of them regained their bearings and stepped further into the room. Susan opened a set of doors to reveal a bathroom with a double shower, twin sinks cut from marble, and fluffy, white linen towels. Andy walked through a spacious living room and opened another door, revealing the master bedroom and the king-size, honeymoon bed. Patio doors led to a balcony overlooking the water.

"Fancy a walk on the beach?" Andy called to Susan, who entered the bedroom after him, a hand cupped over her mouth in shock. "Before the weather sets in and the others get here."

"Only if you're going," Susan joked.

"Only if you want me to go."

They made their way to the ground floor and Andy deposited the room key at the reception for safekeeping.

As they were heading toward the door that lead to the beach, they were stopped by Georgie, Joe, and their respective wives, who had all travelled to the venue together.

"Where are you two going?" Joe asked.

"For a walk on the beach."

"Aw, how romantic." They all laughed.

"Be back soon." Andy chuckled.

As Andy and Susan walked hand in hand along the beach, they breathed in the sea air and enjoyed the slight spray from the water.

"May I ask you something, Andy?"

"Sure."

"Yesterday, what you said to my mum and dad, were you telling the truth about how you feel?"

"Yes, very much so."

"Well, just so you know, I feel the same about you."

Andy put his arm around her shoulders and pulled Susan to him as they strolled further down the beach.

They returned shortly after four o'clock, and by this time the reception area was awash with partygoers. A large queue of guests stood at the reception, while others were exploring the hotel.

"Key for Room 304, please." It was the same receptionist who had checked them in.

Handing over the key, she asked if the room was to their liking.

"Oh yes, very much so!" Susan exclaimed. "Thank you so much."

"No problem at all." The receptionist was visibly pleased.

As they turned away from the reception desk, Andy saw June enter the hotel. He assumed her companion was the friend she said she was bringing with her.

"Hey, June. You made it then."

"Good observation, Andy. You'll make a great cop yet." June rolled her eyes before approaching Susan for a hug. "Hello, Susan. So good that you are here. Someone needs to reign in the big man. Andy, Susan, let me introduce my friend to you both. This is Sheena Gough.

"Pleased to meet you, Sheena." Andy shook her hand.

"Sheena!" Susan squeaked as she pulled her into a hug, earning bewildered looks from Andy and June. "Long time no see!"

"Let us get booked in and we'll catch up shortly," Sheena purred.

"Sure, no problem. We are heading for the gym and pool area.".

"What room are you guys in?" June prompted as Sheena approached the reception.

"304."

"Can't be. All our numbers start with two."

"I'll explain later."

"Okay, see ya."

Andy and Susan headed to the pool area, where they enjoyed a swim before Andy headed to the sauna.

"You not coming in, Susan?"

"No chance. The steam will play havoc with my hair."

Andy shook his head as he entered the sauna alone.

"Susan, where's Andy?" shouted June from the entrance to the pool area.

"In the sauna!"

"We're in room 206 for pre-drinks! Mega booze carryout in the bath. Loads of time! Dress casual!"

"Okay!"

A short time later, Andy and Susan had changed back into the clothes they had arrived in and were about to head to room 206 for pre-drinks. Andy asked Susan how she knew Sheena.

"We were at uni together, I remember that Sheena really mature for her age."

Susan ended the conversation on that note, and they made their way to room 206, the room occupied by Danny Boyle: the only other guy on the shift that was still single. Andy and Danny were rarely paired together during his probationary period. So, although they were on the same shift, they did not know each other. Now was a good time to change all that.

Susan was introduced to all the guys and they, in turn, introduced her and Andy to their wives and girlfriends. There was a knock at the door, and in came Margaret.

"Last but not least" Danny cried, who was at the back of the room. Everyone cheered. "Drinks in the bath Margaret! Don't get in, lift the drink out."

Hi, I'm Margaret." She stuck her hand out to Susan, who took it gladly.

"I'm Susan. We spoke over the phone."

"Is this your first Christmas night out?"

"Yes!"

"Okay, so, coming from a veteran of these nights, the secret is to pace yourself," Margaret advised before she headed to the drinks tub.

Upon her return, Susan realised that Margaret was at the party on her own. "Margaret you can sit with Andy and I. You can be my mentor!" She raised her glass in a toast.

Margaret laughed and agreed with pleasure.

As the pre-party got into full swing, the chat and booze were flowing. It followed a natural rhythm, the ladies gathering in one part of the room, and the men spread between the balcony and other parts of the room.

The wives, who had known each other for years, gathered around Susan.

"So, are you guys thinking of marriage yet?"

"How long have you two been an item?"

"Where do you work?"

The questions were fired at Susan from all directions, but she didn't feel overwhelmed or that the ladies were being nosey. Instead, she felt the chat was more supportive of her presence.

Diane Black, the Sergeant's wife and probably the oldest in the group, came over to sit with Susan. She put her hand on Susan's and, in her distinctive island lilt, whispered, "you are going to be fine my dear. You handled that so well." Susan smiled in response.

As Susan got up to walk over to Andy, she eyed June and Sheena talking, away from the main body of the party.

"Folks!" June suddenly bellowed. "It's six-thirty and dinner is scheduled for eight o'clock. Table twenty-one is reserved for us, so don't be late!" She and Sheena left the room.

"We are out of here as well guys," Andy announced. "For a rest before dinner."

"Depends what you call a rest Andy," shouted Joe, to loads of laughter.

At seven-thirty, Andy and Susan were ready to make their way to the function suite. Andy was in his best, dark blue suit, a brand new crisp white shirt adorned with a blue, Paisley-patterned tie, and black shoes. Susan wore a long, midnight blue dress with thin shoulder straps and matching, open-toed high heels.

"You look stunning, Susan Berger. But something is missing."

"What's missing?" She turned in a circle before feeling at her neck. "I am wearing the pendant you gave me."

Andy proceeded to open a box and present Susan with a pair of sparkling diamond earrings.

"I was saving them for Christmas, but tonight is as good a time as any."

"Oh Andy, but you are saving for a flat."

"Well, it's now a one-bedroom flat." He laughed.

Susan went over to the mirror to put in the new earrings. Once they were in, she stepped back to admire them. Then, she went over to Andy and kissed him.

"To you, from me. You deserve that, Andy Blackmore."

"Let's go show off your beauty, Miss Berger."

Before Andy could open the door, Susan stopped him. "There is something you should know before we go down there."

"Okay." Andy frowned. "Go for it."

"June's friend, Sheena. We were at uni together."

"Yeah, you said."

"She was married at the time and had an affair with a lecturer which broke up her marriage. The scandal broke that only married to please her parents, and so that they didn't discover her secret. You see, her lover was a woman."

"So, what are you saying? Were you involved with her?"

"Oh my God, no!"

"Sorry."

"No, it's okay. I understand."

"Am I missing something here?"

"Is June gay? Or is it just a coincidence that she happens to be a friend of Sheena?"

"Haven't a clue. Can we go now?"

"Yes, sorry I brought it up. I just thought that you should know."

"Maybe just as well. You know what I'm like."

"Yes, I do know what you are like, and you are so right." She laughed.

Once everyone was properly seated, the four-course meal of typical Christmas Faire was served, with wine to accompany it. At nine-thirty, dinner was finished and the plates were cleared, just in time for the guests to go to the various bars while the dining room was transformed into a dance floor. Small cocktail tables were set up, as well as a stage for the DJ.

The lights were dimmed and music boomed from the substantial speakers. Everyone contributed ten pounds to ensure that the cost of drinks at each table was evenly split.

"First-timers, listen up!" June yelled over the music. "When a certain song plays, you cannot dance with your husband, wife, partner, or whoever you are with! And a forfeit is a straight shot down the neck!"

"What's the song, June?" shouted a voice in the dark room.

"Madness, House of Fun."

As the night went on, Susan was not short of dance partners, since Andy hated dancing. When House of Fun was on the decks, he grabbed Margaret and went straight to the dance floor, ending up next to Susan and Joe.

"Susan, can you spare him for an hour later?" Margaret shouted.

"An hour?" Andy scoffed, before laughing. "Not worth the bother."

"You have to consider my age now, Andy."

Once the dance was finished, everyone was sweating profusely, but smiling. There had been no forfeits, which Andy reckoned June found disappointing.

Andy and Margaret sat down at a table whileSusan headed for the loo. She was promptly followed by Sheena.

"Aaaandy." Margaret smacked her lips. She was a little worse for wear. "If I was younger, we wouldn't be down here dancing. I—" She burped. "I can tell you that."

"Oh, Margaret, you may regret saying that in the morning." He chuckled.

Susan was washing her hands when she saw movement in the mirror. A cubicle door opened and out walked Sheena.

"Hello Susan." She saluted. "How is life treating you?"

"Very well, and you?"

"Good, good.

Do you have a teaching job?"

"I do, at Bankvale"

"What are you teaching?"

"I'm Deputy Head."

"Ah, you were always a flyer, even at your young age. I'm pleased with you." Sheena paused to take a deep breath. "I need to get out of this heat and noise. Fancy a short walk with me?"

"Sure." Susan recognised that there was more to this request as they made their way to the patio.

"Do you remember what happened to me at university?" Sheena spoke up as soon as they were outside.

"Yes."

"It cost me my marriage, it cost me everything. Even my family."

"I know, and I am so sorry. It must have been devastating for you. I cannot imagine what it would be like to lose contact with my parents." Susan paused for a moment, considering if she should ask the question she had been pondering all night. "What, what is your connection to June, Sheena?"

Sheena laughed heartily.

"I knew when you saw me you would be thinking that."

"Whoa, Sheena, I am not judgmental, you should know that. What you do with your life is your choice."

"Yes, but June is not part of my life. I love her to pieces, but June is not a lesbian."

"You don't have to explain anything to me Sheena."

"Ah, but you were wondering, weren't you? What I can tell you is that she thinks the world of your Andy. That should tell you she's straight."

"Come on you, let's go inside. It's getting chilly." Susan wanted to end the conversation. She was harbouring serious doubts about that last remark.

Andy saw Susan and Sheena coming back into the function suite together and went immediately over to Susan, taking her hand and leading her onto the dance floor. Andy held Susan tightly and whispered, "is everything alright?"

"Oh yes, it is now." She melted into his arms.

June approached Andy and Susan.

"Hey, so why are you not on the second floor with us?"

"Somebody wrecked our allocated room last night," Andy explained. " Naturally, it wasn't available today."

"So, where are you?"

"Room 304, the honeymoon suite."

"Christ. That's brilliant. Practice run for the future," June winked before walking away, laughing.

"Hopefully," Susan whispered into Andy's ear.

The evening ended chaotically: some three hundred guests gathering on the dance floor to the sound of Runrig's Loch Lomond. The crowd joined hands, swaying to the music before rushing towards the centre at the appropriate verses, virtually crushing each other.

"Room 206 open for service again!" yelled Danny, who stumbled toward the lift. Susan and Andy decided to forgo the invitation.

the lift was extra busy, blocked by the queue of partygoers too inebriated to take the stairs. Andy and Susan decided they were fit enough. As they rounded the landing on level two, they saw, through the glass fire door, June entering Sheena's room, their hands linked. Andy and Susan continued up the stairs to their suite in silence.

Andy poured Susan and himself a brandy and opened the balcony doors. They sat looking out over the water and the lights of the surrounding islands. Andy got up and switched off the bedroom lights, revealing the stars in the clear night sky.

"It feels like we're the only ones here." He whispered, looking upwards.

"I wish we were."

The balcony doors were closed, the curtains drawn. Andy drew Susan close to him in bed.

"Andy," Susan whispered, stroking his upper lip with a finger. "Do you see us together, in the future?"

"Yeah, I do. I've never felt this way before."

Andy could only barely make out her smile in the dark.

"Breakfast is served no later than eleven, you know," she whispered, before kissing him on the lips.

Chapter Twenty-Two

A ndy refused to move so asked. "What time is it, Susan?"

"How should I know? Enough time for a cuddle, that I do know. Can you stop time?"

"Sadly not. You stay there, I'll get a shower."

"Yes. After one last cuddle."

Susan rolled over onto her front and raised herself on her elbows, bleary-eyed, her hair all over the place. She looked into Andy's eyes.

"Andy Blackmore, look at me," she demanded. He obliged. "This is how I look first thing in the morning after a night out. Tell me, what are you thinking right now, looking at me?"

"That I love you, and I am mad for you, no matter how you look."

"Satisfactory answer."

"Behave," Andy mouthed against her lips as they disappeared under the king-sized duvet. "Do you know there is a double shower in there?"

"Uh-huh. That can wait a little while." Susan pulled him closer to her.

Having dressed for breakfast, packed the bags, and checked the room for anything that might have been left behind, they finally trooped along to the lift to head to breakfast.

The lift stopped on the second floor, where June and Sheena were waiting.

"Good morning ladies," Andy greeted.

"Hi girls," voiced Susan.

"Good morning," they replied in unison as they stepped into the lift.

June turned around and smirked at the couple. "Did you two enjoy yourselves last night?"

"Yeah June, it was a great night," Andy chirped. "And thanks for organising it all."

"No problem, big man. Any advice you need organising next year's night out, just ask."

"Do you two always look this good after a night out? Sheena mused.

"Depends on how we start the day, Sheena." This earned Andy a sharp dig in the ribs and a laugh.

"True Andy, so true."

They all dumped their bags in the baggage room for collection, having planned to leave after breakfast, and headed to the dining room. The substantial buffet offered fry-ups, fruits, grains, and toast. Canisters of tea and coffee were laid out, as well as an array of juices.

"Geez, they must have a lot of chickens in this area," commented Andy.

"We have," responded a stone-faced young lady behind the buffet counter.

"How do you like your eggs in the morning?"

"Preferably unfertilised." Her face remained unchanged, causing hysterics at the counter.

"Andy Blackmore, speechless?" cried June. "Would not have believed it if I hadn't seen it for myself."

"I can't believe you just asked that," Susan wagged a finger at her boyfriend. "Well, you got more than you bargained for."

Once the four of them sat down, they watched the troops file in for breakfast in pairs. Some of the ladies straggled behind them alone.

Margaret came into the room with Daniel, looking bright and breezy. Daniel looked a wreck.

"You are looking well this morning, Margaret," Andy commented.

"It all depends on how you start the day."

Sheena shot a knowing glance at June and Susan before they all collapsed into heaps of laughter. Everyone but Margaret.

"Did I say something funny?" inquired Margaret, her pencilled eyebrows raised.

"Andy will explain," June offered.

"Well Andy, I'm waiting."

"Nothing better than starting the day with a bit of physical activity, Margaret."

"I agree. But bedroom Olympics with a younger man is not all it's cut out to be. Danny fell at the first hurdle, and I am more used to a marathon myself. A half marathon would have done me just fine. As for the pole-vault, that snapped in the run-up. Enjoy breakfast folks." She marched towards the buffet area.

The four of them looked dumbfounded, unsure if she was joking, and unsure what the joke was. Danny walked by.

"Danny," June called.

"Shut it," he grumbled, dragging himself to the coffee machine.

After they finished their enormous breakfast, Andy announced, "Well, we're going to make our way back up the road, ladies."

"Okay," replied June as she bit into the last bit of toast.

"Nice to have met you, Sheena."

"You too."

"Let's not leave it so long next time Sheena." Susan smiled at her old classmate. "Maybe have a coffee and catch up?"

"That would be great. You two take care."

Before leaving, they went around the tables, where other members of the shift were sitting among other revellers from the night before, saying their goodbyes. While collecting their bags, they met Sergeant Black and his wife, Diana.

"Nice to have met you." Sergeant black did his version of a smile.

"You also." Susan smiled.

"Is Brian Berger your father by any chance?"

"Yes, he is."

"Ah... I worked with him years ago. Please give him my regards."

"I will."

"So lovely to have met you both." Diana gave them a warm smile.

On the drive home, Andy and Susan discussed how the move to the CID for six months would affect their relationship, especially with the change in hours for Andy's work.

"If we are strong enough, and this relationship is strong, then we will survive," Susan affirmed.

Only got Christmas and a couple of shifts before the big move, Andy thought as he drove. As for June and Sheena, just what was going on there?

Chapter Twenty-Three

T he weeks leading up to the festive period were nicknamed the Turkey Patrol. Shops selling turkeys were likely to get a late-night visit by the local housebreakers, who then sold the stolen turkeys on the cheap. The stock in these shops was plentiful, since many families had their turkeys pre-ordered. Special attention was always given to the local butcher, a favourite of Andy's office for the large bacon rolls he prepared in the early mornings.

By eleven o'clock on Monday night, those who did not have a spare day off presented themselves for duty, as this was the start of their last night shifts of the year. There seemed to be an air of resignation: now that the Christmas night out was over, there was not much to look forward to except parties in hotels in the outlying areas.

"June," Sergeant Black barked. "Take Andy out and keep him out of trouble before he moves on."

"Oh, Andy, see any outstanding paperwork you have to do? Try and get that finished this week. Georgie, Joe, you two together. Billy, Stevie, Spill Hill, keep an eye on the shops. Danny the village, the same remit for you."

"Yes, Sergeant," Danny replied, knowing he was the spare man going out on his own.

"To your duties. Fall out." He started heading towards his office when he quipped, "Oh, and Danny, hope everything is back in working order today."

Danny shook his head as he followed the others to get his radio.

"Never mind him, Danny." June hugged him.

Andy and June drove through the winding streets of the village, and checked all their properties: the local shops, the factories, and, more importantly, the butchers' shops. June eventually pulled the vehicle into a suitable parking area for a break, allowing them a full view of the street.

June politely asked Andy about Susan and her days at university.

"To be honest June, I don't know a great deal about her uni days. She finished with an honours degree, then went back and got a masters." He paused for a moment. "I suppose that is how she has her current job. Why are you asking?"

"No reason."

"June, you never ask anything without reason." He leaned his head against the car door and watched June stare out of the window and slowly tap a the steering wheel. "Okay, let's try this. What is said in here stays in here."

"Okay." She continued to tap the wheel and stare straight ahead.

"I knew Sheena when she was married. We actually knew each other before that for a long while. She decided on a career change and went to university to get a degree to teach English and History. She met someone there, and they became very close. It wasn't long before that friendship became a full-blown affair. In the end, it cost her marriage, and I was left to pick up the pieces. I had, and still have, my place, so I let Sheena move in with me until she got herself sorted out. I assumed it was a guy she had been seeing and, me being me, decided to go and see her husband Jeff, whom I had also known for years. He was in pieces. As we know, it turned out it was a woman she was having the affair with. I thought I was good at reading people and knowing my friends, but boy I got that one wrong."

After a pause, Andy spoke quietly, "June, you can't get everything right all the time. Especially if someone hides something from you and covers it up with a pile of lies."

"Yeah, I suppose so. Once her house was sold, she moved out of mine and into her lover's place."

"Did you ever meet the woman?"

"Andy..." She paused, not sure where to go with this.

He said nothing, waiting on June to continue.

"Andy, all I remember about her was that she was older. Sheena claimed that she seduced her with tuition money. Having said that, I'd had a gut feeling for years that all was not well with Sheena's marriage."

"She must have used her name at least."

"Sandy."

"Am I right in saying she went to City University with Susan?"

"Yes, why?"

"So, you were out with her on Saturday at her school night, then?"

"Yes."

"It's good she still has you as a friend."

"She was desperate to meet you on Saturday."

"Oh? Do you know why?"

"She wanted to meet the guy I fell for the first time I laid eyes on him, despite knowing in my heart it would never work between us. The reason I am telling you all this now is that, when you finish your secondment, I doubt you will come back. Besides, Sheena felt threatened by you."

"Threatened? I had never even met her."

"One night we'd been out drinking. Drinking a lot. When we went back to my place, we ended up in bed together, and it led to a brief affair. I was lonely, she was lonely. It just happened. It ran its course, until one Saturday night. Andy, I am not a lesbian, but it made my feelings towards you confusing. And if it ever got out, I didn't want to hurt you. That's why, when I thought you were about to ask me to go away with you, I said no. Angela's inquiry was my saving grace as it was when you met Susan after all those years."

"Well, it is thanks to you we're together."

"And I'm happy for you."

"Thank you. You know you're right June, I was going to ask you to go away with me."

"What did concern me was us working together after we got back, not to mention the rumour mill."

"What is meant for you will not go by you, June. As for this discussion, it never happened."

"Thanks, Andy." She was relieved at how easy the conversation ended up being.

They both sat in easy silence for a few moments.

"Before we get back to work," Andy started at last, "I have something to tell you. Although I'm with Susan, I want you to know that you'll always have a special place in my heart for all the help you've given me over the past few years."

Starting the engine, June smiled at him. "I'm glad big man."

They headed towards the office through the empty streets of the village.

The second half of the shift followed the pattern of the first half. All the properties were checked a second time, and all appeared to be in order. They saw Danny walking around on his own and picked him up.

"Getting cold out there, Danny?" Andy tried to make conversation.

"Aye, sure is. My feet are freezing."

June turned on the heater.

"Aw thanks, June, I need that."

"Control to Zulu 1," a composed voice spoke over the radio.

"Go ahead," June affirmed.

"There is an anonymous report of banging noises from behind the butchers on the Main Road."

"Roger, we're near there. We'll go on foot." June turned to Danny. "You coming with us?"

"Sure I am."

The three officers left the vehicle, making sure to close their doors quietly behind them. They scurried to the shop. Andy made his way to the back of the other shops, while June and Danny chose a tenement each, cutting off all escape routes.

Initially, they could not see anyone. Then they heard noises from inside the freezer, which they knew was not alarmed. They waited as Danny went back into the common close and, from the upper window, saw a large hole in the roof of the freezer.

He went straight back downstairs and joined the others, pointing to the roof. Andy and June gave a thumbs up.

"Right folks!" June's voice was hoarse, but it carried. "This is the police! Come out of the freezer, now."

"Is that you, Mary?" A gruff voice echoed from the freezer.

"Nah, it's June."

"June, is that bam-stick Andy wae you?"

"Not just Andy, but Danny as well."

"Aw, alright June, fair's fair."

"Is it Boab I'm speaking to?"

"Aye."

"Do you want us tae bring you out a Turkey fur yir Christmas?" A different voice called from the freezer.

"Boab? Who else is with you?"

"Daft Maggie is wae me."

"Right, out you come."

"We cannae. The ladders are outside."

June sighed as she pulled out her radio.

"Zulu 1 to control."

"Go ahead, June."

"Can you get the key-holder out, please? We have two persons in the freezer that can't get out."

"Roger, standby."

"Control to Zulu 1?"

"Go ahead."

"ETA thirty minutes, June."

"Roger, thanks." She put the radio away. "It will be thirty minutes before we can get you out," June called to the housebreakers. "Tell Maggie to keep you warm in there." June laughed.

"Aye, okay June, thanks." The three officers smiled and shook their heads.

Tommy Arnold, master butcher and key holder, arrived disgruntled and angry. He was mad at being called out, madder that his sleep had been disturbed, and maddest of all at the damage to the freezer. It would have to be repaired quickly, and the contents of the freezer would need to be moved to another shop before everything had time to defrost. Tens of thousands of pounds of food could be lost. As he opened the freezer door, Maggie was finishing off keeping Boab warm.

"Aw Maggie, for God's sake pull your trousers up," June groaned, shielding her eyes with a hand as she tried to stifle her laughter. "You too Boab. Put that away before it gets frostbit."

Back at the office, June and Danny took the lead, leaving Andy free of more paperwork, using him only as a witness.

Sergeant Black appeared at the charge bar." What have you got this time, you two?"

"Housebreaking with intent to steal, Sergeant," June announced. "We'll have to see if Tommy Arnold can rescue the contents of the freezer. Could be a huge loss for him."

"We can get the early shift to check that out."

"As you can see, we have Bobby Cullen and Maggie McLeod in custody."

"You will need to get Maggie's mother down here. She's only fourteen."

"No," June gasped. "Bobby was… giving her one when we opened the freezer door!" She whispered harshly.

"Oh well, June, I am sure you can sort it all out before you finish." He patted her on the shoulder.

"Mhm."

Zulu 2 was dispatched to pick up Mrs. McLeod and bring her to the office to collect her daughter. She arrived in her dressing gown and slippers, with a coat wrapped around her shoulders.

"Where is she?" Mrs. McLeod bellowed as she came down the corridor. Then, spotting June, she pointed a long, red fingernail at the police officer. "June, where is she? She's not been in all night!"

"She's in the detention room." June started walking and didn't look back, assuming the mother was keeping pace.

"What has she been up tae?"

"Housebreaking at the butchers."

"Ach, no."

They reached the detention room.

"Maggie, out you come." June pounded on the door. "Your mother is here to collect you." After a brief pause, she opened the door.

"Maggie, listen…" June trailed off as she looked at the girl, only a child "You're going to be reported for housebreaking. So will Bobby."

"Bobby? Bobby Cullen?" Mrs. McLeod set her hands on her hips. "Where is that little git? You know they have been seeing each other? He's seventeen."

"Well, that brings me onto something else," June started.

"Whit?"

June turned to Maggie and tried to offer a reassuring smile.

"Maggie, your mother has to know about what was going on in the freezer."

"Know what?" Mrs. McLeod's eyes jumped between the officer and her daughter. "Ach June! Are you havin' a laugh? Am ah thinking right, what you are gonna tell me?"

June nodded.

"C'mere ya dafty." Mrs Mc.Leod's hand made contact with her daughter's face. "Doctors for you later, and the pill. Wait until yer faither hears about this! He'll kill wee Boab, but not before he rips off hi—."

"Mrs. McLeod," June interrupted, clearing her throat.

"Call me Jeannie, love."

"Jeannie, Danny and I'll take you home."

"Thanks, hen." She smiled brightly, before turning back to her daughter with a scowl. "Right you, ya wee tart. Let's go"

"God help her when she gets home," June murmured to Danny. "Oh hey, come to think about it, Boab has done better than you this week."

"Haha!" Danny clapped his hands, before muttering, "bitch."

Upon his return to the office, Andy completed the relevant paperwork so that June and Danny could finish on time. Robert Cullen was charged with housebreaking, as well as unlawful sexual intercourse. Once that news hit the streets, his life would be a misery.

Andy stood facing June as she leaned against the door of her car, arms folded, legs crossed in front of herself. The rest of the shift made their way to their respective cars, and Andy could feel their eyes dart to the pair of them.

"June, earlier tonight I said something—"

"We said lots."

"I said that I was seriously attracted to you. Do you remember?"

"No, you said you were going to ask me to go away with you."

"Well, I always have been. But there is one thing I won't do and that is cheat on Susan. I just wanted you to know that our feelings for each other were mutual."

"Thanks, Andy. You're very special to me and I hope you know that." June rolled her eyes, and they chuckled quietly. "Hey, I never asked, where is your night out on Saturday?"

"I forgot to ask Susan!" Andy slapped his forehead and laughed, feeling better now that they had truly cleared the air between them.

"Where's your party?"

"I think that it's at the Hilton Hotel."

"Oh, how posh! Anyway, see ya tonight Constable June Brown, the one that got away." He smiled.

"See ya tonight, Constable Andy Blackmore, the one I let go."

"I gotta say June, life with you is never dull, that's for sure. I'm gonna miss you next year."

"Andy," she sighed, "get in your car and drive away, please."

He nodded, got in his car, and waved towards June as she drove off, feeling his heart getting torn. His thoughts turned to Sandy, the woman who had seduced Sheena. Susan would know who she was if she was a lecturer at university. Yet, Sandy was nothing to him and neither was Sheena. So why even bother?

Andy had no idea what he would soon be unravelling, how tight and twisted it all was, and how it affected the people he thought he knew.

Chapter Twenty-Four

A t 18:00, Andy dragged himself out of bed. The night shift was not his favourite. While people were having dinner around their table, chatting about the day's events in the surrounding flats, he was sitting in his dressing gown, alone, having breakfast, eating porridge and banana for a slow release of energy in the winter darkness.

He knew that his fellow emergency service workers in the Fire and Ambulance Services were in the same situation as he was. They did fourteen-hour shifts in comparison to his eight. There is a standing joke understood by emergency service workers that they could go to bed and get up if they got a call to go out, but in all seriousness, the firemen probably had the most dangerous job of them all. The guys in the ambulance depot in Bankvale were good colleagues. Andy always made it a regular port of call for a cup of tea or coffee. The great thing about the ambulance depot was that they had a colour television which was always playing a live game of football during the late shift. You could count on seeing a police car in their garage on those nights. This created a sense of camaraderie among those in the emergency services. There was something unique about everyone. Depending on what shifts they were working, some would miss Christmas and even New Year. Some would miss special family birthdays. Many would miss hearing their sons and daughters first words or seeing their first steps.

I have almost another thirty years of this. It's getting near Christmas. The school will close shortly for the holidays, but Brian and Sandra Berger are retired, so Susan will be with them. I might as well go home to the east end, see Mum and the rest of the family at Christmas, and my mates.

Andy reviewed his shifts for the holidays, the last day of work before going on Secondment was Boxing Day.

At eight o'clock that night he called Susan's number.

"Hello, Sandy speaking. Who's calling?" A voice intoned playfully.

"Sandy?" Andy was confused.

"Oh, hi Andy! Sorry, it's Sandra." She laughed. "Sorry about that, I was expecting a call from an old friend."

"No problem." He recovered quickly. "A quick call from me instead."

"Susan went over to a friend's house earlier. Shall I get her to call you?"

"Yeah sure, if she's in by ten. I'm on the night shift."

"Okay Andy, no problem."

"Thanks, Sandy— erm Sandra." He laughed.

"Oh, Andy, you are a bad boy! See you soon, I hope."

He hung up the receiver, wondering why her tone changed from a playful greeting to a forced niceness. He decided he had better start getting ready for the nightshift. He set the coffee to bubble away in the percolator and headed for the shower. As he stood under the hot water, he realised that all he was looking forward to, even at this early stage in the week, was time with Susan.

As he towelled himself dry, the phone call echoed in his mind, Hello, Sandy speaking. Who's calling?' Sandy, Sandra. Sandra, Sandy. Nah, no way. It was just a coincidence.

The phone rang in the living room and interrupted his questioning thoughts.

"Hiya." Susan's voice was jovial.

"Hi Susan. Can I tell you something? I miss you, so very much."

"Really?"

"Yes, and hey, I have something to ask you too. Where are we going on Saturday night, so I know what to wear?"

"Hilton Hotel, city centre," she began. "Starts six-thirty and finishes about one in the morning. Then we head back to yours to get under your duvet by two o'clock." She laughed.

"Hilton Hotel? Are you sure?"

"Yes, why?"

"Well, you'll never guess who else is going there."

"Who?"

"June and Sheena."

"Oh, that's great! I do like them."

"I thought so too. Look, I have to get ready for work. Can I call you tomorrow night?"

"I'll think about it."

"I love you, Susan Berger."

"Love you right back, Andy Blackmore."

"Hey, you want a laugh before you go?"

"Yes."

"I called for you earlier, as you know from the message. I got a surprise when your mum answered the phone and said, 'Hello, Sandy speaking'."

"Oh, she must be reliving her mad City University days when she was a History lecturer. She hasn't been called Sandy since."

"You never said anything about that. Your mum is a brain-box then?"

"She is. You watch out," Susan admonished before laughing.

"Now I know where you get your looks and your brains."

"Oh, you stop it! Now get to work, have a good night, and take care." She hung up.

Andy replaced the receiver and sat in stunned silence. June had said Sheena's lecturer was called Sandy. Could it be?

"Right folks," announced Sergeant Black at the muster. "I have not sorted out the Christmas and Boxing Day shifts yet. So, my offer is, sort it out yourselves. I know some of you have young children, so come back to me before we finish. I need a minimum of five on duty both days. One in the office, two double-manned cars. Remember, check the shops again tonight." He paused. "Good captures last night. Wee Boab was released for a report. He did the CID a good turn this morning for a case they are working on. Same teams as last night. Hopefully it will be a peaceful one."

As the team were handed their radios, they quickly sorted out who was working Christmas Day. Andy volunteered, to allow someone with children the day off, and June did the same. But his shift insisted he spend his first Christmas with Susan. They both agreed to take Boxing Day off. In this way, everyone got a crack at the double-time over the holiday period.

"Well, Miss Brown," Andy started as the pair made their way to the carpark, "looks like you and I may get one last waltz before I leave the shift for a while."

"And how do you figure that?"

"Because I spoke to Susan earlier tonight and Bankvale staff are heading for the Hilton Hotel too."

"You're joking!"

"Nope."

"Fabulous. I look forward to that dance then."

"So do I, to be truthful." He looked into June's eyes, not flirtatiously, but with true caring.

June returned his state, but in a more quizzical way. Her head was in a turmoil, torn between thoughts about Sheena and unrequited feelings for Andy.

She hated Christmas; her family was a fractured one, and not on the best of terms with each other. Christmas Day was usually her worst nightmare, so she was glad to be working. After Christmas, she would follow her usual routine and see her mother before the late shift, then spend Boxing Day with her.

"What are you doing over the Christmas period, Andy?" June asked as they climbed into Andy's car: she needed the small talk to distract herself from her thoughts.

"I'll see Susan in the morning at her parents, then see you in the afternoon. On Boxing Day, I'll go see my mum and brother, then spend some time with Susan over my days off after New Year's. Christmas Day is my last shift before I move on. I must admit, I'm looking forward to the change."

"I know," June spoke quietly.

"Come on, we should get going. This is boring."

Andy started the car and drove off. He made his way through the village and stopped at the main roundabout at the dual carriageway. Buses passed them by as they carried Christmas revellers from the local hotels back to their pick-up points: most were heading into the city. City dwellers and workers loved travelling down to hotels around the loch-side for their party nights, while those that worked away from the city filled up the big hotels there. It was like a festive migration.

Just as they were about to leave the roundabout, a car travelling south sped past, clipping the kerb of the roundabout without slowing down.

Andy reacted immediately, manoeuvring his marked police car smoothly behind the speeding car. The driver did not appear to be in full control: the vehicle drifting from side-to-side on the roadway. June turned on the blue lights and siren and sent a radio message to the control room.

They quickly found out that the vehicle was registered to a local female who lived along a farm road. Control room staff relayed to June that a traffic car was heading her way to assist and intercept it safely.

"Vehicle stopping, " reported June to the control room.

"Roger."

Andy stopped behind the car, the blue lights flashing in the darkness, illuminating the trees and steep grass embankment with a strobe effect. As Andy and June approached the vehicle, the driver opened her door and tried to alight from the vehicle, only to slump back in her seat.

"Ishh there uh — hic — problem?" she slurred.

"Yes, there would appear to be," replied June. "What's your name?"

"Ermmm… Anne!"

"Does Anne have a surname?"

"Aye."

"Anne, listen to me. I need you out of the car."

"Okay, cutie, any — hic — thing for you."

"Aw, Anne, you're stinking of alcohol."

June produced a breath test and warned Anne of the consequences of a refusal. A traffic car arrived at the scene.

"Geez, she is well gone," commented Willie, a traffic officer with years of experience.

The breath test proved positive. Shocker.

"If you guys want, we can see this one through if you bring her car back to the office."

"Is that okay with you, Andy?" asked June.

"Sure. No problem."

"Okay. I'll get her car, you take ours. I'll see you back at the office."

As the suspect was driven off in the traffic car, Andy returned to the office and waited for June's arrival. Not long after, he heard the back door crash open.

"Andy Blackmore!" she shrieked. "Where are you?" June stormed in, face flushed in anger. "Next time I say I'll take a drunk driver's car, ignore me and you do it!"

"Eh?" He inquired innocently.

"She pissed. All over the seat. I'm soaking."

"Well, you better go change your trousers, cause it looks like you were the one who pissed herself." Andy tried in vain to hold back his laughter.

She frowned, "I don't have any in my locker."

Sergeant Black came to the charge bar from the front office to see what was going on.

"Pissed yourself, June?" he barked.

June pinched her nose and sighed.

"Well, you ain't coming out with me like that," Andy remarked. "If you want, I'll go out alone and you get dried off, if it's okay with the Sergeant."

"Aye, fine by me. Just do me a favour and stay out of trouble. And pick up Danny."

"Okay, Sergeant."

Andy had not been driving long before he spotted Danny walking slowly along the road, diligently checking his property. Andy rolled down his window.

"Hey Danny! I'll give you a lift."

Danny jumped, startled. When he craned his neck to look inside the car and spotted Andy, he relaxed.

"Where's June?"

"Drying off."

"What?"

"She wet herself."

"Oh," he sniggered, "that's a shame."

On the drive back, Andy and Danny chatted away about their mutual interests; they had never really gotten a lot of time together since Andy joined the shift. Danny asked if he spent a lot of time in the gym on his martial arts skills, to which he answered that it had taken years of dedication to get to where he was today. Had he been in this job instead of bricklaying, he probably would not have reached his current level, due to the shift patterns. Andy enquired why Danny was so curious.

"It was something I always wanted to try but never got around to."

"If you want, you can come with me after New Year's, once I find out my shifts."

"Yeah, thanks Andy. That sounds great."

Andy sensed that there was something else on his mind.

"You okay Danny?"

"Yeah… listen this is nobody's business but yours, but there are a few on the shift wondering what is going on between you and June. You guys seem close. Everyone met Susan at the Christmas Party, and we all think she is cracking. You are so well-suited together. "

"Okay, let me set the record straight. Nothing is going on between June and me. We are work colleagues and we happen to get on great. Thankfully, since we spend a lot of time together." Andy drew a deep breath and continued, "I will always be grateful to her and others on this shift for getting me through my probation. That. Is. It. End of story. By the way, what raised this suspicion? Because I don't think I have ever done anything wrong."

Danny explained it was June's demeanour since the news came out about Andy's secondment. "Also, people noticed she was giving you glances during the night out."

"Right, well I am seeing her on Saturday night. We happen to be going to the Hilton Hotel."

Danny's eyes widened.

Andy continued, "You can tell everyone that, and, oh, that I am going with Susan. It's her school staff night out and it so happens June is also going with a friend. That is the reason we are both off."

"That's good, Andy. I'm pleased to hear that."

"Do me a favour Danny. Don't let June get wind of this, please."

"No problem. I will kill it stone dead. By the way, do you know if her pal Sheena is available? She's lovely."

"I'm not sure Danny, you'd better ask June."

Break time was over, and June had a few hours to run down on the clock before she finished. June had dried off as best she could, Andy had returned, and the two of them were back out on the street.

"I made sure I didn't pee on the seat, June."

"Gee thanks, Andy, you're a real pal."

"Just a heads up, apparently there are a few on the shift that thinks we have something going on. Also, Danny has an interest in Sheena, which he is going to ask you about."

"You're joking."

"Nope, just letting you know. And I never mentioned this to you."

"Cheers."

"Well, tomorrow night is our last before it's party time again."

"Yeah. and my last waltz with you, Mr. Blackmore."

The remainder of the night shift drifted to a slow halt at seven o'clock in the morning, and everyone headed home. Andy remained wide awake until nine o'clock and then went to the gym. The swimming pool called out to him for an hour's workout. Since he had been seeing Susan, memories of Catherine had begun to hurt less and even to fade a bit.

As he dressed in the changing room, a male voice behind him queried, "Andy Blackmore?"

"Who wants to know?"

"That doesn't matter, and don't turn around." Andy stood still. "Christmas Eve. Take care, at the bank. Just before it closes."

"Meaning what?"

"It's an early Christmas present to you from a friend. I'm just Santa's little helper."

Andy waited until he heard the door to the changing room close. He finished dressing, went home, and headed straight to bed. But he struggled to sleep as his mind spun. Who is Santa's little helper? And why me?

Chapter Twenty-Five

A ndy walked into Headquarters via the public office, which was buzzing with activity. He did not have the code for the back door, so it was his only way in. He saw a small queue of people waiting to be seen by — what appeared to be — the only officer on duty, despite the place being filled with officers of all ranks.

"Next," the officer shouted after a fifteen-minute wait. Andy walked up to the officer and cleared his throat.

"Hi, can I speak to Detective Inspector O'Dowd?"

"Name?"

"Andy Blackmore."

"Is he expecting you? He is a busy man."

"No."

"Tell me what you want to see him for and I shall contact him."

"Tell him Andy Blackmore is here. That's all."

At this point, the Divisional Commander entered the office and was heading to the public reception desk when he saw Andy, looking frustrated.

"Do you have a problem, Constable Blackmore?"

"No, sir, I am just trying to get to see Detective Inspector O'Dowd."

"Constable Johnston, open that bloody door and let Andy through to the DI."

"Yes, sir." Constable Johnston pressed a button below the counter and the door swung open.

"Thank you, sir." Andy nodded at the officer.

Andy did not have a clue where he was going as he walked down the corridor finding a maze of offices. He'd better learn quickly where everything was after the turn of the year. He soon found an office with the nameplate stating Detective Inspector.

Andy knocked on the door.

"Come in." Andy opened the door and walked in.

"Do you have a few minutes for me, sir?"

"Sure, I wanted to see you anyway. What can I do for you, Andy?"

"Well, sir, at the end of my shift this morning, I decided to swing by the gym on the way home for a workout."

"Mhm." The DI had put his pipe in his mouth and was trying to light it.

Andy related the incident and then sat in silence while the DI inhaled the sweet ingredients of his pipe and rocked in his chair.

"Tell me this, Andy. You have been in this job just over two years, why are you getting the turns and the success?"

"I don't know about the turns, sir. I have no idea. As for the successes, they have been down to being with a good shift where we all muck in together. One for all, all for one."

"So, it's the bank this time? Allegedly?"

"Yes, sir."

"Anything else to go with the cryptic message he gave you?"

"No, sir. What I know you know."

"Thanks, Andy."

Andy stood up to leave the office, only for the DI to motion for him to sit back down.

"We might as well have a chat while you're here, Andy. As I said, I wanted to see you before you start in January." Andy sat back down. "Your reputation as a fighting machine proceeds you. Some of the guys are wary about you coming into the department and causing unnecessary problems."

"Okay."

"They are all aware that you can be outspoken and that you fear nobody, no matter the rank. They are also aware that you have very little, if any, court experience, since everyone you have done has pled guilty, for some reason or another."

"Okay?" Andy had to bite his tongue, remembering June's advice to reign in his east end manner.

"The older detectives are aware that you are seeing Susan Berger."

"What has it got to do with anyone who I see?"

"A lot of them knew her father in the old days, and let's just say he's a bit protective."

"And your point is what exactly? Sorry, sir, but this is not on. Can I suggest, with respect, that you have a word with them all before I start in January? Otherwise, I will. But I do not want to get off to a bad start with anyone. Whatever gripe or obligation they have with her father has nothing to do with Susan or me, so tell them to draw their horns in."

"You are just what I heard you are. I'm glad to not be disappointed." He extended his hand in greeting. "Welcome to the CID, Acting Detective Constable Andrew Blackmore. Now get to your bed and leave everything else to me. Oh, and say nothing to your shift. And I mean nothing. I'll be in touch."

"Thank you, sir. Before I leave though, there is something that is bothering me. How did anyone know I was at the pool this morning? Do you think I'm being watched?"

"Hmm. Be careful Andy, whatever you do, wherever you go, until we get this sorted."

The only way out was back through the front office, past the officer at the front desk. Andy walked into the foyer and glanced at the officer as he tried, in vain, to keep the public happy. Just as he placed his hand on the glass of the door, he heard a voice shout,

"Hey, are you Blackmore?"

Andy turned in the direction of a different officer, while a member of the public burst out laughing.

"What are you laughing at?" The Station Constable scoffed.

"Imagine that, the Station Constable not knowing Andy Blackmore," declared the seated man. "Constable, everyone knows Andy. We wish there were a lot more like him."

"I don't know him," muttered an elderly lady sitting across from the man.

"Thanks, Pat," Andy waved. "And hey, have a merry Christmas with your family. See ya soon." Andy left the office.

The night shifts were quiet, until Friday. There were the usual calls for disturbances: loud music blasting from pubs and clubs with open windows. Even the control room was used to Andy's responding to calls he attended with the quick result of "matter resolved" This was a lesson he learned from Joe in his early probationary days.

Near two o'clock in the morning, the radio burst into life.

"Control to Zulu 1."

"Go ahead," Andy responded. It was June's turn to drive in the first half of the shift.

"Loch Hotel. Alleged serious assault. Ambulance attending and en route."

"Roger."

June drove up the side of the loch, its winding road leaving little room for error. The blue light of the ambulance speeding ahead of them reflected off the calm water. The ambulance then slowed down, allowing them to pass. They would meet at the scene shortly.

When they arrived, they saw Christmas partygoers spilling out of the premises, heading for their buses, while others were still inside. June looked at Andy, who nodded. June blocked the only exit from the car park with the police car. The buses were going nowhere for now, much to the annoyance of both the drivers and revellers.

Andy and June walked inside and were taken to the function suite, where they saw a young man lying on the floor. Gary and Craig, from the ambulance depot in Bankvale, arrived in their green coveralls with medical bags and immediately got to work on the victim.

"Andy, radio for urgent assistance," ordered Gary. "We need a bit of help here." Andy obeyed.

"Gary, what's happening?" Andy asked once he was done.

"He's been stabbed, mate. We have to get him down the road."

"Okay. Hopefully, we have guys coming up here. June, what are you thinking?"

"Lockdown."

"Agreed."

"Who is the manager here?" June shouted.

"I am," answered a man nearby, dressed in a smart black suit and bow tie.

"Lock all the doors here."

"Are you joking?"

"Listen, pal," Andy pointed at the man. "Lock the doors now or the next lock you will hear will be the one on your cell door. Get it? Oh, and another thing. Get a member of your staff on each door. I want nobody in, nobody out. Understand?"

"Yeah, yeah, I get it," he replied immediately before setting off to organise the demands.

Gary and Craig were working furiously on the victim, who was lying on the floor and trying to stem the flow of blood coming from his side.

"Andy, June," Craig shouted, "time to move." The paramedics carried the victim out of the function suite on a stretcher to the waiting ambulance, which then sped into the night towards Bankvale hospital.

Through the large window they saw the flashing blue lights of arriving police cars, containing a combination of uniformed and plainclothes s CID officers.

Detective Sergeant Anderson took the DJ's microphone and asked everyone to take a seat: each person would be seen as soon as possible.

"Hey pal, how long is this going to take? " asked a man who had been attending the private function.

"All night and all day if necessary," the DS replied.

"You're joking, man."

"Do I look like I am joking?" barked the DS before turning around to shout, "is the general manager here?"

"I am," responded the young man near the bar.

"Okay, keep the bar open for as long as this takes. Do you understand?"

"Christ," Andy murmured to June. "We'll be lucky if we get out of here for our night out."

"Tell me about it."

"June, ladies, meet me in the lavvy," said a Big Jessie, who was on a night out with her pals.

June went into the toilet while Jessie kicked open the cubicle doors, making sure nobody was inside. June turned around and saw that another woman had followed her inside.

"Haw you," Jessie exclaimed upon opening the door on one startled woman. "Shut yer legs and come back in five minutes. Now beat it."

The woman scrambled to get off the toilet and sprang out the door. "June, at the top, right-hand corner, there's a young man in a black suit and shirt, grey tie, with blond hair. The blade is down the back of his trousers. He's looking for a way out of here. Merry Christmas to you and Andy."

June went back into the function suite, looked around, and identified the suspect. She observed how casual he was.

"You okay, June?" Andy hissed.

"Follow me."

"Nope, not until you update me."

"Male," June whispered, leaning in to Andy. "White. Black suit and shirt, grey tie and blond hair. The blade is allegedly down the back of his trousers."

"Got him."

They wandered over to a nearby corner in order to get a better view of the male, but failed to spot the knife.

June called out. "We are here to interview everyone."

"Piss off, I'm going home," blurted the suspect.

"Really?" Andy's voice was deadpan.

June knew, by the tone of Andy's voice, that all hell was about to break loose.

"Listen, sir," June intoned. "Please sit down. We have a job to do, so let us do it."

"Screw you, bitch. I'm leaving."

"Sit," Andy spat.

"And you are?"

"Your worst nightmare." Andy placed one hand over the other.

"Andy, chill," June hissed, cringing.

"Hey, what is your bitch talkin' about?"

"Last call," Andy warned.

As the man made to leave, Andy rushed up to him, reached around the waistband of his trousers, and removed a blade from the inside of his trousers. Then, he placed his hands on the man's shoulders and shoved downward, hard.

The man collapsed into his seat.

"DS Anderson, I believe this is what you are looking for." Andy handed him the blade. "June, detain him, would you?"

"Thanks," DS Anderson huffed, his eyes wide.

"Sergeant, me and June have a night out tonight. Can we head out?" requested Andy.

"Just leave statements for me before you finish."

"No problem."

"See you in January," DS Anderson said, clapping Andy on the shoulder.

"Maybe." He turned to June. "Our last waltz is pending."

The two of them left together, leaving behind a stunned crowd.

"Andy?" June piped up once they were outside. "What did you mean when you told the DS maybe?"

Andy didn't answer her, and stayed silent the whole way back to the office. Once they had completed their statements back at the office, Andy and June put them in an envelope for DS Anderson.

"Where are you two going tonight, then?" Joe asked them.

"If the rumours around here are correct, then for a night of debauchery," replied June. "Sadly, they're not. Andy will be with Susan, and I'll be out with a friend. We'll all be at the Hilton Hotel in the big city."

"Well done again," Sergeant Black commented. "You two have a great night."

"Thank you, Sergeant."

"Now you two are finished. Head home and get some sleep before your night out."

"See ya tonight, June?" Andy asked.

"Absolutely, Andy." They made their way out of the office.

"Oh, this might sound a bit mush, but I have a request for the DJ tonight for us."

"And what is that exactly?"

"See ya!" He drove off, leaving behind the usual wave of exasperation.

"Good morning, may I speak to Miss Berger, please?" Andy spoke in a terrible French accent.

"Who is this?" Susan answered.

"Susan, it's Andy."

"Oh Andy, see you and your terrible sense of humour, you make me laugh.

"Susan just before I go for a sleep, I just want to double check the travel arrangements. I'll pick you up at five-thirty, tonight, yeah?"

"Are you not drinking then?"

"Not a lot. But I have managed to get us a room in the Hilton. If that's okay with you?"

"Lovely. Now, get to bed."

"Okay, see you later."

Andy, punctual as usual, arrived at precisely five-thirty to pick up Susan. Sandra answered the door and beckoned Andy in.

"Susan! Andy's here!" she called into the depths of the house. "Wow, Andy, you look so handsome. I wish I was going tonight." She ran a finger down the lapel of his grey suit jacket as Susan entered the room, wearing a long, pink evening gown.

Andy was gob smacked: all he could do was stare.

"Well, say something," demanded Susan.

"What can I say? Other than stunning."

Sandra looked at them both, "Right, you two get going."

As Susan was picking up her small clutch bag, she asked Andy if June and Sheena were going to the Hilton.

"Yes."

"Good! I'm looking forward to seeing them."

"Oh, do you know someone else that is going tonight?" Sandra asked.

"Yes," Andy replied, "June Brown, who I work with, and her friend Sheena Gough, a teacher."

"Sh-Sheena Gough?" Sandra stared at Andy, her eyes wide.

"Do you know her, Sandra?"

"N-no, no. Not at all."

"Sorry, it was just something about the way you said her name, I thought you may—"

"No," she repeated and promptly opened the door. "Enjoy your night." She practically pushed Andy and Susan out the door, her cheeks red and eyes bright.

At the reception of the hotel, Andy and Susan checked themselves into their room before making their way to the pre-dinner drinks reception. Susan introduced Andy to her friends and colleagues.

"Andy, this is Anne Banks. Anne helped me so much when I started school and we have become good friends." Andy shook her hand.

"So you're Andy Blackmore," she commented with a wide smile. "Well, there isn't much I don't know about you already."

"Meaning?" He returned the smile.

"You have no idea."

"Anne," Susan jived, swatting at her friend. She turned to Andy. "She is going to get me into trouble with you if she keeps going."

The staff from Bankvale found their assigned table. Dozens of circular tables and most fully occupied. Each bearing Christmas crackers and lit candles in a central display on a red tablecloth. Buckets of ice contained bottles of Pinot Grigio

Andy remarked how subdued this evening was in comparison to his shift's night out. They'll warm up later.

"Andy!" a familiar voice called, June. "Susan! Hi! You look good tonight. See you guys later?"

Andy gave her a thumbs-up as Susan responded, "yes, look forward to it!"

 Andy leaned into Susan and whispered, "you do look stunning."

She gazed up at him and smiled. When he looked up, he saw that June and Sheena's table was directly opposite theirs..

A flurry of waitresses descended upon the guests and took their orders. It was like a military operation: the waiters were uniformed in smart black trousers and shoes, white aprons and bow ties, and small white towels draped over their arms. Like clockwork, all the starters were served at once, as was the dinner shortly after. Ninety minutes later, the plates were cleared away, and the waiters retreated to bring out the next course. Cake with coffee, tea was served for dessert.

"Ladies and Gentlemen," boomed the DJ over the speakers. "This is Christmas. It's time to party, don't you agree?"

"Yes!" The guests answered in unison.

"So, let's partyyyyyy!"

Merry Christmas Everybody was put on full blast, and everyone sang along. Andy knew this would be a loud night.

Anne, sitting on Andy's left-hand side, leaned over to whisper, "Susan is besotted with you, do you know that?"

Andy's only response was a wide smile.

"You came to the school a while ago on an inquiry, I believe, and she immediately recognised you. She hasn't shut up about you since."

"She's a very special woman, and that's all I'm going to say."

He turned to Susan and grabbed her hand. "Susan, although I hate dancing, I think it's dance time."

"I agree."

"Let's go." He pulled her onto the dance floor. While dancing, they heard a shout.

"Andy!" It was June. "Don't forget our last waltz. You promised."

"What does that mean?" inquired Susan.

"Well, as you know, I'm finishing up at the office, and I promised June one last waltz tonight."

"Oh, Andy." Susan laughed." What are you like?"

"All I have to do is find a song to request."

"I'll help!"

"You don't mind me having a dance with June?"

"Why should I?"

"No wonder I love you to bits."

As the night was in full swing and the bar staff were kept busy, the DJ lowered the music and made an announcement.

"If there is an Andy Blackmore here this evening, please go to the reception. Thank you."

"Andy?" Susan tried to catch Andy's eye, but he was looking at June, on full alert.

"Haven't a clue."

As he got up from the table, Andy noticed June was also looking at him. He quickly walked to the reception desk.

"Hi. I'm Andy Blackmore."

"You received a telephone call," the receptionist reported. "The caller left a message for you. They said to tell you to have a good night."

"Did the caller say who he or she was?"

"Em… Santa's little helper. They insisted it wasn't a hoax." The receptionist did not look convinced.

"Can I have the number, please, and access to a private telephone?"

"Sorry, Sir. I cannot do that."

Andy thought fast, reaching into his wallet to produce his warrant card.

"I need his number and a private telephone, now."

"Come with me."

As he started to follow the receptionist, Andy glanced back and saw Susan and June observing him from the foyer. "Girls, go back to the party."

The women crossed their arms, and June quirked an eyebrow.

The receptionist held the door open to a small office and closed it behind him.Andy dialled the telephone number. After a few rings, someone picked up. It was silent.

"This is Andy Blackmore."

"Andy. How's your night out going?"

"Fine, thank you. Who am I speaking to?"

"Santa's little helper." Andy recognised the voice from the dressing room. "Christmas Eve, two cars, two drivers, four shooters, prepared to go all the way to get the big delivery from the security guard delivering the festive cash to the bank. Santa says take care, Andy. Oh, and enjoy your night at the Hilton."

He hung up before Andy could respond. What the hell? He dialled another number.

"DI O'Dowd, please. It's urgent."

"Who's calling?"

"Andy Blackmore."

"Andy? I thought you had a night out."

"Yeah."

"Okay, mate. Hang on."

There was a rustle and some murmuring before the DI answered, and Andy explained what happened.

"Thanks, Andy."

"No problem, sir."

When Andy returned to the function suite, he saw June, Sheena and Susan chatting at a table. As he was walking over, a hand suddenly grabbed his shoulder. Andy turned sharply.

"Andy Blackmore!" Angus smiled at him. "How are you doing mate?"

"Angus, long time no see, mate. How the hell are you?"

"Fine Andy, just fine. Who are you here with?"

"My girlfriend, please come meet her."

"Sure, mate."

"Excuse me, ladies, this is a very special friend of mine, Angus MacAleer. We served our apprenticeships together in the building trade."

"Hello Angus," the girls spoke in unison.

"Andy, is it okay if we leave the girls for just two minutes? There are some people you should meet."

"I have to get permission, Angus." He laughed.

"Yes, go ahead," Susan bantered. "Just don't be too long."

Susan watched him approach a nearby table full of men. They embraced each other like long lost friends. She turned to June and noticed she was watching him too.

"Susan," Sheena spoke, startling Susan out of her thoughts. "When we met last week, did I catch that your last name is Berger?"

"Yes, it is."

"When I was at uni I had a lecturer, Sandra Berger. I knew her as Sandy. Do you know her?"

"Yes... I do, Sandra is my mother. She went by Sandy at university."

"Your mum was my history lecturer I'm sure, years ago."

"Possibly. She's retired now, but is still in touch with a few of her students and colleagues."

"Small world huh?"

"Sure is."

"Would you tell her I was asking for her? I would love to see her again."

"Sure, we can even arrange something and all meet up."

"I would love that."

June sat silently, taking everything in. As Sheena went off to the ladies room, Susan leaned over towards June.

"June, can I ask you something?"

"Sure."

"Are you in love with Andy?"

"Susan… he's in love with you—"

"That is not what I asked you."

"I-I am very fond of him and we work together. That's it."

"Alright."

"So, what have you two been talking about while I have been gone?" Sheena interjected when she returned.

"Being in love," muttered June.

Susan and Andy danced the rest of the night away. During a slow dance, Susan whispered in Andy's ear,

"We need to talk later."

Andy did not have time to answer before the DJ blared over the speakers,

"The moment has come for Andy and June to have their last dance to The Last Waltz by Engelbert Humperdinck. Sorry man, it was the only one I could find."

Andy nodded at Susan before going to grab June. He swung her onto the floor as The Hump began belting out the song. Andy was no dancer, but he managed to get through his last waltz with June without crippling her. At the end of the song, Andy kissed June's hand and led her back to her table.

"Thanks, Andy," She kissed his cheek.

Andy went back to his table and sat next to Susan,

"It's the end of a chapter, Andy," she commented. He smiled at her. "But not the story." She sounded bitter.

"Sorry, you've lost me."

"Doesn't matter, it's just me being insecure."

"I don't know who this Blackmore is," announced the DJ, "but now he demands I play My Love by Lionel Ritchie, for Susan. Only another hundred and fifty songs and he'll have danced with every girl in here. Respect."

"Come on." Andy got up and extended his hand to his partner. "This is for us." He led Susan onto the dance floor once more.

Andy held Susan close as they danced slowly. Susan placed her head on his shoulder and her arms around his waist. "You're safe with me, Susan."

Although she smiled so wide a tear dislodged from her eye and sprang down her cheek, Susan could not help the sinking feeling in her stomach.

"Ladeeeees and gentlemen, the evening is drawing to a close, and it has been a pleasure for me to DJ your Christmas Party. Let me wish you all a Merry Christmas, so will you all join hands in a big circle in the centre of the floor. IT IS TIME — DRUM ROLL PLEASE — FOR LOCH LOMOOOOOD."

As Runrig struck up the opening notes, the floor was instantly crammed with bodies.

"Oh hell, here we go again, Susan."

"Indeed!" she gasped as they whirled around the floor.

As the music faded away along with the night, Andy thanked everyone at the table for their hospitality and warm welcome.

"Oh, we shall see you again Andy, that is for sure," one of Susan's colleagues promised before she sauntered away.

Andy approached the DJ.

"Hey man, thanks for that Lionel Ritchie song."

"No sweat man. Oh, by the way, this got passed to me to give to you."

He handed Andy a note which read, Merry Xmas! Love, Santa's Little Helper. XXX.

"Who gave you this?"

"Don't know man, people dump stuff on my desk all night."

Andy put the note in his pocket before doing a quick search around the venue for any familiar faces or clues as to the identity of Santa's little helper, but came up with nothing.

"Well, Susan we are residents tonight. Shall we retire to the bar for a nightcap?"

"Yes please," she replied. "I need to speak to you anyway."

"Two large brandies, please," Andy ordered at the bar. "One with ice, one without."

When he had laid down the brandies on the table, Andy sat beside Susan.

"Susan this has been a cracking night. Thank you for inviting me."

"Yes, it has. You've been a hit with the staff, but that's Andy Blackmore. Everybody loves him."

"As long as Susan Berger does, Andy doesn't care."

"Does that include June Brown?"

"Eh, what do you mean?"

"She's in love with you, you idiot."

"Susan, how many times do I have to say this? June and I work together, that's it."

"Not for her. And it's funny, she said the exact same words."

Just then, Sheena and June approached the table.

"Hey, are you guys staying the night?" June smiled.

"Yeah," replied Andy.

"Why don't you come up to our room? We have some drinks, and a few others are coming up."

"Would you mind if I pass tonight?" Susan said morosely.

"No, sure, we understand. See you in the morning." They said their goodbyes before making their way to the lifts.

"Right," said Andy. "There is something I want to say to you, Susan Berger—"

"Andy, big man," interrupted Angus, approaching from behind and placing his hand on Andy's shoulder. "We all wish you all the best in your future, you and yer missus here. Can we get an invite to the wedding, whenever that is?"

"Angus!" Andy spun around in his chair and exclaimed, Tommy Tim! All you guys will get an invite, if she ever asks me to marry her and I say yes."

"We'll be there, that's for sure."

"Haw Tommy, nae Sel'ik songs or yer banned."

"Sure, Andy. Don't want you to lock me up."

"Would be my pleasure, Tommy," he said, laughing and initiating the hugs and back slaps specific to grown men, before his old friends left one by one.

Andy was struck by how much he missed those guys and the freedom he had back then that they still had. He preferred when he was 'Andy the brickie', a rocker who was always good for a bit of madness, rather than 'Andy the cop'. For ten years they were a team, brothers in arms.

"Sorry about that," Andy murmured as his past walked out the door.

"You miss them, don't you?"

"Badly. Seeing them makes me realise just how much."

"Andy Blackmore, is that a tear in your eye?"

"Nah, don't be silly." He wiped it away and chuckled. "These guys helped shape who I am today. I'll always be grateful to them. Anyway, back to where we were, wherever that was. I want you to listen to me. It is easy to love someone, but to be in love with them is different, right? And I can tell you for sure that I am in love with you. Someday soon, I might just ask you to marry me."

"Why?"

"Why? Because I want you to be mine, to have and to hold, a-nd... and at this moment I can't think of anything else."

"Well, don't expect an answer immediately. I might have to think about it." Susan winked.

He laughed. "Oh, I would give you a minute. But if there's no answer after that, the proposal is off the table." They laughed, but Andy could tell Susan was still tense. He paused. "Pick up your glass, Miss Berger. Let's head to our room."

Andy pushed back his chair and stood up, but when Susan raised a finger to stop him, he sat back down.

"There is one more thing before we go upstairs," he said softly. "When you got the call to go to the reception, what was it about?"

Andy glanced at the room from the corners of his eyes before returning his gaze to Susan. "We're in a public place and I don't know who is sitting nearby, but all I can say is that it was office related."

"Okay, no problem." Being the daughter of a police officer, she knew better than to ask anything further.

This is not the time for work, Andy thought. It's time to enjoy the company of a lady who I'm deeply in love with and want to be with for a long, long time.

Chapter Twenty-Six

The following morning, Susan and Andy made their way to breakfast where they joined some of Susan's colleagues. They had decided to stay overnight, despite the fact that most of them lived on the outskirts of Glasgow. It was leading up to the festive period, and the school holidays were now on. No such luxury awaited Andy and June, who still had a few days to go.

"Hey Andy," piped up Anna. "Can we expect to see Susan wearing something special when we return to school?"

"Possibly, but I don't— well, I can't say much about it in public. You'll understand."

Susan knew something was coming out 'Andy style'. She looked down at the floor with dread.

Andy leaned back in his seat, echoing the mannerism of Sergeant Black.

"Now let me see," he mused, staring at the ceiling and holding the attention of the whole table, especially the women. "I was thinking, should I get her something special? And to be truthful, I did. I've got her a T-shirt that says 'I have survived Andy Blackmore' with my picture on it."

"Are you winding us up, Andy?" said Anna. He shook his head.

"I got him one too," Susan retorted. "It says 'I survived this man and it has my dad's photo on it. He'll have to wear it everywhere for seven days solid or he is banned from you-know-what for six months."

"Go Susie!" squealed Anna. "Andy Blackmore, you have more than met your match." She fell into a fit of giggles.

"Morning all," June croaked, entering the dining room with Sheena in tow.

"Morning guys," responded everyone at the table.

"What is all this hilarity so early in the morning?" asked Sheena.

"Susan just got one over on Andy," announced Anna, "and the betting is that she wins."

"Oh Hell. I give up, honestly," Andy stated. "This is gang warfare, and I'm not participating."

"Andy, are you working tonight?" asked June.

"Yeah."

"I want to speak to you before then."

June headed to the toilets and was immediately followed by Susan, who had picked up on the comment. Susan waited as June came out of the cubicle.

"Right, what was that all about?"

"What?"

"Your comment."

"Susan, think about it. The public announcement to go to reception during a night out, and the note handed to him by the DJ. What is happening with your man?"

"June, you love him," Susan insisted softly.

"Yes, okay, yes, and I will not see anything happen to him, alright?"

"Okay, you and I, let's go find out, now."

They walked back into the function room where Andy conversing with several people, including Sheena. June sat at a spare table as Susan went over to Andy and beckoned him to sit beside her and June. Sheena also rose to join them. Susan raised a hand to stop her.

"Not you, Sheena."

"Okay, what is this all about?" Queried Andy. "Is Santa's due soon?"

"Andy this is serious," Susan spoke. "June wants to speak to you, remember?"

"Susan, what the hell has gotten into you?"

"Go ahead June," said Susan, avoiding eye contact with him.

"Andy, the first time you walked into our office you blew me away. I know there is — what, ten-twelve years between us? — but there was just something there. Over the years, we've spent loads of hours together. The inquiry into Angela Johnstone, the situation with Catherine…" June eyed Susan and decided to stop. "I could go on and on." Unspent tears made her eyes bright. "I-I fell in love with you. I am so sorry. And I feel so pathetic about it. Like I'm just one more woman infatuated with the oh-so-great Andy Blackmore to add to the list. And I've tried to push it down, but I can't."

June sighed then continued. "When you met Susan again at the school after all those years, I knew then that you were gone, just by the way you looked into each other's eyes. And as much as I hate Susan for taking you away, I love you both." She chuckled through the tears and took a deep breath. "So, now that I have that off my chest, what was that call for you to go to the reception? And the note left with the DJ? I saw it. You might be smart but I'm smarter. Don't you ever forget that, Blackmore." June wiped her eyes with a slight laugh.

"Wow." Andy sighed. "Hell, my head is buzzing." He leaned forward, elbows on his thighs, chin in his hands. Susan watched closely with bated breath.

Andy looked up at June and held out his hand. She placed hers in his.

"June I owe you, Joe, Georgie, Sergeant Black and the other guys on the shift a lot. But even though I'm moving on, I'll be back. Those early days were challenging for me. They were an adjustment. The cases I was doing were difficult for me, to say the least. As for the way I handled those cases… I'll admit it was a bit unorthodox. I got into trouble, thanks to you. But I would do it all again, even knowing you'd rat me out, and do you know why? Because, as a mate, I love you to bits. Now, as far as this lady is concerned," Andy said, gesturing towards Susan, "I love her. June, you are my mate, but she is my soulmate. In time, I will want to marry her."

"That was corny, Andy Blackmore," June winced.

"I could say the same to you, June Brown." As if switching channels on a TV screen, he changed the subject. "As for the call and note? I'll get into it, but not here. Not now."

"June," Susan spoke up, "if you love my Andy like I know you do, look after him. He needs someone out there."

"Yeah." She laughed. "To wipe his arse."

"Exactly."

"What about you and Sheena?" asked Susan.

"Who knows?" She shrugged, but Susan thought she say the hint of a smile.

"Time to hit the road? " Andy asked Susan, who nodded. "See you later, Miss Brown."

"Maybe."

Andy reported for duty the following evening and was immediately dispatched to the Divisional HQ. There was no briefing, just a confused-looking Joe driving him there, fast. He was shown straight in through the back door.

"Joe, what's going on here?" Andy asked.

"Don't know, big man."

"Seriously?"

"Seriously! Looks like you got yourself in over your head. Not to panic, I've been there. CID. I hate it."

"Meaning?"

"You've got information they haven't."

"I don't know this week's lottery numbers, honest."

"Do you ever take anything seriously?"

"Nah, Joe. I'm just a brickie."

As soon as Joe and Andy entered the general CID office, three officers in casual gear entered the room. They are not local cops, Andy thought.

"Blackmore?" one growled.

"Who's asking?"

"Me."

"And you are?" enquired Andy.

"We were warned about your attitude."

"Cool your jets mate," Joe hissed.

"Who are you?" the officer nodded at Joe.

"Joe McGrath."

"Beat it."

"No chance."

"Okay, we seem to have a situation here," Andy said calmly. He paused. "You have a seriously bad attitude, so—"

"Ha!" the officer interrupted. "We have a bad attitude?"

"Besides," another officer interjected, "you are in no position to deal."

"Gentlemen, gentlemen," Andy said, waving his hands, unfazed, "Joe and I are two of the three musketeers, so think of us as one."

Andy stood, removed his baton and handcuffs, and finally his jacket. He placed his right hand over his left and stared at a wall.

"Listen, guys, please don't annoy him," Joe begged. "See, when he goes like that, it's game over."

The three officers started to look uncomfortable. A door opened and in walked the Divisional Commander with DI O'Dowd.

"What's going on here?" the Division Commander barked.

"Em, well," Joe began, "I think Andy is about to wipe out these officers."

"Oh for Christ's sake, I should never have brought you in for this. Sit down you three. Andy, you too."

"Yes, sir."

"Right, Andy, what's going on?"

"Can I stand now or have I still got to sit, sir?"

Joe buried his face in his hands. "We are never going to change him," he moaned, voice muffled.

"Good," replied the Divisional Commander.

"Anyway," started Andy, "as I was about to say, this is everything I have up to the early hours of this morning..."

Andy related everything regarding the gym incident, as well as the information he had been given at the hotel the previous evening. Everyone was silent.

"Who is Santa's little helper?" piped up one of the officers finally.

Joe knew exactly what was coming and shook his head.

"I don't know."

"And why you?"

"Same answer."

"Gents, get to my office now," the Divisional Commander bellowed at his three officers. Once inside, he asked them about their impressions.

"No wonder they call him the Iceberg," one said. The others grumbled agreement.

"Are you in?" the Divisional Commander challenged them.

"We're in," they said.

"Okay. If this is a goer, it's a cracking turn."

"Yes, sir."

Andy partnered with Joe for the rest of the night while June tidied up her paperwork. At the end of the shift, everyone wished Andy all the best on his new venture, and he thanked them for what they had done for him as they left the confab room.

June and Andy walked down the corridor together for the last time in a silence broken intermittently by best wishes from the early shift.

Andy closed his locker for the last time in Bankvale, taking what he needed. June closed hers, and they walked out of the office as they had done for the past couple of years. Together they crossed the street towards their cars, which were parked side by side.

"Hey, you," said Andy.

"What?"

"I am not going to let you down, you know."

"I know."

"June Brown, you are very special to me. Always will be."

"Hey, sorry for the meltdown the other night, but Susan caught me in a... moment. But I have to say I'm glad it's out."

They got into their cars. Andy drove off first, followed by June. As they drove along the dual carriageway, Andy was first to peel off towards his flat before June headed to the city as she always did.

Andy parked in his bay, pulled the keys out of the ignition, opened his door, and got out. As he locked the door and was about to head into the close, a car pulled up behind his and the drivers' door opened.

"Andy Blackmore," called a voice from the car.

"Yes?" Andy smiled.

" I have a message for you. I love you, Andy Blackmore."   Susan wrapped her arms around him.

"What are you doing here?"

"It's Christmas Eve, and this is the only place I want to be."

Andy stepped back, grabbed her hand, and led her up to his flat.

Chapter Twenty-Seven

A ndy opened the door with a sleepy greeting. "Why are you here? And at this time? It's half-past seven in the morning."
"I need you right now. Hold me?" she uttered so quietly Andy barely heard her. He pulled into an embrace.

"What's wrong?"

"I don't know where to begin. I know I shouldn't have just showed up at this time. You need your sleep. B-But I really need you."

They sat down on the couch, and Susan curled up into him. It seemed to be their special haven, where they could share anything. Andy decided that once he got his own place, the couch was going with him.

"I am going to get a couple of hours sleep," Andy said after a minute of silence.

"Can I come with you? I have been out all night."

"What?"

She didn't answer him. As Andy brushed his teeth, he could see her reflection in the mirror: fingers fidgeting with her hair, her eyes darting around the room. Once they were in bed, neither of them could sleep. Andy knew that whatever had happened was a major event.

"Andy," she whispered finally. "I want you to be honest with me, because... because she is June's mate, so I don't want you covering anything up if you know anything."

"Okay." He wondered if his worst fears were about to emerge.

"Has June said anything to you about Sheena?"

"Yeah, lots. They're mates."

"Has she said anything about her being married?"

"I think that was years ago, if I remember correctly. When she was at university."

"So you know?"

"Know what?"

"Please don't make me say it." She sniffled. "Do you know anything about Sheena having an affair with a woman named Sandy while she was at university?"

"Yes. June said she always had suspicions that Sheena was never into her marriage, and that she always had a leaning towards women. Susan, remember when I called your house, and your mum answered? She referred to herself as Sandy, saying she was expecting a call from a friend. Then you said she taught history at the university." He hesitated. "Please tell me I am so wrong about all of this."

"I can't, Andy, because… it's true. My mum and Sheena had an affair at university." Andy reached for her hand. It was wet. "I don't understand any of this. I am sick with worry a-and I'm confused. I don't want to go home."

Susan laid her head on his chest and Andy could feel her tears soaking his T-shirt. He held her close and stroked her hair. It was all he could do.

When Susan calmed down, he asked, " who knows about this?"

"I don't know."

"Your dad?"

"Oh Christ, I hope not!"

"How did you find out?"

"When I got home today, I went to my room to wrap presents. I heard the phone ring and Mum answered. She sounded pretty angry, so I opened my door and I heard her say, 'Sheena, I told you never to call me at home'. I was about to shut my door when I heard her say, 'does anyone know about us?' I realised she did not know I was in my room. Then I heard her say, 'did you see Susan and Andy last night?' Mum said that if anyone ever found out about them, she was finished. And then she hung up.

"Then I went to the kitchen. She was shocked to see me. I told her I heard everything. 'Sorry darling, you were never meant to know about this', she said. I asked her if she'd had an affair with Sheena Gough. She said she had, but hadn't seen her in years. I knew you were working the nightshift, so I just drove around, hour after hour, mile after mile, stopping at petrol stations to eat, before coming here this morning. Can I stay for a while?"

"Of course. In fact, I'll get some keys cut today. Mi casa es tu casa."

"Thank you."

They dozed off for a while in each other's arms and were awakened by the telephone ringing. Andy looked at the clock. It was approaching noon. They had been sleeping longer than he thought. Andy's saving grace was the late-night hours of shops on Christmas Eve.

"Hello," Andy grunted into the receiver.

"Andy, it's Sandra." Andy was suddenly more alert. "Is Susan there?"

"Yes."

Andy pointed at the receiver and mouthed 'your mum'. Susan shook her head from side to side vigorously.

"Can I speak to her?"

"Sorry Sandra, she doesn't want to speak to you right now."

"So, you know now as well."

"Let me speak to her about it. We'll get this sorted."

"Okay." She hung up.

"Jesus, what a mess," Andy commented. Susan humphed in reply. "Where do we go with this?"

"Phone June, would you? See if Sheena is there. I want to meet up with her today."

Andy dialled June's home number.

"Hello?"

"June?"

"No, it's Sheena. Who's calling?"

"It's Andy."

"Hi Andy, June is asleep right now. Do you want me to have her call you back?"

"No, it's actually you I'm wanting to speak to."

"Oh, Andy, you devil."

"For once I'm not having a laugh. I have Susan with me. She wants to meet up with you today, and I think you know why."

"Oh no."

"Oh yes."

"Okay, how about The Caffé Bean on Sauchiehall at two?"

Andy held up two fingers and Susan nodded.

"Done." He hung up the phone and looked at Susan, who had stood up and shucked on his dressing gown. She was leaning against the wall.

"She wants to meet at The Caffé Bean."

"Good." She squinted at Andy. "I don't want you there."

"No problem."

Andy drove to the city centre and parked in a multi-storey car park. They walked down to The Caffé Bean, but before Susan could go in, Andy put a hand on her shoulder to stop her.

"Susan, let's stay outside where we have a clear view of the door."

Two o'clock came and went with no sign of Sheena. She appeared ten minutes later, went into The Caffé Bean, and sat at a window table which overlooked the pedestrian precinct, its throngs of Christmas shoppers carrying last-minute presents as they rushed from shop to shop.

"You okay?" Andy asked.

"Yeah. Time to go in."

Susan went in and took her place next to Sheena.

An hour later, Andy arrived back at The Caffé Bean, as agreed with Susan. Susan sitting alone so Andy went in and joined her. "Coffee?" he asked.

"Black, please. Small."

"You okay?"

"Not really. Maybe. I suppose so."

"How did your meeting go, then?"

"We got a lot sorted out and I understand a bit better now what happened. But I have to get Mum's side of the story."

"I understand."

"Three hundred and sixty-five days in a year and this all had to blow up now. How do I face Dad?"

"What we can do is continue as normal. Christmas dinner as arranged, as if nothing happened."

"It's going to be difficult, sitting there with both of them."

"To distract her Andy handed Susan a copy of his house keys. "Merry Christmas. Early present for you."

"You are mad, Andy Blackmore. Which is one of the reasons I love you."

They sat by the window, drinking their coffee, and watched the world go by, for some fun they started making up stories about people who caught their attention.

"Oh, I had a thought," Andy spoke up after a particularly odd-looking lady has summoned a fit of laughter.

"Okay, go ahead."

"You know how tomorrow is Christmas Day?"

"Really?"

"Stop it." Andy wagged a finger at her and clutched his stomach. "Anyway, I'm thinking of doing the right thing and asking Mr. Berger if I can marry his daughter."

"What if he says no?"

"I'll say 'okay, no problem. It's gonna happen anyway. Like it or lump it.'"

"Right, there's just one problem. Have you asked his daughter?"

"Shit, never thought of that bit!" He took her hand. "Susan Berger, will you marry me?"

"Yes! I will!" she exclaimed hugging him. Does this mean we're engaged?"

"Yes, I just like a bit forward-planning."

"Oh right," she replied, as if a marriage proposal was a daily occurrence.

"Is being engaged not a bit old-fashioned?"

"No, Andy. It's nice."

"Where do you want to go, Susan?"

"Back to your place, so I can get my car and go home. Better to face this now."

On the way back to Andy's flat, they listened to the news on the radio.

"Two men were shot dead and two seriously wounded by police officers in Bankvale following an attempted raid on an armoured security vehicle delivering cash to a local bank. Two others are in custody. It would appear that the police had been tipped off about the robbery and were lying in wait for the robbers. We shall update you as soon as we get further news about the incident."

Susan looked at Andy, who was ashen.

"Do you believe this?"

"I know," he blurted out.

"How terrible is that?"

"Bad."

Andy continued the journey in silence. She hadn't been brought up in a police household without learning something along the way, quiet and observe. Susan had enough to deal with without taking this on as well, but when Andy was ready to speak, she would be there to support him. Susan got in her car and went home.

Andy sat on his couch, staring at the unwrapped presents on the floor but thinking about the shootout. Between what was happening with Sandra and Susan, as well as the news of the robbery, the Christmas spirit had deserted him.

He turned on the TV and, while he waited for the news to begin, started making dinner. The Divisional Commander, accompanied by the Force Press Officer, was issuing a statement on the robbery

"Hello everyone," the Divisional Commander began. "At eleven o'clock today, a vehicle delivering a large sum of cash to the bank arrived in Bankvale. Two vehicles followed carrying four armed men intending to rob the courier. Armed police officers confronted the men. Regrettably, shots were fired and two men died, while two others were seriously wounded and are in critical condition. Two others have been arrested in connection with this incident and police inquiries are continuing. I shall not be taking questions at this time."

At that point, the Divisional Commander and Press Officer left the stage at the press conference.

Andy stared at the TV screen and did not even notice as his pot of pasta boiled over. Only when the water sizzled on the hob did he awake his dream-like state. He decided he no longer had an appetite, and abandoned dinner in favour of wrapping his presents for family and friends. At seven o'clock, the telephone rang.

"Hi, " he answered.

"Can I stay with you tonight?" Susan blurted. "I want to bring in our first Christmas together."

"As I've said, mi casa es tu casa. You have keys."

Shortly after, they were huddling together on the couch. Susan told Andy there was one thing they had to sort out going forward; she had to stop wearing his dressing gown in the morning.

"Are you hoping Santa might bring you one?"

"If that's all Santa brings me, you are gone."

"Yeah, right."

"Yeah. Right!"

Two glasses of wine later, they listened to music. There had been an awkward silence between them for a few moments.

"So—" Andy began.

"Andy I—" Susan started at the same time.

They laughed.

"You first," Andy ceded.

"I can sense when something is wrong. My dad was a police officer. And today you went very quiet when the news came on. You don't have to answer this, but did you know anything about the attempted robbery?"

"Yes."

"How much did you know?"

"Everything."

"Did you share it with anyone?"

"Yes."

"Who?" she pressed.

"Those who had to know, Susan." Andy gritted his teeth. "I was warned not to discuss it."

"I knew that you knew something about it."

"What about you?" Andy was eager to change the subject. "Was everything okay when you got home?"

"I told Mum I had met up with Sheena and she just crumbled, asking me why I did that. I told her I had to. I needed to understand why everything happened the way that it did and what caused it from her side."

"How are you feeling?"

"Confused. Hurt, I suppose. Wondering if my family life has been a lie all these years. I fell this is real, especially after this last week - I feel lost - except with I am with you."

"So, what are we going to do tomorrow?"

"Play the part of a happy family, I suppose."

"We could go to my family. It's probably time for them to meet you, I think. No better time than Christmas Day."

Chapter Twenty-Eight

A ndy awoke before Susan and lay gazing at her. She looked so peaceful for someone whose life had been turned inside out. All because of a telephone conversation she should never have heard.

"Why are you watching me?" Susan croaked.

"I was wondering what you would like for Christmas breakfast?"

"Tea and toast, please. Nothing changes for me, even at Christmas."

"Breakfast in bed it is then. And I'll see if Santa has been in."

"You're such a big kid."

"Yep."

Andy went to the kitchen, boiled the kettle, and popped bread in the toaster, before slipping back into bed.

"Well, has Santa been then?"

"Yeah, and there is one big parcel for you."

"Lovely." She rested her head against his shoulder.

When they went into the living room, Andy handed his gift to Susan, who promptly opened it.

"Ah, my dressing gown."

"Try it on. You never know what else is in there."

Susan slipped on the gown and shoved her hands into the pockets. She pulled out a long, slim jewellery box. Susan opened it to reveal a diamond bracelet.

"Merry Christmas Susan."

"Oh my gosh! It's stunning! You know you have the best taste?"

"Especially in women. I'm glad you like it."

"I love it!" She covered his face in kisses.

Andy and Susan pottered about the flat until it was time to head homewards. Andy drove to his brother's house, where his mother also lived. Afterwards they would go to Susan's.

"Hey, Ricky," Andy said once his brother opened the door. "Merry Christmas." Andy walked inside, trailed by a shy Susan. "Hi kids, Alice, Merry Christmas. Hello Mum. Merry Christmas." He hugged her tightly. "I want you all to meet Susan."

"Welcome," Ricky said and shook her hand. "Nice to see you, Andy. How's the job?"

"All good at the moment."

"Who did you say this is, Andrew?" croaked Andy's mum.

"Susan, Mum."

"Hello, Susan."

"Listen, guys, we are just stopping by en route to Susan's parents for dinner. I just wanted to drop these presents off."

"Thank you, Uncle Andy," one of his nephews piped up.

"No problem."

"Andrew, who is this?" his mum asked again, pointing at Susan.

"Susan, Mum."

"Andy, we have to meet up and have a chat, mate," Ricky suggested.

Andy looked at his mum, then back at his brother. "Sure. I'm off over the holidays. I'll call you."

"Thanks."

"Nice to meet you all," Susan half-shouted over the buzz. "Hopefully we get longer next time."

"That would be great. Maybe even dinner some night?" Alice invited.

"Bye, Mrs. Blackmore." Susan waves Andy's mum.

"Oh, goodbye, my dear."

As they drove off, Susan put her hand on Andy's arm and squeezed gently.

After parking his car, Andy turned to Susan. "You ready?"

"As ready as I'll ever be."

"We'll do this together."

Following the typical Christmas greetings and an exchange of gifts, dinner was served: the traditional Christmas helpings of turkey, roast potatoes, boiled potatoes, and Brussels sprouts.

"Beautiful bracelet, Susan," Sandra exclaimed, gasping.

"Thanks, Mum."

"You are good to her, Andy."

"Well, she deserves it, Sandra. She has been good to me."

"I see you had an attempted robbery down your way, Andy," remarked Brian.

"Three dead and one critical."

"Three?"

"Yes, another died last night."

"Can we change the subject please?" appealed Susan. "It's Christmas."

"Susan, give me a hand to clear the table," Sandra ordered.

"Sure."

"Tea or coffee anyone?"

"Small coffee please."

"Coming right up."

Once Sandra and Susan were in the kitchen, Brian started quizzing Andy about the attempted robbery, but Andy responded merely with vague answers or silence. Brian was suspicious about Andy's silence, and wanted to quiz him relentlessly on his intentions but his thought was focused. I know I should be able to let her go, but I can't it's just too painful. He refocused on Andy realising he could not show his hatred.

Andy read all this on Brian's face but before he could say anything Susan came back into the room with Andy's coffee, and her father stopped talking immediately.

"Well, that was a sudden silence. What were you guys talking about?"

"Nothing."

"He was asking about our future," offered Andy.

"Oh really, and you said what?"

"Nothing. I never got the chance."

"Okay, now is your chance."

"Fine, I was going to ask him if I could marry his daughter someday."

"And if I say no, what would you say?" Brian demanded.

"I'd respect that, but it would happen anyway."

"No wonder they call you the Iceberg." Brian forced a tight smile.

"Loosen up guys," Sandra implored, strolling in from the kitchen. "It's Christmas. No more police talk."

Andy went into the kitchen, picked up the dish towel, and started to dry the plates and cutlery next to Sandra.

"Alright Andy?" Sandra muttered.

"Yes."

"Good. Stay strong."

Sandra placed her hand on Andy's and gave a nod. "I'll come down to see you sometime when Susan is not there. We need to talk."

Andy gave a slight nod. "Well folks, that was a fantastic dinner and a lovely day," Andy announced. "But I need to make tracks."

"My car is at your place, I'll come and get it, then come back up the road."

"No problem."

"Susan, just stay there and come back in the morning," urged Sandra.

"Is that okay with you Andy?"

"Of course! No problem."

"Goodnight," Andy cut in, waving at Susan's parents as he opened the door and stepped out.

"Goodnight Andy," Brian huffed. "Glad Santa was good to you."

Andy stopped in his tracks, turned, and stared straight at Brian. But Andy did not have time to ask him what he meant before Susan dragged him out the door and closed it on her parents.

"Can't stand being in there any longer," Susan explained, but Andy was not listening.

What the hell was that all about? wondered Andy as he turned the ignition. This is beginning to stink to high heaven.

"Andy?" Susan piped up after ten minutes. Andy realised she'd been speaking the entire time. "Once a cop, always a cop," she muttered. You're not the Andy I knew from school. You will always be Andy the cop from now on, even if you quit." She sounded bitter. Andy knew this really had nothing to do with him.

"Neither your dad nor his friends will interfere with us, Susan, and that's a promise. I want to spend the rest of my life with you."

Susan smiled. "And me with you."

I thinking last night," Susan began, "since we have been together, you have never really mentioned your brother Ricky, his wife Alice, their kids, or even your mother."

"It's a long story."

"You know what is going on in my life."

Andy sat beside Susan. "This couch is becoming a confessional."

"I wouldn't know."

"Me neither. Anyway, here we go then."

Chapter Twenty-Nine

Andy began to share his story of when he and Ricky were at school. Ricky was the one with the brains: he flew through his exams with ease and had glamorous, intelligent girlfriends. At the same time, a lot was expected of him. Ricky went to university to qualify as a chemist and now had his own family, a big property complete with their three-story house and a small guest house for their mum built at the rear of the property.

"So," Andy continued, "he has all that and still I sit here wondering if he's happy. I know I am, and you cannot buy that." Andy continued with the fact that Ricky also followed in the family footsteps, becoming a Freemason and earning the title, 'Master of his Lodge'. He was also connected to the Grand Lodge of Scotland.

Andy paused and took a sip of tea before continuing to say that, unlike his brother, he was not intelligent and had hated exams. One day in his teenage years he had helped his mate's father, a bricklayer, who told him he should think of bricklaying as a trade. Sports-wise, he had been into his football and rugby, as well as various martial arts. He had kept the latter quiet from everyone.

"When I became involved in the Angela Johnstone inquiry, I remembered you instantly. I remembered that when I was in the Boys Brigade, you were in the Girl Guides. I remembered that I fancied you like crazy but hardly spoke to you. You had guys surrounding you all the time. I left school early, as you know, went to college, and became a brickie, while you went on to university. It was a major shock to my family that I refused to join the lodge. From that day forward I was blackballed by the family: I'd broken a chain that had been linked for over seventy-five years. Mum always stood by me and supported me though. She knew I was suffering in Ricky's shadow. I think working with people from so many different backgrounds, and having a tight-knit group of friends, stood me in good stead for this job. If there is one thing that I learned at the Christmas night out, it was to never become part of a culture where my job is the be-all and end-all in life. I am going to keep my friends. And I'm going to keep you. It took me thirteen years to get near you, Susan Berger. But They do say that all comes to those who wait." Andy and Susan smiled at each other. "Anyway, as you saw yesterday, and this breaks my heart to be honest, Mum's memory is fading. I think that's why Ricky wants to speak to me. Well, I hope it is, and that nothing more sinister is wrong."

A comfortable silence fell between them after; Andy had shared more in an hour than he had in all the time they had been together.

Susan considered all he had shared before suggesting, "Why don't you call him? There's no time like the present."

Andy brushed her cheek with a kiss and went over to the phone to dial his brother's number.

"Hi Ricky, it's me... Yeah, hi. Is today convenient for us to meet up? Good. Do you want to come here, or shall I come to you? Okay, see you in a couple of hours." Andy placed the handset back on the cradle and turned toward Susan. "Sorted. And... thank you."

"Nnew year, new beginnings." She smiled.

"Maybe."

"So that's the story behind Andy Blackmore then, is it?"

"It's the first time I've told it to anyone. Even my close mates don't know all that."

"I'm honoured."

"Why?"

"Because it's a sad story - and you are actually opening up to me. Something I feel you don't do easily, if ever."

"You are more than welcome to do that." Andy returned the smile.

"I also agree with you about friends. Since my dad retired, all he has is his old colleagues. He rarely associates with the neighbours, or anyone that is outside the lodge or police. He does not do anything out-with that circle. It drives Mum crazy."

"Speaking of your mum, and please don't mention this to her, she said yesterday that she wants to come here and talk to me, alone."

"Why?"

"If I knew that, there would be no point talking to her."

"That is my mum you are talking about." She slapped his thigh.

"Oy, that hurt."

"It was meant to."

"What age is your mum, by the way?"

"Fifty-six. Why do you ask?"

"She's a fine-looking woman for fifty-six." Andy gave her a slow wink.

"Do you want another slap?"

"Hmm, how much would that be?" He playfully tickled her.

"You are impossible!" she shrieked. She smacked his hand away, and, once she had gotten her breath back, murmured, "it is probably home time for me. And you should get yourself to your brothers' house. I'll call you later."

"Yes, ma'am.."

Susan kissed Andy on his cheek.

Andy swung his car towards the large iron gates as they slowly swung open, their twisted, ornate spires slicing viciously through the sky. He entered the driveway and parked behind a Mini Cooper that was parked behind a Mercedes.

The front door was at least three meters tall and half of that in width, made from grey, smoked glass. It lay open, awaiting his entrance. Andy knocked anyway.

"Come in and shut the door behind you," Alice's voice called from inside the house.

"Hiya Alice," Andy greeted her as he entered the living room. His nephews bounded up from a leather couch to tug on his hands and show him their new toys. "Hey kids. I see Santa was good to you this year."

"Yes, Uncle Andy! We'll show you later what we got."

"I would love that."

"What did Santa bring you, Uncle Andy?"

"Em, nothing. I must have been bad, or he just forgot me."

"Oh, that is sad. You have to be good this year, then!"

"Oh Andy, stop winding them up," Alice chided him.

"Well, if a little white lie keeps them good all year, it works," he whispered and laughed. "Besides I got the best present of all."

"What's that?"

"Susan."

"No wonder you look so different, Andy. Happiness suits you."

"Nope, but they do help."

"If you could get your brother to go, that would be grand."

"If you want."

"Yes, I want."

"Want what Alice?" enquired Ricky, entering the room.

"You to get a body like Andy's."

"But I've been building this up for you and the kids for years!" He grabs his belly.

"What good is all that if a workaholic like you drops dead?"

215

"Oh give it a rest, woman. Andy, let's go to the other room."

Andy glanced back at Alice as he left the room, giving her a reassuring wink, to which she smiled.

Ricky and Andy went into a massive lounge: a common feature in a stone villa such as this, with a fire blazing in a marble fireplace and large bay windows looking out over a sprawling and manicured front garden. Andy wondered how stunning it must be in the summer months. Andy relaxed into a red, leather Chesterfield chair with a studded back and rolling arms.

"Where is Mum?"

"In her wee villa. She has to keep her independence while she can."

"I noticed she was off yesterday."

"That's because you are hardly here."

"Yes, and that's my fault. Now that my probation is over, I want to get some normality back."

"Good idea." Ricky paused, seeming to hesitate as he stared at the roaring fire.

"Right, Ricky, spit it out. There's something on your mind."

The door to the lounge burst open and the kids ran in. "Dad, Dad come and see this!" screeched their daughter, Annie. "Alfie's riding his bike!"

"That's great!" Ricky ruffled Annie's hair. "I'll be there soon. You should know not to interrupt me when I am speaking to Andy."

"Ricky, it's Christmas. Two minutes won't make much difference." Andy requested.

"Sure."

"Andy," Alice called from the doorway, "would you like to stay for dinner? Leftovers from yesterday."

"Do I get a doggy bag too?"

"I am sure we can manage something." She smiled.

"Right, where were we?" asked Ricky.

"The next time Alfie or Annie ask for something special like that, just do it, Ricky. Life is too short."

"Are you a parent now?"

"Ricky, I didn't come here for this. I thought you needed to speak to me."

Slumped back in his chair, Ricky explained that over the last months he had noticed a decline in their mothers' mental health, so he had taken her to the doctor. They diagnosed her with Alzheimer's. It was unlikely to improve. When she sold her house to move in with him and Alice, the money was used to build the extension she occupied. It was his opinion that the time had come for him to apply for control over her money and assets. That was the best way forward. There was a likelihood that, in the not-too-distant future, their mother would have to receive specialist care in a nursing home, as he and Alice were both working and would not have the time to care for her on a full-time basis.

Andy sat there in silence, taking everything in, bit by bit.

"So Andy," sneered Ricky, "is this relationship with Susan serious? Or is she another one of your flirtations as you wander down the road, casting women aside?"

"We'll see what happens." Andy did not want to share his true feelings. Instead, he was watching his brother closely.

"Tell me, is she the daughter of Brian Berger?" Andy nodded. "And what's his wife's name again? I can't remember."

"Sandra."

"Yes, that's it. Sandra."

Andy knew from his brother's demeanour that something was bubbling under all this. He was waiting for his brother to burst, like a criminal under investigation. Ricky likely thought he was being nonchalant: he had always underestimated Andy's intelligence.

Andy was leaning back, his arms resting on the rolling arms of the chair, his right ankle resting on his left thigh. But as his brother stayed silent, Andy became overwhelmed with the urge to change his position.

Finally, Andy sat up, leaned his elbows on his thighs, and clasped his hands. He was determined to make Ricky break. Slowly, he circled his thumbs around each other, all the time staring at his brother.

After a while, the door opened, and Alice looked in. She sensed the tension in the air.

"Em, would you boys like tea or coffee?"

"I think your husband needs a strong coffee," replied Andy. "Mine not so strong, please. Black, two sugars."

"Coming right up."

Silence reigned until Alice came in and served the coffee.

"Thank you, Alice," Andy murmured, smiling up at her.

"You're welcome."

She served Ricky his coffee, and lingered only for a moment before he spoke sharply,

"Leave us now, Alice."

Alice flinched and stood up straight. She slowly turned her gaze on her husband and squinted at him before obeying.

"You are a total asshole," Andy muttered harshly, his voice low.

"Who are you to talk to me like that? Remember, you're in in my house."

"I'm your brother. I mean listen to you. You have a beautiful wife, and two great kids, and you treat them like shit. "

"Back off."

"Back off? I'm just warming up. Let's wind the clock back. Whose idea was it for Mum to sell her house and move here?"

"Mine. She wasn't coping on her own and you weren't about a lot. Actually, you weren't around at all."

"Strange, she never mentioned it to me."

"She has Alzheimer's Andy! Who sounds like an asshole now?"

Andy ignored him. "How much did you get for her house?"

"Not a lot."

"Try again."

"One hundred and fifty."

"Thousand?" Ricky nodded. Andy sat back and unclasped his hands, tapping one finger on the arm of the chair. "So, what is left of that?"

"Somewhere between fifty and sixty thousand," replied Ricky.

"So, ninety to a hundred thousand to build the extension to your house?"

"Yeah, thereabouts."

"Does Alice know about the gambling?"

"Know what?"

"About all this, what you've done?"

"No."

"Why not?"

"I've never told her."

"Are you in trouble?" Andy's voice was filled with concern.

"No."

"You might have the brains of the family, but you were always a shit liar. Tell you what, Ricky, let's get Alice in here and we can sort this."

"No!" Ricky blurted. Then, catching himself, whispered harshly, "no way!"

Ricky was silent for a moment or two before admitting that he thought his marriage was in severe trouble and that he was terrified of losing everything. He owned four shops and forty employees: some full time, most part time. Due to escalating costs in the shops, he was heading toward financial ruin.

Andy looked away from his brother and took a long, deep breath.

"For God's sake, say something!" Ricky pleaded.

Seconds later the door to the lounge flew open.

"Is everything okay in here?" Alice demanded.

"Ask your man."

"Ricky, what is going on?"

"Nothing," Ricky spoke through clenched teeth.

"Give us a few minutes, please?" Andy nodded at her.

"Sure. But dinner is almost ready."

"Thank you," he replied.

She exited the room once again, leaving the two brothers in tense silence. "I think we should go for dinner." "Then, I am going to tell you what will happen." His tone was grave and unrelenting.

Alice watched Andy roll about the dining room floor with Alfie and Annie and warned him not to kick over the table. The kids were screaming and laughing as he tickled them, and they climbed all over him, trying to get him back.

"Right, you three children. Dinner's on the table."

"Uncle Andy says we can eat on the floor!" Alfie exclaimed.

"Yeah Mum, down here!" Annie added.

"No chance," she responded jovially.

"Aw Mum, do we have to go to the table?" Andy whined, laughing.

"Yes Andy."

"Aww, okay Mum."

"She's not your mum," Annie cringed.

"Where's Granny?" Alfie asked.

"Your dad is getting her," Alice said as she put the dinners on the table.

"Thanks, Andy. You've made their Christmas."

"Don't be silly."

"Presents. Being here. Wrestling on the floor. I hope that you get the chance to do this with kids of your own."

"Yeah, would be nice I suppose. But, at the moment, I can hand yours back."

"Well if you and Susan ever want to get some practice in, you're welcome to childmind for us. We rarely go out now. All he does is work, go to the lodge, and have late-night drinks with his mates."

"And you, Alice?"

"Well someone has to take care of the kids!"

Alice's hands were draped over him. He reached up and took her hand in his.

"Alice, look at everything you have here, two great kids—"

"Two great kids and nothing else."

Andy felt a kiss on his neck from Alice. "Dinner?"

Andy greeted his mother as she entered the room and held out a hand, which she shakily accepted. "Hi Mum."

"Hello, son."

"Come over here and sit beside me."

"Thank you. That would be nice. Where is that other girl?"

"What girl?"

"The one you were with yesterday."

"Susan? She's with her mum and dad today."

"That's nice."

"Second-day turkey and stuffing. Can't beat it!" praised Andy.

Following dinner, Andy went to the kitchen and hugged Alice, thanking her for the invite.

"Ricky and I are going back into the lounge for a chat," Andy commented on his way out the door.

"No problem, I'll bring the coffees out."

Andy returned to the lounge with Ricky, closing the door behind him.

"Andy, listen," Ricky implored as soon as they had sat down.

"No, you listen to me for a change. My days of walking in your shadow are over.. Yous ell Mum's house, you build yourself a big fancy extension, and you want Power of Attorney over Mum's affairs? Did she not give you enough when we were children, seeing you through university? Now you're draining everything?" Andy was shouting at this point. You're in big trouble."

Just as Ricky was about to answer, the door to the lounge opened. Alice handed out the coffees and left just as quietly, feeling the familiar tension in the room.

"You're right I'm in trouble. The gambling hasn't gone my way. I've been on a losing streak for a while and the more I lose the more I think I can recover it by betting more."

"Does Alice know?"

"No. I just told her things weren't good at the shops just now."

"Well, you two will have to address it at some point."

"That's not all." Ricky gulped. "I think Alice might be having an affair."

"What makes you think that?"

"I don't know, she doesn't act like she used to. She nags when I drink, so I go out, and then she nags about that. But she doesn't try to keep me at home."

"Maybe you're looking for an excuse for your behaviour."

"Maybe."

Andy brought up the potentially explosive subject of their mother, her future, and where Ricky saw her going in the coming months. He also wanted to know more about the gambling debts and how he would repay them in the event of their mother's death. He knew about her will.

"How do you know about the will?"

"Because I was there the day it was prepared and signed. Oh, and by the way, Power of Attorney? That was also arranged that same day. I have that."

"Are you joking?"

"No Ricky, I'm not. Looks like your troubles are about to continue, Brother." Andy stood up to leave. "Tell you what, I'll be back in a couple of days. You better have answers ready for me and Alice."

He walked into the dining room. "Alice, I'm off. Thank you for everything. See you in a few days."

"Bye Andy." She hugged him and patted him on the cheek. "Love to Susan."

"Night kids," Andy yelled.

"Andy they are in bed," Alice whispered harshly.

"Oh, sorry."

"Night, Uncle Andy! Love you!" A high-pitched voice squealed above them.

"Your kids talk in their sleep?" Andy teased before opening the door to leave. He smiled at Alice before closing the door behind him.

When he reached his car, he heard the door open again behind him. Andy turned and watched as Ricky approached.

"Goodbye Brother."

Ricky held out his right hand. Andy looked down for a few moments, debating whether or not to return the gesture. He looked his brother in the eyes and saw a hint of sadness and resignation. He drew his hand from his pocket and gripped Ricky's hand tightly.

"Listen," Ricky said and cleared his throat. "There's a couple of other things you should know."

"Look, it's late. Can we leave it for next time? I will see you in a couple of days. We can sort this together then."

"Nah, listen, it's now or never. The rest will sort itself out. I understand that you feel you lived in my shadow years, but it hasn't exactly been easy being your brother either. So much was expected of me, but nobody expected you to make much of yourself. You got to have a normal teenage life, the oneI wanted. The pubs, the gigs, the fun. What I would have given to have that time back and join you. And now look at you, a police officer with a beautiful girlfriend."

Andy could only stare at Ricky.

"Now," continued Ricky, "the other thing." Andy crossed his arms and waited. "Brian Berger is watching you. There is something in his past that he is terrified that you'll uncover. Something that has been going on in his family for years. He's waiting for you to slip up and then the brotherhood will come down on you like a ton of bricks." Ricky pulled Andy into an embrace.

Over Ricky's shoulder, Andy saw Alice silhouetted in the doorway, lit from behind.

"Hey, you take care of your lady over there," Andy murmured, "and those little demon kids of yours."

"If anything happens to me, please look after them."

"Of course."

Ricky watched as Andy backed out of the driveway and sped away. Andy headed back to his flat, this time to an empty bed. Susan was at her parents' house for the night after seeing some friends.

As Andy drove, the evening with his brother played back in his mind like a video. He was concerned, to say the least, about his brother's behaviour, but put it down to him being under immense pressure, from work and from their family.

As he opened the door to his flat, he heard the telephone ringing. He rushed to answer.

"Hi."

"Hey, how are you?" It was Susan.

"I'm good."

"What's wrong?"

"Not sure. Nothing."

Susan decided to change the subject. "How was your day at Ricky's?"

"Alice and the kids were great. She invited me to stay for dinner. The kids got me into a lot of trouble, we were rolling about on the floor, causing chaos." He started laughing.

"Oh Andy, trust you! And what about Ricky?"

"Well, to be truthful, that was a whole different kettle of fish."

"In what way?"

"It's far too much to get into right now. This is one for the couch, if you know what I mean."

"I get it." Susan paused. "Dad was asking about you when I said you were over there tonight."

"Asking what?"

"Why I was not there with you."

"And you said what, exactly?"

"That I thought you were trying to get your mum's future sorted, due to her condition."

"Susan, listen,. You have to stick to that and not waiver from that story. Understand?"

"What the devil is going on?"

"I don't know," he lied. "Something is, and I have a feeling it's serious."

"Have you seen the news today? The last man alive from the robbery died in hospital. That is all four dead. There was an interview with the consultant in charge of his case."

"I'll try to catch it. The late-night news is on shortly, then I'm off to bed. Night, Susan. I love you loads."

"Love you too. Hopefully, see you tomorrow."

"Hopefully."

Andy switched on the news. The death of the robber was the second story broadcast. It had slipped down the order of importance. He watched as the Consultant Surgeon, Mr. James Massey, gave a prepared statement to the media. When Mr. Massey raised a hand to scratch his cheek, Andy immediately locked onto his pinkie ring, which bore the Masonic symbol of a Square and Compass. Andy slumped onto the couch, feeling shattered by the situation with his brother Ricky and the news about the robber.

As he fell asleep, Andy had no idea of the rude awakening he was to get the following morning.

Chapter Thirty

Somewhere in the waking world, Andy could hear the telephone ringing. He ignored it several times, but it persisted. Soon he began to rise from the depths of slumber. His body felt like he had been kicked from pillar to post, and only when he reached for the receiver, rolled over and hit the floor did he realise he had fallen asleep on the couch.

"Hello," He winced.

"Andy?"

"Yeah, who is this?"

"It's Alice." Her voice was quiet, almost timid.

He eyed the clock. It was just after seven. "What's wrong?"

"Sorry to bother you so early.I It's just that, after you left last night, Ricky left and I don't think he's been home all night."

"What do you mean you don't think? You must know if he went to bed or not."

"No, I don't know, Andy. We haven't shared a bed for over a year, and I can't find him anywhere in the house. I even checked the kid's room, but they're both still sleeping."

"Is his car there?"

"No."

"Okay, check everything again. Check the garage and extension. If you have a shed, check that too. Then call me back. I'll get dressed and head over."

"Thank you. I didn't know who else to call."

"It's fine, we're family. Just check everywhere."

The phone rang just as he was looking for his car keys.

"Andy, he is not here, and I'm really worried."

"Okay. At this time, I should be able to get there in about thirty to forty-five minutes, depending on the traffic."

"Thank you." Her voice broke as the call ended.

For the second time in less than twenty-four hours, Andy's car swung through the gates and into the driveway of his brother's house. From his car, Andy carefully viewed the scene. No sign of Ricky's Mercedes in the driveway or anywhere near, that was for sure. When he had been there earlier, the Alice's Mini Cooper was parked behind the Mercedes.

Looking at the gap between the Mini and the curbed garden, it would have been tight to get out, but manageable.

Alice opened the door and beckoned him inside. She pointed upwards and put a finger to her lips, indicating that the children were asleep. Andy nodded his understanding. He entered the kitchen and heard the kettle boiling. Alice poured two coffees. She was in her dressing gown, its matching belt loosely tied around her waist, leaving the top half partially open to reveal her cleavage. If she was not his brother's wife, Andy would have considered it seductive. However, it was not just her state of undress that caught Andy's attention, but the way she walked around the kitchen, her long, black, unbrushed hair adding to her tempting appearance.

"Has this happened before?"

"No. Never."

"Okay, so this is out of character?"

"Absolutely! Andy, what did you guys talk about yesterday? Because after you left, he was very distressed. I've seen him act out in a million ways, but I have never seen him like that."

"After I left, did he talk to you about anything?"

"No."

"Anything at all? Think!"

"He said 'love you all' and then went out the door.

"Alice, call the police. Tell the operator you want to report a missing person considered vulnerable, possibly suicidal."

"Are you having a laugh?"

"Just do it."

Alice obeyed. Halfway through her report, Andy took the receiver from her and informed the operator that he was a serving officer and that he had serious concerns for the welfare of his brother. The operator said a car was being dispatched to them immediately.

"Alice, can I suggest that you get some clothes on before they arrive?"

"Yeah sure." She bit her lip. "When this is all over would you like to see me like this again?"

"Absolutely not."

"Pity."

Two officers arrived shortly after, and Andy let them into the house. Alice came downstairs dressed in a loose sweatshirt and tracksuit bottoms, though she had left her feet bare.

"Hi guys."

"Who is reporting who missing?"

"I am reporting my husband missing."

"Why?"

"What do you mean why? Because he's missing! He hasn't been home all night."

"Well, normally we wait twenty-four hours before taking a report of a missing person."

This is not the way we do things, Andy thought, and it is not happening here.

"If you would like to call back tomorrow, Mrs. Blackmore," continued the officer, "then we will return. If your husband has not come home by then, we can start a missing person inquiry."

Alice looked at Andy. "Do you agree?"

"Em no, I think it should be done now."

"Well as I said, sir, we normally wait twenty-four hours."

"Really? Well, in this case you are not going to wait twenty-four minutes."

"Sir, we are leaving now."

"Then you might as well head straight to the Complaints and Discipline office and tell them Andy Blackmore sent you for neglect of duty."

The uniformed officers sighed and were about to leave before one of them tilted his head, as if recalling something. "Wait a minute, is your husband Richard Blackmore? The Chemist?"

"Yes," replied Alice.

Immediately, the officer turned to his colleague and pointed at him.

"Get writing. We're filing a missing person report." He turned to Andy. "What's your relationship to Richard?"

"Brother."

"And you said you're a cop?"

"Yes."

"Where?"

"Z Division."

"I'm sorry, but twenty-four hours are the rules here man."

"Really?"

"Oh hang on, do you know Brian Berger?"

"Never heard of him." Andy replied cooly.

"Oh, okay." The officer suspected he was being lied to.

"Tell you what, give me your notebook and I'll write you out my details and a brief statement, save you asking questions. How about that?"

"Sure, thanks, mate."

"I am not your mate."

As the officers were leaving, their radios activated and an operator asked them to attend a report of a car lying in a field.

"Roger. We're currently attending a missing person report. It will be submitted for the last call."

"Noted. The vehicle in the field is a silver Mercedes, registration number Romeo Bravo 465."

"See that registration number they just broadcast? That's my brother's car."

"Do you want to come with us to identify it?"

Andy turned to Alice. "You should stay with the kids. I'll be back soon."

"Okay." Alice gulped.

As they drove toward the incident, a voice came over the radio again, "Control to Alpha 4."

"Go ahead."

"The car is registered to a Richard Blackmore, same address as the missing person."

"Roger," confirmed the older officer, "we have his brother in the car."

"Andy Blackmore?"

"That is a positive."

"Then you've got the Iceberg in your car. Be careful."

"Roger."

"Iceberg?" The younger cop scoffed.

"Forget it," Andy grumbled.

They pulled up beside a gate and got out of the car. Andy followed the officers into the field. As they approached the car, Andy noticed a hose pipe sticking out of the exhaust and leading into the vehicle through a slightly open window. The engine was running.

"Christ," one of the officer's said and turned around, walking straight up to Andy and blocking his view. "Would you like to wait here? We shall see what we have."

"I think I know what we have. But please, on you go."

Andy watched as the older of the two officers cupped his eyes and pressed his face against the glass. Then he pulled the driver's door open and switched off the ignition. He saw the officers speaking to each other in low voices, blocking his view of the car's inside.

"Mr. Blackmore," one of them called, beckoning him towards the vehicle. "It's—"

"Empty," Andy finished for him. Where he had been dreading seeing his lifeless brother, there was only air and expensive leather.

"He is not in there."

"Check the trunk, I'll look around. He must be somewhere."

Andy scanned the area around the car. He had only walked a few paces before he noticed something sticking out of the long grass a few metres away. It looked like a hand. He ran over to find his brother in a heap on the grass. He turned him over onto his back and felt for his wrist. There was a slight pulse.

"Get an ambulance here immediately!" he cried.

Within ten minutes, an ambulance was on the scene. Within another five, Ricky was loaded onto a stretcher and into the ambulance, which sped away, sirens blaring and blue lights flashing.

After moving Ricky's car to the police compound for safekeeping, the police returned to visit Alice at the house to deliver the news.

Andy called Alice from the hospital and informed her that Ricky was in serious but stable condition. Alice asked him to wait at the hospital for while she contacted her her parents to mind the children and his mum.

Alice arrived at the hospital about an hour later. Andy took her into a side room he had been given.

"So what happened? The police officers just said Ricky lying in a field. Where is he?"

"He's in intensive care. Alice, sit down." She did as she was told. "It looks like he tried to commit suicide." Alice gasped and put a hand to her heart. Andy continued, "but he changed his mind in time. He had fed a hosepipe from the exhaust of his car through the window. He's suffering from carbon monoxide poisoning, and it will be a while before we know what damage he's done to himself."

Andy watched Alice, who was staring at the spotless hospital floor, eyes wide, head shaking.

"Can I see him?" she asked finally.

"I'll get a member of staff to speak to you."

Andy left the room, and a few minutes later, he returned, followed by a nurse.

"Mrs. Blackmore?" she spoke softly. "Follow me please."

Once they reached Ricky's room, Alice staggered a little at the sight of Ricky lying there: all the medical apparatus surrounding him, enabling him to breathe pure oxygen so as to get rid of the poison circulating his body.

Alice took a seat by her husband's side and lay her hand over his. Ricky looked like he was sleeping peacefully, his head resting on the pure white pillowcase. Andy stood silently at the foot of the bed, wondering why his brother would go to this extent instead of seeking help.

The door opened and a nurse entered. She performed the usual duties of checking all the readings on the machines and adjusting the drip.

"Nurse, can I speak to a doctor, please?" asked Alice. "I need to know what's going on."

"I'll see who is available," she said as left the room at a brisk pace.

A few minutes later, the nurse returned. "Mrs. Blackmore, would you like to come with me please?" Alice hesitated, looking between the nurse and Ricky. "He's in good hands."

"Andy, come with me?" she requested, waving Andy along just as she was leaving. He followed, and they were both shown into an office. Inside, a smartly-dressed man sat behind a large oak desk.

"Mrs. Blackmore," he started, "I am Doctor James Grady, your husband's medical consultant at this time."

"Pleased to meet you, I'm Alice. This is Andy, Ricky's brother." Andy nodded as Alice took a seat.

"How can I help you?"

"I need to know what is going on with Ricky. How he is, what will happen to him. We have two small children at home who I have to try and explain things to."

Ricky was suffering from medium carbon monoxide poisoning. He was being treated with pure oxygen and so far the treatment was working and keeping him alive. The long-term effects would not be known for a while, but Doctor Grady was hopeful Ricky would recover sufficiently to have a reasonable lifestyle.

"Can I ask what you mean by reasonable lifestyle?"

"Well, that depends on how much of the exhaust fumes he managed to inhale."

"I'm sorry, I'm not following you."

"I am not saying this is going to happen, but you would have to be prepared that things might not be quite the same in the future. Is your husband employed?"

"Yes, he is a chemist. He owns four shops."

"Oh." The consultant considered this, glancing at Andy before continuing, "Mrs. Blackmore..." he rolled his pen between his fingers. "Have you any idea why your husband would want to take his own life?"

"No, absolutely none at all. He is a successful businessman. We have a large villa, two cars, two great kids. We want for nothing."

"Mr. Blackmore, do you have any idea what may be going on with your brother?"

Andy stared at the consultant. "Nothing that could not be sorted in time."

"What does that mean?" Alice turned around in her seat to glare at Andy.

"I'll speak to you back at the house," Andy uttered.

"When he's up and about, he will have to be psychologically assessed and then we'll go from there," Doctor Grady interjected.

"I understand," said Alice, turning back to the doctor. "May I see Ricky before I leave?"

"Certainly. Stay if you wish. Mr. Blackmore, do you have a minute? I need some details about the events earlier today."

"Certainly. Alice, on you go. I'll catch up."

"Mr. Blackmore," Doctor Grady intoned once Alice had stepped out of the room.

"Call me Andy, please."

"Andy, do you know what is going on?"

"He has severe financial problems. Gambling. And he told me that he thinks his marriage is falling apart. Also, he was annoyed that our mother handed over Power of Attorney to me. That means he cannot access the remainder of her cash. Only I have control over that. Doctor, does this remain confidential?"

"If you wish."

"I want to be the one to tell Alice."

"As you wish."

"Thank you. Now can I ask you, what are the best and worst case scenarios for Ricky?"

"Best? Really good recovery and back to work. Worst? Memory impairment, mental deterioration, emotional instability. Short-term exposure will cause certain changes in his intellectual functioning, but we don't know how long he was exposed to the gas in the car."

Andy joined Alice at her husband's bedside.

"Is there anything I can get you, Alice?"

"Answers. I need answers. The truth." She turned to Andy then, lips pursed, eyes wet and red. "And I believe that you have them both."

Andy put a finger to his lips to silence her. Then he then placed his one hand on top of the other to shape the letter 'T'. Alice nodded and kissed Ricky's forehead before they left.

Alice and Andy sat at a round white table in the busy, volunteer-run hospital cafe run.

"Have you called Susan today?" Alice asked.

"No."

"Don't you think you should?"

"My priority at the moment is you, your kids, and mum."

"Then could you please tell me what is going on? Do not hide anything from me. I am fed up being excluded and treated like I don't matter. Do you know something? I don't think your brother loves or even cares about me anymore. Money is his god, that's the truth."

Andy stared at Alice.

"Who looks after the kids? Me! Who looks after your mum? Me! Who cooks at all hours of the day, and at night when he finally decides to come home? Me! Truth be told, I just want out, but I stay for the sake of the kids. Is that not a horrible thing to say at this time, in this place, when my husband might not come out of here alive? I could walk out of here and not come back, but I don't. So, tell me the whole truth."

"Okay, first things first, call your parents and update them. I'll call Susan and say I am with you and Ricky. Agreed?" Alice did not look happy at the diversion, but she relented.

"I know a place we can both go where we won't be disturbed, hopefully."

As they finished their relatively short telephone calls, Andy led Alice to, of all places, the hospital chapel, where relatives of the sick and dying could find peace in moments of need. The chapel was non-denominational and therefore open to all; the statue of Christ on the Cross was the only giveaway that they were in a place of worship. The chapel was adorned with beautiful ornamentation that offered a serene atmosphere.

Andy and Alice took a seat on a pew at the back, trying not to disturb the one other person sitting at the front, head bowed and hands clasped together in prayer. Andy stared at the statue and found some solace in the silence of the chapel.

"Okay, I am ready," Alice whispered.

"Are you sure?"

"Please."

Quietly and slowly, Andy shared the information that Ricky had given him the previous day: the sale of their mother's house, the true cost of the extension to Ricky and Alice's house, the decision to seek Power of Attorney over their mother's affairs, his gambling addiction, and the effects his debts were having on his business and were about to have on the house.

He also explained how Ricky reacted when he found out he could not get Power of Attorney. Andy went as far as telling her about Ricky thinking that she was having an affair and that their marriage was about to end.

When he had finished, it dawned on Andy that he had not looked at Alice once, nor she at him. They had stared straight ahead.

They sat in silence for what seemed a long time. First to react was Alice, who shuffled into a more relaxed position and slipping her arm under Andy's, drawing him close. She laid her head on Andy's shoulder before breaking the silence.

"This whole thing is just so unreal." She went silent for a while longer. "I want to stay here with Ricky, but I have to get home to the kids."

"I understand."

"I want to check with the nurses that nothing is likely to happen to Ricky soon if we leave."

"I'll wait here for you."

Arrangements were made with the nursing staff that, should there be any sign of a deterioration in Ricky's condition, then she would be contacted immediately. She would also get updates by telephone, and visiting hours would be suspended to allow her to visit whenever was convenient for her.

Since he had travelled to the hospital in the ambulance, Alice drove Andy back to the villa.

"Andy, you should call Susan again and update her about what is going on."

"Okay."

Andy went through to the lounge where he and Ricky had spoken only the day before. He lifted the phone and dialled Susan's number.

"Hello," answered a deep, gruff voice.

"Brian?"

"Yes"

"It's Andy,"

"Oh, Andy, how is your brother, Ricky?"

"Can I speak to Susan please?" There was an uncomfortable silence, and then he heard a muffled shout, "Susan, Andy is on the phone."

"Andy?" Susan sounded out of breath.

"Yes."

"What is going on? I've been trying to get hold of you all day."

"Ask your father, Susan. He seems to know."

"Stop it. What does he know? And where are you?"

"I am at Ricky and Alice's house."

"Why are you back there again?"

"Do you have the telephone number for this house?" Andy gave Susan the number. "Susan, can I call you back? I am with Alice at the moment."

"Why?"

"Ask your dad." Andy was unable to keep the anger out of his voice. "I'll see you soon. Love you, bye."

Andy went back through to the living room, where Alice was sitting with her parents. Her father looked up as he came in said,

"I am sorry about your brother."

"Thank you, Albert, but I am more worried about Alice and the kids. He almost left two kids without a dad. If anyone knows what that is like he should. What an idiot."

Headlights lit up the living room as a car came up the driveway. The light and engine were switched off and the doorbell rang.

"I'll get it," Andy said, springing out of his seat almost as soon as he'd sat down, "in case it's a reporter."

Andy opened the door to find Susan standing there.

"Come here," she said as she wrapped her arms around him. "I am so, so sorry."

"Everyone is through here in the living room." Andy lead her in. "Albert, Mary-Anne, this is my fiancé, Susan."

"Pleased to meet you, Susan."

"Likewise. Alice, how are you?"

"I am okay for now. Just waiting to see what is going to happen."

"We'll go home now," Alice's father cut in. "Call when you need us." Alice showed them out.

As soon as she came back, the door to the living room burst open.

"Mummmmmy," cried Alfie and Annie as they charged in. They thew themselves at their mother before turning to the guests. "Uncle Andy! Aunty Susan!"

"Hey guys," Andy greeted them with a forced positive tone. "Why are you not in bed? It's getting late."

"Can you put us to bed, Uncle Andy? We have a police book you can read us."

"Yeah, I have always wanted to do that. But no carry-on tonight."

"Awwwww, okay Uncle Andy."

Andy turned to Susan. "Aunty Susan, eh?" He looked again at the terrible twosome and said, "I am a police car chasing you upstairs. Get into bed to escape! Memaw, memaw, memaw!" They began to run to their room, giggling all the way.

"I'm in bed, Uncle Andy," shouted Alfie.

"Me too," added Annie.

"Oh, I have to search then." Andy placed a hand above his eyebrows and pretended to search for his nephew and niece. "I can't find you! You win."

Andy took a seat at the end of Alfie's bed and read them the police book. It wasn't long before their eyes were droopy.

"Night kids," He whispered as he turned out the light and made his way out.

"Night, Uncle Andy."

"Shhh, I might find you if you talk."

Andy returned to the living room.

"Alice, we have had virtually nothing to eat all day," Andy said. "How about a takeaway?"

"Indian or Chinese?"

"Chinese?"

"Yeah."

"Susan, what about you?"

"Indian."

"China two, India one. Chinese wins."

"Aw Andy, please," Susan begged sarcastically, pouting her lips.

"Let's phone for both. My treat."

After they'd finished eating, Andy and Alice explained the events of the day to Susan.

"This whole day is going to change things drastically, Alice," Andy proclaimed. "No matter what happens to Ricky, I have to look at Mum's situation and what it will mean for her when Ricky gets home."

Alice nodded her head and turned to Susan. "Would you have any objections to Andy staying here to give me a hand with the kids and his mum, until we get a shift system going for visiting?"

"You have to ask me that? Of course he can stay here to help you out. I will see him whenever."

"Thank you."

"You can stay over too. We've plenty of room."

"I appreciate the offer, but I am a phone call away if you need me."

"Thank you. Oh God what a way to end the year!" Alice exclaimed suddenly. "Welcome to the Blackmore family, Susan."

They chuckled half-heartedly.

"Alice," Andy spoke after a moment. "Do you want to phone the hospital and get an update or should I?"

"I'll do it, if that's okay?"

"Oh yes, for sure."

Andy and Susan sat together as Alice made her telephone call.

"Ward ten, ICU, please. Hello, this is Alice Blackmore. I am enquiring about my husband, Richard Blackmore. My brother-in-law, Andy Blackmore and I spoke to Doctor James Grady earlier today." Alice listened for a few seconds. "Yes, yes, I understand. I forgot to ask today when I can see my husband in the morning? Oh, yes okay. If there is any change in his condition, would you please call me? Thank you so much. Goodnight."

Alice told Susan and Andy that Ricky's condition was still serious but stable. "The nurse said that visitors are restricted to immediate family at this time, and visiting time is from eleven o'clock in the morning. There is no change in his condition, but if there is, they will call immediately. Hopefully, I won't hear from them."

The living room door opened to reveal Andy's mother.

"Hey, Mum."

"Hello Andy. You are Andy, yes?"

"Yes, Mum.

"And who is this?"

"This is Susan."

"Hello Susan. Pleased to meet you."

"Mum, you met Susan a couple of days ago."

"Yes, I know. Do you think I am stupid or something?"

"No."

"Where is your brother? I need to speak to him."

"Em, he had to go to the shop to give out medicines."

"That boy is always doing things he doesn't know anything about."

"Mrs. B.," Alice piped up. "It's time for bed, don't you think?"

"Really? Okay then, goodnight Susan."

"Goodnight Mrs. B.," she said, following Alice's lead.

"Night Mum."

"Yes, night son."

"What time is it?" Alice asked once Andy's mother had left the room.

"Almost half past ten," Susan answered.

"Hell, where has the time gone?"

"Time waits for no-one, Alice."

"That is so true."

"Call me if you need me to watch the kids or do anything else."

"Thank you, Susan."

Alice watched from the window as Andy led Susan to her car, kissed her gently, then closed her door. He stood back, letting her manoeuvre her car and head slowly towards the gates before driving through them and away.

Andy returned to the house and made his way to the living room, which was now empty. He sprawled on a couch and stared at the open fire, watching the flames dance in the dark. Fires had always fascinated Andy, even as a small child when he watched the coal burn in his grandparents' fireplace, lying on the floor on his side, head resting on his hand. He had never had the opportunity to do that again since his grandparents died.

"Would you like a drink?" Alice asked, coming in from the kitchen.

"Yes, please," Andy murmured, his back to Alice.

"What would you like? We have everything here, courtesy of the reps Ricky deals with."

"Do you have Brandy?"

"Yes, loads. Ricky hates the stuff."

"I'll have that then, with loads of ice, please. What are you having?"

"Same as you. Some things never change."

"Some things never change, but some things do and life goes on."

"What is that supposed to mean?"

"I remember that was your favourite tipple years ago."

Alice left to get the drinks and came back promptly with two brandies in hand.

"Why are you lying on the floor?"

"Childhood memories."

"Of what?"

"Watching the flames in the big coal fire at my grandparents' house."

"Can I watch them with you?"

"Sure." He sat up, drawing his knees up to his chest.

Alice sat beside Andy, adopting the same position. Two brandy glasses lay on the hearth next to each other.

"Andy, do you have any idea how much debt Ricky has gotten us into?"

"No."

"I have to find out for myself. He has control over all our financial affairs, even the bank books are in his name. He gives me housekeeping money every week. I know this is something you don't want to hear, Andy, but living with your brother can be a nightmare at times."

"Well, on Christmas Day I gave him a row for speaking to you the way he did."

"That was nothing compared to some of the things he says."

"Why do you stay?"

"No place to go, and it would kill Mum and Dad if I left him. Also, concerning what you told me today, I am not having an affair. I never have done since the day we got married. Do you know that he sleeps in the spare room? Has done for just over a year now. No love, no tenderness, no cuddles, absolutely no sex at all. I am only thirty-five years old. Don't get me wrong, I have thought of having an affair, but I hardly get out, so who would I meet to have an affair with? It would only be sex and that's not me."

"To be honest, I am a bit uncomfortable hearing this. This is for you and Ricky to sort out."

"I have tried everything, to be honest, but nothing works," she continued, ignoring Andy. "I have tried to instigate sex, I bought sexy underwear... I even offered him a threesome to see if that sparked interest, but nothing! Am I ugly? Is that it?"

"No."

"Am I attractive?"

"Yes."

"Thank you." She kissed his cheek.

As they cupped the brandies in their hands, Andy felt Alice's head rest on his shoulder.

"Do you mind?"

"No, it's okay."

"Do you think that you could ever be unfaithful to Susan?"

"Honestly, no I don't. Never even been tempted since I met her."

"That is a lovely thing to say."

"Alice, why did you give up a glittering career?"

"To be a wife, and to be a mother. Anyway, I can always go back when the children get older."

"True." Andy yawned. "It's probably late, and I think we have a long day tomorrow."

"This has been lovely sitting here with you. I am sorry if I embarrassed you tonight."

"No, you didn't at all. As I said, it is something you and Ricky have to sort out. I will tell you something and it is full of ifs. If you were not married to Ricky, if you were single or divorced, if I was not with Susan, then I would be seriously attracted to you. You're a beautiful woman, Alice. Don't let Ricky ever take that away from you."

"Even though I am older than you?"

"Oh yes."

"Andy, we have a spare room. The bed is always made, so you can use that tonight or until we get things sorted with Ricky."

"Thank you."

"Goodnight."

They laid their empty brandy glasses on the nearby table. The dim lamplights were extinguished on their way out of the room as they made their way to their respective bedrooms.

As Andy got into bed there was a quiet tap on the door.

"Come in."

Alice opened the door slightly and looked in. "Everything okay?"

"Yes, thank you. All is good."

"Do you need pyjamas or anything?"

"No thanks," Andy said, laughing. "Who wears them nowadays?"

"Ricky."

"Oh, okay."

"Goodnight Andy."

"Goodnight Alice."

Andy heard the door of the adjoining bedroom closing. He heard Alice shuffling around as he drifted off into a deep sleep.

About seven o'clock in the morning, Alice awoke to her alarm. She had decided to send the children to the school kids club as usual and maintain their routine as best she could. She got out of bed and pulled on her dressing gown, wrapping it tightly and tying the cord around her waist. Within minutes, the coffee percolator was bubbling.

She went to the room where Andy had spent the night and knocked gently on the door. There was no reply so she tried again. Still, there was no reply. She opened the bedroom door to see Andy lying there with a single sheet partially covering him. She eyed his naked torso as he slept peacefully. Her eyes started to move downwards, admiring his muscular body without an ounce of fat.

As Andy stirred slightly, but kept sleeping moving onto his back. The outline of his manhood was now visible under the sheet and was proportionate to his body. She could not move from the doorway, an erotic surge taking hold of her body, her nipples becoming erect. She knew she had to leave the room immediately before she did something she would regret forever.

She returned to the kitchen and sat at the table, thinking about Ricky. No news is good news, she thought. The phone had not rung during the night.

"Good morning," Andy greeted her from the doorway, startling her. "Any coffee available?"

"Oh hell, Andy. I was a million miles away there."

"Sorry. I thought you would have come in to wake me."

"No, thought I would just leave you for a while."

"How about I take the kids to school for you?"

"That would be great, thanks. But it's the holidays. They go to a kids club instead."

"Oh, okay. After that, I'll go to the flat."

"Are you coming back tonight, Andy?"

"Do you want me to?"

"Yes, please."

"I will be at the hospital to see Ricky at some point today, but I'll give you space to be with him."

"Thank you. Will you see Susan today?"

"Hopefully."

"She is so lucky to have you."

"Please remind her of that." He laughed. Then with a more serious expression, he asked, "what about Mum?"

"I'll see to her. She will get picked up at ten o'clock today and taken to her club until five tonight."

Alice got the children up, dressed and fed. She packed their bags and their lunches. Annie was five years old, and Alfie was seven. They both loved going to their club, where they got to play games with their friends until the three o'clock. They worshipped their parents, as kids that age often do, but their dad was their hero, because he gave medicine to people to save their lives.

"Right guys, here is the score," Andy announced to the kids. "I am taking you to your kids club today because Mum and Dad are busy, so you have to show me where your school is 'cause I don't know. Who knows where your club is?"

"Me, me, me," they shouted in unison, bouncing up and down.

Alice walked Andy and the kids to the door. "Bye guys," she said with a smile that looked more like a frown.

"Bye Mum," the three of them called.

"Andy, come here, please." He saddled back up to her, and she placed her hands on his shoulders and kissed him on the lips. "Thank you from the bottom of my heart for being here for us."

"Em, yeah, no problem." He flushed. "Honestly. See you later, yeah?"

"For sure."

She looked on as Andy drove down the driveway and out of the gates with her children. She went back in and sat at the kitchen table, thinking about the past twenty-four hours. The information she had from Andy, wondering if she had any money or not, her husband's secret gambling debts, where this was going to leave them all. At least she had a career, even if it had been put on hold for the children. But she would not be destitute as she was a qualified lawyer. She could start on her own if necessary and she would always have a place for her and the kids while her parents were alive.

Then there was Andy. She knew that he was in love with Susan and that Susan felt the same about him, yet she knew that her crush from years ago was bubbling to the surface. She had once had strong sexual feelings for him: something that she had hidden all through her courtship with Ricky.

Alice's head was in turmoil. How can I control my feelings and urges for him? She recognised that these urges were partly because she received no intimacy from Ricky, and she missed the warmth of an embrace. She knew it was wrong, but she also knew it was normal, the need to feel loved. Alice considered how her early life with Ricky had been and how different it was now.

Was it the right thing to do, inviting Andy to stay here while Ricky is fighting for his life?

Chapter Thirty-One

The 29th of December, 1982 was rapidly approaching. Andy packed an overnight bag to go back to Spring Mount. He showered and changed, throwing on his black t-shirt with a motif of a clenched fist on the chest, a pair of light blue jeans, and white baseball boots. He was freshly shaven and groomed, having been to his Italian friend Giovanni. Andy smelled like a bottle of Brut aftershave, a favourite that Giovanni never seemed to run out of. He called Susan to update her.

"Good morning, Miss Berger."

"Hey Andy, how is your brother?"

"Well, we got through the night without a phone call, so I would say he's stable."

"That is good news. What are your plans today?"

"Just about done everything that I needed to do today."

"Are you staying overnight again tonight?"

"That's the plan, unless you have something arranged for us?"

"No, nothing."

"Tell you what, let me go see Ricky at the city hospital. Then I'll come take you for something to eat, away from everything. I miss you."

"I miss you and I know this is a trying time for everyone. I am sorry."

"See you later. Love you."

"Love you too."

Andy hung up the phone, locked up the flat, and made his way to the car.

Once he was on the road, Andy glancing in his rear-view mirror and noticed a vehicle following him, which had been parked in the street only moments ago. Andy adjusted his mirror as they drove through the busy West End, keeping an eye on the car, a black Vauxhall Astra GT. It had two male occupants.

He saw a Shell garage ahead and pulled in there, despite not needing petrol. The car following him pulled onto the forecourt to a pump on the opposite side. Andy unhooked the nozzle, inserted it into the filler of his petrol tank and went back to the pump. The driver of the vehicle exited his car and leaned against it, staring at the pump. Andy approached him, grabbed him, and dragged him between the pumps, slamming him against the side of his car. The second man got out of the car and came towards them.

"Tell your mate not to come any closer, or you're gone," Andy spat.

"Nah, he is going to destroy you, Andy."

Andy pulled the petrol hose from his car and held it to the man's body.

"Okay, tell him to get back in the car, or I am going to cover you in petrol and... have a smoke."

The man's eyes widened.

"Davy, get back in the car. This nutter is going to set me on fire."

"He's bluffing!" Davy squealed.

"Really? I'm gonna start a countdown, and if I get to one, he goes up in flames."

"Dare you."

"Hey Andy," someone shouted. "You got a problem?"

How are there so many people who know my name here?"Andy, it's us."

And there they were, three of Andy's favourite poachers from the river.

"Hey, guys, how you doing? Yeah, I could use some help. Any of you got a lighter?"

"Sure, here you go mate." One of them reached into his pocket and handed Andy a lighter.

"Cheers, can I suggest you all stand back? This is gonna be a hell of a show."

By now the staff in the petrol station had called the police. Other drivers stood aghast, watching the proceedings unfold before them. One smart woman drove off without paying for her petrol.

"Okay, where were we? Oh yeah, reaching number one."

"Can we do the countdown?" one of the poachers piped up.

"Are they being serious?" whined the man Andy was holding.

"Hey boys," shouted Andy, "this guy wants to know if you are being serious about this?"

"Hey mate," goaded one of the boys. "Do you know Andy Blackmore? He's a nutter. He will do you."

"L-listen, mate," the hostage stammered. "What you gonna do?"

"Well, if you don't tell your gorilla to get back in the car, I'm gonna tell my boys to start the countdown."

"Davy, get into the car now," he screamed.

Andy watched as his companion obeyed.

"Now, part two. Who sent you and why?"

"I can't tell you."

Petrol shot from the nozzle over the male's clothing, causing him to fall backwards onto the petrol pumps.

"Oops, sorry," Andy jeered. "Didn't mean to do that."

"Oh, Christ!"

"Okay, let's try again. Who sent you?"

Silence was the only reply

"Right boys, party time."

In the distance, police and fire brigade sirens could be heard.

"Five," the poachers started. "Four. Three. Two–"

"Okay, okay! Stop," he screamed. "I'll tell you, I'll tell you."

Andy waved at the poachers to stop. "Now I make it you have one second left."

"Okay, we're retired cops who do private investigations. We were asked to make enquiries into your private life. See who you are with and what you are doing."

"And you were hired by who, exactly?"

"I can't tell you."

"Ready boys?"

"No, no, no! I'll tell you. All I know is that we were subcontracted and had to report back to Brian on this phone number." He handed him a small commonplace book, open to a page with the number scrawled in smudged ink.

"Brian?"

"Berger."

"Good man." Andy smiled. "Have a long and happy retirement." Andy patted the man on the shoulder and watched as he joined his partner in their car and drove off.

"Thanks, guys," Andy addressed the poachers and tossed the lighter back to its owner. "That's one I owe you, now get out of here."

Andy went into the petrol station and paid for the petrol he used to dowse the man with. "Do me a favour," he said to the man behind the counter, who shakily accepted the one pound coin. "Those guys just saved my life. Forget you saw them."

"Sure," he agreed, nodding vigorously.

"As for me, there is twenty quid. Merry Christmas mate."

"M-Merry Christmas."

Andy got back in his car and drove off as the police and fire brigade arrived. He headed to the hospital to see his brother. He knew the phone number given to him off by heart. That was to be dealt with later.

Andy arrived at the city hospital and parked. He went to the intensive care unit and pushed open the blue door leading to the nurses' station.

"Hi, I'm here to visit Richard Blackmore."

"You are?"

"His brother."

"Oh, please wait here a minute. We've been expecting you." The nurse rose from the table and went to a room close by.

"Please come in here, Mr. Blackmore."

Andy entered the room and saw his brother Ricky sitting with Alice. He was wearing a respirator and was barely able to speak. Ricky had been moved late last night to a room further from the nursing station as his life was out of immediate danger. For now.

Alice looked up at Andy and smiled. Ricky just sat there, looking embarrassed. Andy was in no mood to be messed about.

"You Goddamn dickhead," he said in a low, menacing tone. "What are you playing at? You almost left a beautiful family without a husband and father. Fatherless like we were. All because of what? Do your wife and children mean nothing to you?"

"Andy, relax," pleaded Alice. "Now is not the time."

"Sorry Alice, but now is the time and place." He exhaled loudly. "I'm going to see Susan. I'll see you later."

Andy continued his journey into the east end to Spring Hill. His next target was Brian Berger.

Pulling up outside the Berger household, he parked his car and went to the door, praying Brian would open it.

"Andy," Sandra exclaimed when she found him on her stoop, come in. Susan is upstairs."

When Andy walked into the living room, he saw Brian Berger sitting in his armchair reading the paper, ignoring him.

"Brian," Sandra intoned. "Andy is here."

"Oh, hello Andy. Didn't see you there."

"That's okay."

"Tea or coffee?" Sandra interjected.

"Let's go for tea today, please."

"No problem, on its way." She left for the kitchen.

"So, Brian," Andy started, "how are you today?"

"Fine, thank you. Are you here to collect Susan?"

"Yes. We are going for something to eat before I go back and see my brother's family."

"How is he?"

"I am sure you are well acquainted with his condition."

Brian raised an eyebrow.

"Well Andy, I hope your last date with my daughter is a good one. I can't say it has been nice knowing you."

"The last date?" Sandra said incredulously, reentering the living room.

"Yes, apparently so. Andy was just saying, new year new beginning. He's going to tell her over lunch but wanted us to know first."

"Andy?" asked Sandra inquisitively, staring at him with wet eyes.

"Hey babes, how is your brother?" asked Susan as she entered the room.

"Well, he was sitting up when I left him with Alice."

"What about the kids?"

"They're at their club, while Mum is at hers."

Andy realised he was being watched by both Brian and Sandra for different reasons. He was ready to pounce. "I have not planned this at all Susan, but due to circumstances beyond my control, your dad was saying this is our last date, for reasons best known to him. I was going to leave this for a few months until we went on holiday to Tenerife in the summer, which was supposed to be a surprise. I planned to get you alone on a beach at sunset and ask you to become my wife. But, here we are." Andy got down on one knee. "Susan Berger, will you marry me?"

Susan said nothing for a moment, only glancing at her father to shake her head. Then, she turned to Andy, tears in her eyes.

"Andrew Blackmore, I love you so much, I would be proud to be your wife."

"Is that a yes, then?"

"Of course it is."

"Now, I think I am supposed to give you a ring at this stage, but, due to the circumstances—"

"Hey, not a problem," Susan interjected. "Tomorrow we go get one."

Suddenly, Sandra shrieked gleefully, bouncing in her heels and waving her hands in the air, no longer able to contain herself. "Congratulations you two!" She pulled her daughter and Andy into a tight hug.

"Thank you so much for your daughter," Andy spoke, his words muffled against Sandra's neck.

"Brian," Sandra snapped as soon as she broke out of the embrace, "congratulate the kids."

Brian stood and hugged his daughter, then shook hands with Andy and saying nothing.

"Susan, let's get drinks," Sandra exclaimed, herding her daughter into the kitchen.

"You know this is never going to happen, Blackmore."

"Really? Listen to me you prick. You can hide behind the brotherhood all you like, but I know your secret."

Brian's eyes narrowed in shock.

Andy continued. "I know you are watching me, so the next time you rent a couple of goons to follow me, make sure they know what they are doing. You sent two keystone cops in their sixties to follow me. Next time there will be a tragic accident involving petrol."

Brian, white with rage, said nothing as he sat down. He picked his newspaper back up and opened it.

"You are mental, Blackmore. I heard what you did today," he mused. "Would you have done it?"

"That is for me to know and you to find out. So, don't try that again."

Sandra and Susan reappeared from the kitchen, carrying four glasses of sparkling wine.

"Sorry, I'm driving."

"Oh, Andy. Just one won't do any harm."

"Tell you what, future mother-in-law, you have mine., We'll have one in private soon."

"What does that mean?" asked Susan, laughing.

"Nothing," Sandra chirped. "Here's to Susan and Andy, the next generation of our family. Congratulations!"

Brian stood, held out a glass and muttered, "congratulations."

Andy wrapped an arm around him, saying it will be great having a father-in-law like him and a mother-in-law like Sandra. Sandra and Susan exchanged hugs, and as Andy hugged him, Brian whispered, "be afraid. Very, very afraid."

As they parted, Brian stared at Andy, who just smiled.

"So, what are your plans for your future together, Andrew?" Brian huffed.

"To keep your daughter happy, to encourage and support her in everything she does, to be happy together, and to keep her away from the goons who threaten her future happiness."

"What does that mean?" Susan repeated.

Andy turned to Brian Berger. "Do you want to explain or shall I?"

Brian looked at the floor.

"Dad, what have you done now?"

"Nothing."

"Your nose is growing, Pinocchio," Andy commented. "As I said to a couple of your friends earlier, you have until I reach one to tell the truth."

"Dad, what the devil is he talking about?"

"I don't know."

"That nose is getting bigger and bigger. Five. Four. Three. Running out of time Brian. Two."

"Right. Enough," Brian barked, on the edge of panic.

"Strange. That is the number your mates got to before their bottle crashed, in other words they completely lost it!"

Sandra and Susan stood like giants over Brian, and it struck Andy that this was the first time he had seen him at their mercy.

"I am waiting, Dad."

"So am I," added Sandra, her arms folded.

"Susan," started Brian, "you are my only daughter. What I have done in the past and what I do in the present has always been to protect you from people who were not good for you. All I have ever wanted was the very best for you. All I did was try to protect you from idiots, and can I tell you now that although you are about to marry someone who loves you, he is also probably one of the most idiotic people I have ever met. Which also makes him dangerous."

"Explain," Susan commanded.

"Today he threatened to set fire to a man."

She turned to Andy. "Is this true?"

Andy nodded. "Maybe you should ask your dad why I did that."

"Dad? Don't bother." Susan disappeared from the room, returning a few minutes later with a bag.

"Can I come live with you?" she asked Andy, lips pressed tight together, eyes looking everywhere but her father.

"Yes, of course."

"I mean permanently."

"Same answer."

As Andy and Susan left the house, they received a loving hug from Sandra. Brian was nowhere to be seen.

Once they had driven off, Sandra went back into the living room. "Brian, whatever it is you have done, you have just cost us our daughter. You have always been so possessive over Susan. No one was ever good enough! What is wrong with you? Your daughter, whom you claim to love, has finally found love and happiness and all you want to do is ruin it!"

"He knows about you and your friend Sheena," Brian stated, his calml voice at odds with the vicious look on his face.

Sandra did not reply.

"Sort it," demanded Brian.

"What do you mean sort it?"

"You know what I mean. Sort it."

"No way. He is our daughter's fiancé now," she replied angrily. "And there is nothing you can do about it!"

"Sort it, or we are finished with Susan," he threatened, slamming the door behind him.

Andy drove back to the West End with Susan, before leaving her at the flat and returning to the East End to get Alice's kids from the kids club at the school.

"Hey, guys," Andy greeted his nice and nephew with hugs "How was today?"

"Great, Uncle Andy," Alfie exclaimed. "Love you coming to get us."

"Yeah? I love it too. Before I take you home, let's go to Uncle Andy's flat and see Aunty Susan, yeah? Get fish and chips, and sweets."

"Yeah, let's do that," cried Alfie. "See Aunty Susan."

They crept up the stairs of Andy's flat and knocked on the door.

"Aunty Susan!" They shouted as she opened the door. Andy stood there, holding the fish suppers.

"Andy?"

"We come to see Aunty Susan and have dinner with pish and ships," announced Annie, smiling.

"Geez I can't wait until we get some of those," Andy commented, struggling to contain his laughter.

After dinner, Andy telephoned Alice to let them know that they were all safe and would be back home soon.

"Oh, and I have something to tell you and Ricky, something you won't believe. How is Ricky?"

"Recovering," she said vaguely. "Are you staying over tonight?"

"Yes."

"Good."

After he hung up the phone, Andy turned to Susan. "Right, darling lady, I suppose I better get those little ones back to their mum."

"Are you staying overnight?"

"That was the plan. Then go see Ricky's doctor in the morning."

"Well, I know where everything is, so all is good here."

"You know if you move anything I won't be happy," Andy jested, laughing. "Just don't move you out of here before I get back."

"I won't."

"When I get back, I will tell you everything about today."

Andy set off with the children in the car, heading back yet again to the east end. Checks in the rear-view mirror revealed nothing out of the ordinary. Still, he made sure to monitor it for the length of the journey.

Andy opened the large door to Ricky's house, letting Annie and Alfie run past him. "Mum, Mum, we're back," they shouted.

Alice knelt and hugged them both tightly. "Did you have fun?"

"Yes, and we had pish and ships for tea." Annie beamed.

"Do you mean fish and chips, Annie?"

"Uh-huh."

"I hope to live long enough to tell that story at her wedding," Andy commented.

"You are a bad influence on her, brother-in-law," Alice chided, slapping Andy's bottom as he passed her.

Ignoring the slap he asked. "How is Mum? Is she okay?"

"Yeah, she loved her day at her club. She's in her place, watching TV. I'll see to her after I see to the kids. Make us a drink, would you?"

Within an hour, Alice had the kids in their beds and Andy's mum sorted for the night. She sat down for the first time all day. She lifted her brandy glass to her lips and sat on the seat opposite Andy, who was sprawled on the couch, hand behind his head, and barefoot.

"What?" asked Andy when he noticed Alice staring at him.

"Eh?" She seemed like she was coming out of a trance.

"I get the impression I am under surveillance."

"Oh, I'm sorry. I didn't mean to stare. I was in a dream state." She quickly shook her head. "Right, what was it you had to tell Ricky and I?"

"Ready for this? I asked Susan to marry me today and she said yes."

"Oh Andy, that is wonderful. I am so pleased for you."

"Thank you. You are the first to know. Now for part two. How do I put this? Susan has moved in with me, as of today."

"You are joking! Isn't this a bit sudden?"

"Let's just say circumstances dictated the situation."

"Okay," she replied, more curious than satisfied. "Right, my turn to make the drinks."

"About time, too. Thought I was your slave."

"I wish. Susan is a very lucky lady."

At that point, the telephone rang. Both sat looking at it, wondering who was on the other end of the line. Alice picked it up cautiously. "Hello."

"…yes, it is."

"Sorry, who is this?" she asked in a concerned voice.

Suspicious, Andy beckoned Alice to give him the phone, which she did.

Andy said nothing and listened as the caller spoke, "Mrs. Blackmore, your husband owes us a lot of money. He must not fail to pay us this time. While he is in the hospital, tell him to make other arrangements." The caller hung up.

"Who was it, Andy?"

"I don't know. He was a heavy breather."

"Perv?"

"Sounded that way. You should go ex-directory."

"Good idea. So, you were saying, Susan has moved in. Why aren't you there tonight with her?"

"Because I have to take care of you and the kids just now. She understands. Are you okay?"

"Yes, why do you ask?"

"Just a feeling. Something's not right."

"Can I sit beside you?"

"Sure."

"I'll be back shortly, just need to get out of all this. It's been a long day," she explained, leaving the room. She returned a few minutes later wearing a short kimono and sat beside Andy.

"Just had to get off all those layers. Another brandy?"

"You know what they say about brandy, Alice."

"Yes, and it is working." She giggled.

"Yep."

They sat in silence for a while, letting time slip by until Alice suggested. "Shall I put some music on?"

"It is your house."

"Ricky hates the music I like."

"Okay, go for it. But no rubbish."

To Andy's surprise, she put on the blues. She explained that Ricky hated blues, seeing it as a depressing kind of music. Alice's take on it was it was a part of the struggle of black people in America that they expressed through music. Andy said that he never analysed music because it was there to be enjoyed rather than picked apart.

When the phone rang, Alice went to answer it. Andy heard her say,

"I hear congratulations are in order. I am so pleased for you, Susan. Here's Andy."

As Andy took the retriever and listened to Susan, he responded, "Okay, we can deal with that. Night, night, love you too. See you tomorrow."

"Everything okay, Andy?"

He said nothing and Alice did not push for an answer.

"Right, more brandy."

"Are you sure Alice?"

"Yes, absolutely. I never get a chance to do this with Ricky." She got off the couch to make drinks and returned quickly.

"Jesus Alice, they're getting stronger and stronger," Andy observed.

"So what? Do I not deserve it?"

"Yeah sure," he replied, though he was concerned.

The sound of a blues guitar came from the expensive speakers Ricky had installed.

"Oh my God, I just love this song," purred Alice.

Andy recognised the opening bars of Eric Clapton's Wonderful Tonight.

"Do you know something? Ricky has never danced with me to this song. How bad is that?"

"Alice, you know I cannot comment on that."

"Oh, stop being so prudish Andy. Start that song again. I am asking you to break my dance virginity to this song."

"It would be my pleasure to dance with my sister-in-law to this song."

As the song's intro began to play again, Alice and Andy took to the carpeted floor, Alice in her dressing gown, Andy in denims and t-shirt, their bare feet shuffling across the rug.

"So, how do we do this?" he asked.

"Like this." She wrapped her arms around his waist and laid her head on his chest. Andy placed his arms around her, holding her close to him. As the song's close echoed across the room, Alice looked up at Andy and thanked him, placing a small kiss on his neck.

"Okay you're an angel, so this is for you." She lined up Rod Stewart's Angel as they held each other tightly, moving from side to side in an amateurish waltz. As the song ended, Alice and Andy released their hold on each other.

"Thank you, Andy."

"Yer welcome," he slurred.

Alice looked up at Andy. "Hey man, one for the road?"

"Hey, girl, why not?" he replied as the slow, sultry blues rang out across the room.

"Alice, if anything ever happens to me—"

She put a finger to his lips to silence him. "Can I ask you for this dance?"

It was Alice who lined up Pink Floyd's Comfortably Numb. The deep bass struck up as they held each other.

The dancing seemed to be taking a turn in a direction Andy did not want it to go. As Alice held him tightly, it seemed inevitable.

Maybe she just needs support at this time, he thought. But deep within he felt he needed support. He had been getting so close to her over the past few days, but this was a no-go area.

Two large glasses of brandy sat on the table as Alice and Andy danced slowly, pressed close together while the music oozed through the speakers and swirled around the dimly lit room.

Alice tilted her head back. "Kiss me," she whispered.

"No, I can't."

"Yes, you can." She closed her eyes.

Andy looked at Alice. He closed his eyes and their lips met in a kiss which lingered throughout the song. And it was not until the closing bars sounded that their lips parted and they looked into each other's eyes.

"Alice this is not right." He released his hold on her.

"I know," she replied, giggling as she rested her head on his chest.

"What is happening here?"

"I don't know. But it feels so right."

"No everything is wrong about this."

"Is it?"

"Yes. Of course it is. Ricky is my brother, your husband."

"I've wanted you for years, you have no idea. I thought it was just an infatuation, and it did eventually… go to sleep. But now?" She looked up at him and beamed. "Now it is waking."

Alice pulled Andy's head down towards her and kissed him gently, not sure what response she was about to get until their tongues touched tenderly and their breathing began to alter. Andy drew back, whispering, "Are you sure about this?"

"I've never been so sure about anything in my life."

Andy took a deep breath. Everything was so wrong about this. He ordered Alice to take a seat, which she did. He sat next to her and handed her back her brandy, the one she had poured before they danced. They held the glasses close to each other. Nothing was said. They finished their two very large drinks then laid their glasses onto the small table.

As they reached their respective rooms, Andy held Alice close.

"Goodnight Alice. Do you know that you are a very special person?"

"In what way?"

"You do everything for him."

"Oh, that is just my way of life, Andy." She shrugged. "I am a slave to him."

"Well, in that case, that's something else to sort."

"Night Andy," she said as they stood outside her room.

"Night Alice."

Andy went into the guest room. He lay on the bed, fully clothed, for a few moments, reflecting on what happened. *Bed time for me,* he thought. He felt relieved that nothing further had taken place between him and Alice. Getting between the sheets, he settled down for the night.

A minute later, long light penetrated the room for a few seconds before being extinguished. Andy felt the bed covers being pulled back and someone slip in beside him.

"I need you," Alice whispered. "Please, Andy. Hold me."

"Alice, this cannot happen."

"Yes it can." She turned him onto his back and kissed him deeply.

Afterwards, they lay awake in silence. Alice turned to face Andy and whispered, "are you okay?"

"I feel so guilty."

"Listen, if you want, this never happened."

"Trouble is, it did. And we cannot change that. What is worse is that it felt right."

He soon fell asleep, with Alice wrapped around him.

As daylight flooded his room, Andy's eyes opened slowly. He sensed Alice was not beside him. He got up and pulled on his jeans. In the kitchen, Alice was on the phone to the hospital, getting an update on Ricky's condition. He placed his arms around her waist and kissed her neck. Replacing the receiver, she released his hold on her.

"All good?" he asked.

"Yes, in a way. Ricky is getting out today, so that is good news."

"You sound disappointed."

"No, I'm fine. I'll get the kids up and go see to your mum."

Andy sensed her tone was not right. "How is he getting home?"

"I need to go get him with your mum and the kids."

"I'll get him and bring him home to you." He sighed. "Alice, last night was amazing, but it must never happen again. I am confused, to be honest, about the whole thing. You. Last night. Everything."

"I know, but at least I achieved a long-held dream, getting you for a few hours to myself. Susan is so lucky to have you."

After breakfast, Andy called Susan to give her the news that Ricky would be leaving the hospital and that he was going to collect his brother. When he got home, he would take her out, as the end of the year was fast approaching.

"Hey, kids. I am going to bring you a big surprise when I get back."

"Yay!" Alfie shouted.

Alice walked Andy to the door and kissed him on the cheek.

"Thank you," she murmured.

As he made his way to the hospital, his mind drifted back to the night before; what happened would never be repeated as far as he was concerned. After parking his car in the hospital grounds, he made his way up to the ward.

"I'm here to collect Richard Blackmore," Andy announced to the ward nurse. "I'm his brother."

The nurse looked at him, puzzled, and informed him that Richard had signed himself out of the unit earlier that day.

"What time?"

"Ten o'clock this morning."

"Do you know if he got transport?"

"He said his wife was waiting for him downstairs."

"I take it you know why he was in here?"

"Yes."

"Was he assessed before he was told he could go home?"

"He was, and he was given the all-clear."

Andy requested to use the telephone. He dialled Alice's home phone. The phone rang repeatedly before being answered.

"Hello."

"Ricky?"

"Yes, Andy. I got a taxi home, as I thought Alice was too busy to collect me. I didn't realise you had been staying over."

"Just to help out," he blurted.

"Thank you for everything, especially looking after Alice and the kids."

"Tell Alice I will head home to Susan now."

As Andy went into the flat, he got a huge welcome from Susan. They sat and chatted a short time before going out together for something to eat in a local restaurant.

"Tomorrow we are going to get you an engagement ring," he promised.

"There is no rush for that. We can leave it until the January sales."

"Are you sure?"

"Well, it is only two days away."

"True."

As they set off for the restaurant, they were blissfully unaware of events at her parents' house, where the affair between Sandra and Sheena had resurfaced. Brian and Sandra were concerned about the information being disclosed to others and the damage it would do to their reputations in the community. They also had taken into consideration that their daughter was in love with the very man who could destroy their lives.

Soon, a close friend of Sandra's arrived at the house.

"Hello," Sandra greeted Sheena as she opened the door.

"Hello Sandy, long time no see."

"Please come in. Brian is in the living room."

"Hello Brian," Sheena acknowledged him as she walked into the living room.

Brian Berger stood and placed a welcoming kiss on Sheena's cheek while holding her hands.

"Please take a seat, Sheena, and thank you for coming." He gestured towards the couch.

Once she sat down, Sandra offered her a drink.

"I'm driving Sandy, so just a coffee, please."

A few minutes later Sandra returned with a cup of steaming coffee. Sheena took in the familiar sight of Sandra pouring a large whiskey on the rocks for Brian and making a Bloody Mary for herself.

"Sheena," started Brian, "I take it you know why we invited you?"

Sheena stated that she was not aware of the details exactly, and that she found the telephone call from Sandra surprising. She also informed Brian that Sandra had mentioned Susan's relationship with Andy.

"I believe that you have met Andy a couple of times recently," prompted Brian.

"At two Christmas parties. Andy seems like a great guy and Susan seems so happy."

Sheena sipped her coffee. "What do you both want from me after all this time? "

Sandra said nothing. Sheena flashed a look at Brian, who was tapping the arm of his chair and looking at his wife.

Brian sighed and rubbed his eyes. "The reason why we have invited you here tonight is because Susan left home to live with Andy. And she knows about the sexual relationship you had with Sandra, thanks to Andy." He took a large swig of his drink before continuing, "Sheena, I am not going to stand by and watch as he ruins this family. I will protect my family at any cost."

"So, where do I fit into all of this?"

"Well, you are not averse to a little bit of... fun with the ladies and gents, as we all know. I cannot afford Susan to find out any more about our lifestyle than she already knows, or we will never get her back into the fold. You are also aware of other things we have been involved in over the past few years, and you know what that could lead to should any of that ever come out."

"Stop pissing about and get to the point," demanded Sheena.

Brian could feel the gazes of Sandra and Sheena cutting through him, like lasers through steel.

"I want Andy Blackmore out of Susan's life once and for all. Whatever it takes!" Brian slammed a hand down on the coffee table, his face turning red, a vein bulging in his forehead. "The only two people that can do that are you and Sandra. He's a red-blooded man, and you're both mature, sexually-talented women. There is no way that he would refuse to get sexually involved with either of you. As for gathering the evidence proving Andy's infidelity, that will be up to me. His senior officers will find out what he is up to as well, and that will be the end of any promotion prospects." Brian was breathing heavily by the time he was finished. "Sandra, do you have anything to add? "

Sandra silently shook her head.

"Sheena, what about you?" Sheena sat on the couch contemplating her lingering feelings for Sandra. -But then there was also her current situation with June. She put her coffee cup down on the small table next to her and composed herself.

"Brian," she started, her voice calm but laced with poison. "I can't believe what you are planning in that twisted, sick little mind of yours. How dare you sit there and scheme about how to destroy your daughter's future! All to save your skin. It's not just Susan's future, but Andy's, who happens to make your daughter happier than I have ever known her to be."

"But—" began Brian.

"Shut up! I am not finished. "I'm seeing a colleague of Andy's, June Brown. She loves Andy to bits, and there is no way I am going to forfeit my relationship with her so that you can destroy Andy and Susan's. I'll tell you what, you leave Andy and Susan alone or I will destroy you."

Brian sat in total silence, stunned by the response from Sheena. "I take it then that you will not participate in this scheme?"

His answer showed Sheena that he had not changed one bit in all the years she had known him.

"Brian you better pray to God I say nothing about this to June. She will go straight to Andy, maybe even Susan. This is over. And Sandy, please think seriously before you do anything this stupid."

Sheena rose from her seat and left the living room. Sandra followed immediately and came to an abrupt halt at the door as Sheena turned to face her. The look in her eyes said everything. Opening the door, Sheena disappeared into the night.

Brian knew he had a problem on his hands. It was just a matter of how he was going to deal with it. Him.

The evil inside Brian Berger was rising to the surface.

Glossary of Terms

Bail / Bailed - Released from the police office or court to appear at court on a later date.

Bar Officer - A Police Officer who oversees the daily working of the police office during his shift accepting prisoners into the office, logging property, general prisoner care.

Boab - Glaswegian slang for Bob/Bobby

Bothy - A small hut or cottage

CID - Criminal Investigation Department

Circle the Wagons - Figure of speech for everyone to close ranks around a colleague to protect him or her.

Close – Entrance to a tenement in Glasgow

Crime - A crime is generally at common law against the person, murder, assault, rape etc.

Detained - Being kept for a specific time limit for lawful enquiry but not under arrest

Locus - The place where a crime or offence was committed

Muster/Muster Room - A gathering or assemble of people coming together for a common purpose / the meeting place

Offence – An example would be, Public Order Offences, generated by acts Acts of Parliament etc.

Probation - A sentence handed down by a court as an alternative to jail

Probationer - In this series, it refers to a new police officer who has to serve a two-year probation period before being confirmed in the rank of Constable.

Station Constable - Similar role to the bar officer but with additional duties throughout the office

Suits / Soft Shoe Brigade - Complaints and Discipline Department, Senior police officers, so named because of their mode of dress

Suspect - A person suspected of committing a crime or offence

Tin Pail - Rhyming Slang for Jail

Turnkey - Usually a civilian employee sometimes a police officer charged with the care of prisoners, the origin is, turning the key

Drug Terms - Weed/Marijuana - Smack/Heroin - Coke/Cocaine

Worthies - Usually a group of local older unemployed residents known for their drinking sessions, can also be used for low-level local criminals, but also one worthy of praise.

Japanese Phrases

Karategi … Formal Japanese name for the suit used in competition or practice

Dojo … The room or the hall where martial arts are practised

Sensei … A teacher

Kata … A system of training exercises in karate or other martial arts

Ranking of Police Officers

Con … Constable

Sgt … Sergeant

Insp … Inspector

Ch. Insp … Chief Inspector

Supt … Superintendent

Chief Supt … Chief Superintendent

ACC … Assistant Chief Constable

Dep. Ch. Con … Deputy Chief Constable

Ch. Con… Chief Constable

About the Author

Born in the northeast of Scotland Simpson moved to Glasgow in the late 1950s spending his formative years in the East-end of Glasgow. His working life was spent in the civil service, forming life-long friendships with those in the Emergency Services. It was those friendships and a love of writing that led him to create this series while he enjoys the quiet life he returned to in the northeast of Scotland.

Other Books by this Author

For The Latest Information On

Available Novels

New Releases

&

Coming Soon

Please Visit

JasamiPublishingLtd.com

Simpson Munro

Simpson Munro

Jasami Publishing Ltd
www.jasamipublishingltd.com